Also by Lori Ostlund

After the Parade

The
BIGNESS
of the
WORLD

STORIES

Lori Ostlund

SCRIBNER

New York   London   Toronto   Sydney   New Delhi

SCRIBNER
An Imprint of Simon & Schuster, Inc.
1230 Avenue of the Americas
New York, NY 10020

Copyright © 2009 by Lori Ostlund
First published by the University of Georgia Press in 2009.

All rights reserved, including the right to reproduce this book or portions thereof in any form whatsoever. For information, address Scribner Subsidiary Rights Department, 1230 Avenue of the Americas, New York, NY 10020.

First Scribner trade paperback edition February 2016

SCRIBNER and design are registered trademarks of The Gale Group, Inc., used under license by Simon & Schuster, Inc., the publisher of this work.

For information about special discounts for bulk purchases, please contact Simon & Schuster Special Sales at 1-866-506-1949 or business@simonandschuster.com.

The Simon & Schuster Speakers Bureau can bring authors to your live event. For more information or to book an event, contact the Simon & Schuster Speakers Bureau at 1-866-248-3049 or visit our website at www.simonspeakers.com.

Manufactured in the United States of America

10 9 8 7 6 5 4 3 2 1

Library of Congress Cataloging-in-Publication Data

Ostlund, Lori.
[Short stories. Selections]
The bigness of the world : stories / Lori Ostlund. —
First Scribner trade paperback edition.
pages ; cm
I. Title.
PS3615.S64A6 2016
813'.6—dc23
2015029059

ISBN 978-1-5011-1787-9
ISBN 978-1-5011-1788-6 (ebook)

For Anne, of course

Contents

THE BIGNESS OF THE WORLD

The Bigness of the World

The year that Ilsa Maria Lumpkin took care of us, Martin was ten going on eleven and I, eleven going on twelve. We considered ourselves almost adults, on the cusp of no longer requiring supervision, but because our days were far more interesting with Ilsa in them, we did not force the issue. Her job was to be there waiting when we arrived home from school, to prepare snacks and help with homework and ask about our days, for our parents were deeply involved at that time with what they referred to as their "careers," both of them spending long hours engaged in activities that seemed to Martin and me nebulous at best. We understood, of course, that our mother did something at our grandfather's bank, but when our father overheard us describing her job in this way to Ilsa, he admonished us later, saying, "Your mother is vice president of the bank. That is not just *something*."

Then, perhaps suspecting that his job seemed to us equally vague, he took out his wallet and handed Martin and me one of his business cards, on which was inscribed his name, Matthew Koeppe, and the words *PR Czar*. For several long seconds, Martin and I stared down at the card, and our father stared at us. I believe that he wanted to understand us, wanted to know, for example, how we viewed the world, what interested or frightened or perplexed us, but this required patience, something that

1

our father lacked, for he simply did not have enough time at his disposal to be patient, to stand there and puzzle out what it was about his business card that we did not understand. Instead, he went quietly off to his study to make telephone calls, and the next day, I asked Ilsa what a *czar* was, spelling the word out because I could not imagine how to pronounce a *c* and *z* together, but she said that they were people who lived in Russia, royalty, which made no sense.

Ilsa often spent evenings with us as well, for our parents kept an intense social calendar, attending dinners that were, my mother explained, an extension of what she did all day long, but in more elegant clothing. Ilsa wore perfume when she came at night, and while neither Martin nor I liked the smell, we appreciated the gesture, the implication that she thought of being with us as an evening out. She also brought Popsicles, which she hid in her purse because our parents did not approve of Popsicles, though often she forgot about them until long after they had melted, and when she finally did remember and pulled them out, the seams of the packages oozing blue or red, our two favorite flavors, she would look dismayed for just a moment before announcing, "Not to worry, my young charges. We shall pop them in the freezer, and they will be as good as new." Of course, they never were as good as new but were instead like Popsicles that had melted and been refrozen—shapeless with a thick, gummy coating. We ate them anyway because we did not want to hurt Ilsa's feelings, which we thought of as more real, more fragile, than other people's feelings.

Most afternoons, the three of us visited the park near our house. Though it was only four blocks away, Ilsa inevitably began to cry at some point during the walk, her emotions stirred by any number of things, which she loosely identified as *death, beauty,* and *inhumanity*: the bugs caught in the grilles of the cars that we passed (death); two loose dogs humping on the sidewalk across our path (beauty); and the owners who finally caught up with them and forced them apart before they were finished (inhumanity). We were not used to adults who cried freely or openly, for this was Minnesota, where people guarded their emotions, a tradition in which Martin and I had been well schooled. Ilsa, while she was from here, was not, as my mother was fond of saying, *of* here, which meant that she did not become impatient or embarrassed when we occasionally cried as well. In fact, she encouraged it. Still, I was never comfortable when it happened and did not want attention paid me over it—unlike Ilsa, who sank to the ground and sobbed while Martin and I sat on either side of her, holding her hands or resting ours on her back.

We also liked Ilsa because she was afraid of things, though not the normal things that we expected adults to be afraid of and certainly not the kinds of things that Martin and I had been taught to fear—strangers, candy found on the ground, accidentally poking out an eye. We kept careful track of her fears and divided them into two categories, the first comprising things of which she claimed to be "absolutely petrified," her euphemism for those things that she deeply disliked, among them abbreviated language of any sort. Ilsa frequently professed her disdain for what she called "the American compulsion toward brevity." She did not use contractions and scolded us when we did, claiming that they brought down the level of the conversation. Furthermore, when referring to people, she employed their full names: the first, what she called their "Christian" name, although she was not, to my knowledge, actively religious; the middle, which she once described as a person's essence; and the surname, the name that, for better or worse, bound them to their families.

Ilsa eschewed all acronyms and initialisms, even those so entrenched in our vocabularies that we could not recall what the initials stood for. She once left the following message on my parents' answering machine: "I am very sorry that I will be unavailable to stay with the children Saturday evening, October 24, as I have been invited by a dear friend to spend the weekend in Washington, District of Columbia." My parents listened to this message repeatedly, always maintaining a breathless silence until the very end, at which point they exploded into laughter. I did not understand what was funny about the message, but when I asked my mother to explain, she gave one of her typically vague responses. "That Ilsa," she said. "She's just such a pistol." Something else must have occurred to her then, for a moment later she turned back to add, "We shouldn't mention this to Ilsa, Veronica. Sometimes families have their little jokes." Of course, I had no intention of telling Ilsa, a decision based not on family allegiance but on my growing sense that laughter was rarely a straightforward matter.

My mother and Ilsa met at Weight Brigade, to which my mother had belonged for years, certainly as long as I could remember, though she had never been fat, not even plump. She was fond of saying that she had no "love relationship" with food, lingo that she had picked up at her meetings, sitting amid women who had not just love relationships with food but desperate, passionate affairs on the side. My mother, who kept track of numbers for a living, liked that Weight Brigade promoted a strict policy of calorie counting and exercise, which she thought of in terms of debits and credits, though I suspect that what she liked most of all was the easy sense of achievement that she felt there among women who struggled terribly, and often unsuccessfully, with their weight.

She rarely missed the weekly meetings, but because she preferred to compartmentalize the various areas of her life, she disapproved greatly of Weight Brigade's phone-buddy system, under which she was paired with another member who might call her at any time, day or night, to discuss temptation. I once heard her tell my father that these conversations, mostly breathy descriptions of ice cream that served only to work her phone partner into a frenzy of desire, were akin to phone sex. After several minutes of listening to her phone buddy's chatter, she would hear the freezer door open followed by the rattle of a cutlery drawer, and then her phone buddy would bid her an unintelligible goodbye, speaking through, as my mother liked to put it, "a mouthful of shame."

Over the years, my mother was paired with numerous women (as well as one man), all of whom she alienated quickly, unable to sympathize with their constant cravings or the ease with which they capitulated. Furthermore, when they sobbed hysterically during weigh-ins, she dealt with them sternly, even harshly, explaining that they knew the consequences of gorging themselves on potato chips and cookies, which made their responses to the weight gain disingenuous as far as she was concerned. My mother was always very clear in her opinions; she said that in banking one had to be, that she needed to be able to size people up quickly and then carry through on her assessment without hesitation or regret, a policy that she applied at home as well, which meant that if I failed to unload the dishwasher within two hours after it finished running or lied about completing a school assignment, she moved swiftly into punishment mode and became indignant when I feigned surprise. Among the members of Weight Brigade, her approach won her no few enemies. Eventually, she was no longer assigned phone buddies, and by the time she met Ilsa, the other members were refusing even to sit near my mother at meetings, though she claimed to be unbothered by this, citing envy as their sole motivation.

Ilsa was plump when we knew her but had not always been. This we learned from photographs of her holding animals from the pound where she volunteered, a variety of cats and dogs and birds for which she had provided temporary care. She went to Weight Brigade only that one time, the time that she met my mother, and never went back because she said that she could not bear to listen to the vilification of butter and sugar, but Martin and I had seen the lists that our mother kept of her own daily caloric intake, and we suspected that Ilsa had simply been overwhelmed by the math that belonging to Weight Brigade involved, for math was another thing that "absolutely petrified" Ilsa. When my parents asked how much they owed her, she always replied, "I am sure that you must know far better than I, for I have not the remotest idea." And when Martin or I required help with our math homework, she answered in the high, quivery voice that she used when she sang opera: "Mathematics is an entirely useless subject, and we shall not waste our precious time on it." Perhaps we appeared skeptical, for she often added, "Really, my dear children, I cannot remember the last time that I used mathematics."

Ilsa's fear of math stemmed, I suspect, from the fact that she seemed unable to grasp even the basic tenets upon which math rested. Once, for example, after we had made a pizza together and taken it from the oven, she suggested that we cut it into very small pieces because she was ravenous and that way, she said, there would be more of it to go around.

"More pieces you mean?" we clarified tentatively.

"No, my silly billies. More pizza," she replied confidently, and though we tried to convince her of the impossibility of such a thing, explaining that the pizza *was* the size it was, she had laughed in a way that suggested that she was charmed by our ignorance.

Ilsa wore colorful, flowing dresses and large hats that she did not take off, even when she opened the oven door to slide a pizza inside or sat eating refrozen Popsicles with us on the back deck. Her evening hats were more complicated than the daytime hats, involving not just bows but flowers and actual feathers and even, on the hat that Martin and I privately referred to as "Noah's Ark," a simple diorama of three-dimensional animals made of pressed felt. Martin and I considered Ilsa's hats extremely *tasteful,* a word that we had heard our parents use often enough to have developed a feel for. That is, she did not wear holiday-themed hats decked with Christmas tree balls or blinking Halloween pumpkins, although she did favor pastels on Easter. Still, Ilsa's hats really seemed appropriate only on the nights that she sang opera, belting out arias while we sat on the sofa and listened. Once, she performed Chinese opera for us, which was like nothing that we had ever heard before and which we both found startling and a little frightening.

Later, when we told our parents that Ilsa had sung Chinese opera for us, our mother looked perplexed and said, "I didn't know that Ilsa knew Chinese."

"She doesn't," we replied. "She just makes it up." And then Martin and I proceeded to demonstrate, imitating the sounds that Ilsa had made, high-pitched, nasally sounds that resembled the word *sure.* Our parents looked troubled by this and said that they did not want us making fun of Chinese opera, which they called an ancient and respected art form.

"But we aren't making fun of it," I replied. "We like it." This was true, but they explained that if we really liked it, we wouldn't feel compelled to imitate it, which Martin and I later agreed made no sense. We did not say so to my parents, because about some things there was simply no arguing. We knew that they had spoken to Ilsa as well, for she did not sing Chinese opera again, sticking instead with Puccini and Wagner, though she did not know Italian or German either.

My mother, in sartorial contrast to Ilsa, favored tailored trousers, blazers, and crisply ironed shirts, and when my father occasionally teased her about her wardrobe, pointing out that it was possible to look vice presidential without completely hiding her figure, my mother sternly reminded him that the only figures she wanted her clients thinking about were the ones that she calculated for their loans. My mother liked clothes well enough but shopped mainly by catalog in order to save time, which meant that the UPS driver visited our house frequently. His name was Bruce, and Martin and I had always known him as a sullen man who did not respond to questions about his well-being, the weather, or his day, which were the sorts of questions that our parents and the babysitters prior to Ilsa tended to ask. Ilsa, however, was not interested in such things. Rather, she offered him milk on overcast days and pomegranate juice, which my parents stocked for her, on sunny days, and then, as Bruce stood on the front step drinking his milk or pomegranate juice, she asked him whether he had ever stolen a package (no) and whether he had ever opened a package out of curiosity (yes, one time, but the contents had disappointed him greatly).

Martin and I generally stood behind Ilsa during these conversations, peering around her and staring at Bruce, in awe of his transformation into a pleasant human being, but when we heard her soliciting tips on how to pack her hats so that they would not be damaged during shipping, we both stepped forward, alarmed. "Are you moving?" we asked, for we lived in fear of losing Ilsa, believing, I suppose, that we did not really deserve her.

"No, my dears. I'm simply gathering information." She clasped her hands in front of her as she did when she sang opera, the right one curled down over the left as though her fingers were engaged in a tug-of-war. "It is a very sad thing that nowadays there is so little useless information," she declaimed, affecting even more of a British accent than she normally did. "That is our beloved Oscar, of course," she added, referring to Oscar Wilde, whom she was fond of quoting.

When Bruce left, she first washed his glass and then phoned my mother at work to let her know of the package's arrival, despite the fact that packages were delivered almost daily. My mother, who was fond of prefacing comments with the words, "I'm a busy woman," rarely took these calls. Instead, Ilsa left messages with my mother's secretary, Kenneth Bloomquist, their conversation generally evolving as follows: "Hello, Mr. Bloomquist. This is Ilsa Maria Lumpkin. Would you be so kind as to let Mrs. Koeppe know that the United Parcel Service driver has left a package?" She ended each call with neither a *goodbye* nor a *thank you* but with a statement of the time. "It is precisely 4:17 post meridiem," she would say, for even when it came to time, abbreviations were unacceptable.

Then there were the things of which Ilsa truly was afraid, but they, too, were things that I had never known adults to be afraid of. One night, as Martin and I sat at the dining room table completing our homework while Ilsa prepared grilled cheese sandwiches with pickles, she began to scream from the kitchen, a loud, continuous ejection of sound not unlike the honking of a car horn. Martin and I leapt up as one and rushed to her, both of us, I suspect, secretly wanting to be the one to calm her, though in those days he and I were rarely competitive.

"What is it?" we cried out in unison, and she pointed mutely to the bread, but when Martin examined the loaf, he found nothing odd save for a bit of green mold that had formed along the top crust. Ilsa would not go near the bread and begged him to take it into the garage and dispose of it immediately. He did not, for we both knew that my parents would not approve of such wastefulness, not when the mold could be scraped off and the bread eaten. I do not mean to suggest that my parents were in any way stingy, for they were not. However, they did not want money to stand between us and common sense, did not want us growing up under what my father was fond of calling "the tutelage of wastefulness." They were no longer churchgoers, either one of them, but Martin and I were raised according to the tenets of their residual Protestantism.

Ilsa was also deeply afraid to ride in cars with power windows, which both of ours had and which meant that she would not accept a ride home, even at the end of a very late evening. "What would happen if you were to drive into a lake?" she asked my father each time he suggested it. "However would we escape?" When my father explained to her that there were no lakes, no bodies of water of any sort, along the twelve blocks that lay between our house and her apartment, which was actually a tiny guest cottage behind a much larger house, she laughed at him the way that she had laughed at Martin and me when we tried to explain about the pizza.

Our neighborhood was quite safe, but my father still felt obligated to walk Ilsa home, and while he complained mightily about having to do so, he always returned disheveled and laughing, and eventually my mother suggested that she walk Ilsa home sometimes instead, not because she distrusted my father, for she did not, but because she too wanted to return humming and laughing, her clothing wrinkled and covered with twigs. Martin and I encouraged this as well because we were worried about our mother, who had become increasingly distracted and often yelled at us for small things, for counting too slowly when she asked us to check how many eggs were left in the carton or forgetting to throw both dirty socks into the hamper. Of course most people will hear "twigs" and "clothing wrinkled" and think sex, and while I cannot absolutely rule this out, I am fairly sure that these outings did not involve anything as mundane as sex in the park. My certainty is based not on the child's inability to imagine her parents engaged in such things; they were probably not swingers in the classic sense of the word, but they were products of the time and just conservative enough on the surface to suggest the possibility. No, my conviction lies entirely with Ilsa.

It was my fault that things with Ilsa came to an end. One evening, after my father returned from walking her home, he went into the bathroom to brush his teeth and noticed that his toothbrush was wet. "Has one of you been playing with my toothbrush?" he asked from the hallway outside our bedrooms.

"No, Ilsa used it," I said at last, but only after he had come into my bedroom and turned on the light. "We had carrots, and she needs to brush her teeth immediately after she eats colorful foods."

My father stared at me for a moment. "Does Ilsa always use my toothbrush?"

"No," I said patiently. "Only when we have colorful foods." This was true. She had not used it since we had radishes the week before.

The next morning, behind closed doors, he and my mother discussed Ilsa while Martin and I attempted, unsuccessfully, to eavesdrop. In the end, neither of them wanted to confront Ilsa about the toothbrush because they found it embarrassing.

Instead, they decided to tell Ilsa that Martin and I had become old enough to supervise ourselves. We protested, suggesting that we simply buy Ilsa her own toothbrush, but my father and mother said that it was more than the toothbrush and that we really were old enough to stay alone. We insisted that we were not, but the call to Ilsa was made.

Nonetheless, for the next several weeks, my father was there waiting for us when we returned from school each day. He told us that he had made some scheduling changes at work, called in some favors, but we did not know what this meant because we still did not understand what our father did. He spent most afternoons on the telephone, talking in a jovial voice that became louder when he wanted something and louder again when the other party agreed. He did not make snacks for us, so Martin and I usually peeled carrots and then sat on my bed eating them as we talked about Ilsa, primarily concerning ourselves with two questions: whether she missed us and how we might manage to see her again. The latter was answered soon enough, for during the third week of this new arrangement, my father announced that he and my mother needed to go somewhere the next afternoon and that we would be left alone in order to prove our maturity.

The next day, we watched our parents drive away. Once they were out of sight, I began counting to 280, for that, Ilsa had once explained, was the amount of time that it took the average person to realize that he or she had left something behind. "Two hundred and eighty," I announced several minutes later, and since our parents had not reappeared, we went into our bedrooms and put on our dress clothes, Martin a suit and tie, which he loved having the opportunity to wear, and I, a pair of dress slacks and a sweater, which is what I generally wore for holidays and events that my parents deemed worthy of something beyond jeans. Then, because we did not have a key, we locked the door of the house from the inside and climbed out a side window, leaving it slightly ajar behind us. We knew where Ilsa lived, for our parents had pointed it out on numerous occasions, and we set off running toward her in our dress shoes, but when we were halfway there, Martin stopped suddenly.

"We don't have anything for her," he said. "We can't go without something. It wouldn't be right."

Martin was what some of the boys in his class called a sissy because he did not like games that involved pushing or hitting, preferring to jump rope during recess, and because he always considered the feelings of others. Though I wanted to think that I too considered the feelings of others, I often fell short, particularly when it was not convenient to do so or when my temper dictated otherwise. When it came to pushing and hitting, Martin and I fully parted ways, for I was fond of both activities. Thus, several months earlier, when I heard that three of Martin's classmates had called him a sissy, I waited for them after school and threatened to punch the next one who used the word. I should mention that while Martin had inherited my mother's slender build, I took after my father, a man who had once picked up our old refrigerator by himself and carried it out to the garage, and so the three boys had looked down at the ground for a moment and then, one by one, slunk away. When we got home, I told Ilsa what had happened, and Martin stood nearby, listening to me relate the story with a thoughtful expression on his face. He had a habit of standing erect, like a dancer, and when I finished, she turned to him and said, "Why, it is a marvelous thing to be a sissy, Martin. You will enjoy your life much more than those boys. You will be able to cook and enjoy flowers and appreciate all sorts of music. I absolutely adore sissies."

Thus, when Martin insisted that we could not visit Ilsa

without a gift, I did not argue, for I trusted Martin about such things. We turned and ran back home, reentering through the window, and Martin went into the kitchen and put together a variety of spices—cloves, a stick of cinnamon, and a large nutmeg seed—which he wrapped in cheesecloth and tied carefully with a piece of ribbon.

"That's not a gift," I said, but Martin explained to me patiently that it was—was, in fact, the sort of gift Ilsa would love.

Fifteen minutes later, we stood on the porch of Ilsa's cottage, waiting for her to answer the door. We had already knocked three times, and I knocked twice more before I finally turned to Martin and asked fretfully, "What if she's not home?" To be honest, it had never occurred to us that Ilsa might not be home, for we could think of Ilsa only in regard to ourselves, which meant that when she was not with us, she was here, at her cottage, because we were incapable of imagining her elsewhere— certainly not with another family, caring for children who were not us.

"She must be at the pound," I said suddenly and with great relief.

But Ilsa was home. As we were about to leave, she opened her door and stared at us for several distressing seconds before pulling us to her tightly. "My bunnies!" she cried out, and we thought that she meant us, but she pulled us inside and shut the door, saying, "Quickly now, before their simple little minds plot an escape," and we realized then that she truly meant rabbits.

"Martin," she said, looking him up and down, her voice low and unsteady, and then she turned and scrutinized me as well. Her hair was pulled back in a very loose French braid, and she was not wearing a hat, the first time that either of us had seen her without one. It felt strange to be standing there in her tiny cottage, stranger yet to be seeing her without a hat, intimate in a way that seemed almost unbearable.

"You're not wearing a hat," Martin said matter-of-factly.

"I was just taking a wee nap," she replied. I could see that this was true, for her face was flushed and deeply creased from the pillow, her eyes dull with slumber, as though she had been sleeping for some time.

"We brought you something," said Martin, holding up the knotted cheesecloth.

"How lovely," she exclaimed, clapping her hands together clumsily before taking the ball of spices and holding it to her nose with both hands. She closed her eyes and inhaled deeply, but the moment went on and on, becoming uncomfortable.

"Kikes!" screamed a voice from a corner of the room, and Ilsa's eyes snapped open. "Kikes and dykes!" screamed the voice again.

"Martin, I will not tolerate such language," Ilsa said firmly.

"It wasn't me," said Martin, horrified, for we both knew what the words meant.

"I think it was him," I said, pointing to the corner where a large cage hung, inside of which perched a shabby-looking green parrot. The bird regarded us for a moment, screeched, "Ass pirates and muff divers!," leaned over, and tossed a beakful of seeds into the air like confetti.

"Of course it was him," said Ilsa. "The foul-mouthed rascal. I saved his life, but he hardly seems grateful. His name is Martin."

"Martin?" said Martin happily. "Like me?"

"Yes, I named him after you, my dear, though it was wishful thinking on my part. I dare say you could teach him a thing or two about manners."

"Why does he say those things?" asked Martin.

"Martin ended up at the pound a few months ago after his former owner, a thoroughly odious man, died in a house fire—he fell asleep smoking a cigar. Martin escaped through a window, but it seems there is no undoing the former owner's work, which made adoption terribly unlikely. They were going to put him down, so I have taken him instead." She sighed. "The bunnies—poor souls—are absolutely terrified of him."

Martin and I looked around Ilsa's living room, trying to spot the bunnies, but the only indication of them lay in the fact that Ilsa had covered her small sofa and arm chair with plastic wrap as though she were preparing to paint the walls. "Where are the bunnies?" I asked. I did not say so, but I was afraid of rabbits, for I had been bitten by one at an Easter event at the shopping mall several years earlier. In truth, it had been nothing more than a nibble, but it had startled me enough that I had dropped the rabbit and then been scolded by the teenage attendant for my carelessness.

"I should imagine that they are in the escritoire," she said, and Martin nodded as though he knew what the escritoire was.

"Come," said Ilsa. "Let us go into the kitchen, away from this bad-mannered fellow. We shall mull some cider using your extraordinarily thoughtful gift."

We huddled at a square yellow table inside her small, dreary kitchen, watching her pour cider from a jug into a saucepan, as deeply focused on this task as someone charged with splitting a neutron. "How are you, Ilsa?" asked Martin, sounding strangely grown up. She dropped the spice ball into the pan, adjusted the flame, and only then turned to answer.

"I am positively exuberant," she replied. "Indeed, Martin, things could not be better here at 53 Ridgecrest Drive." She paused, as though considering what topic we might discuss next, and then she asked how we were and, after we had both answered that we were well, she asked about our parents. We were in the habit of answering Ilsa honestly, and so I told her that our parents seemed strange lately.

"Strange?" she said, her mouth curling up as if the word had a taste attached to it that she did not care for.

"Yes," I said. "For one thing, our father is home every day when we arrive from school"—Martin looked at me, for on the way over we had agreed that we would not tell Ilsa this, lest it hurt her feelings to know that our parents had lied, so I went on quickly—"and our mother is gone until very late most nights, and when she is home, she hardly speaks, even to our father."

"I see," said Ilsa, but not as though she really did, and then she stood and ladled up three cups of cider, which she placed on saucers and carried to the table, one cup at a time. She fished out the soggy bundle of spices and placed that on a fourth saucer, which she set in the middle of the table as though it were a centerpiece, something aesthetically pleasing for us to consider as we sipped our cider.

"I may presume that your parents are aware of your visit to me?" she said, and we both held our cups to our mouths and blew across the surface of the cider, watching as it rippled slightly, and finally Martin replied that they were not.

"Children," Ilsa said, "that will not do." This was the closest that Ilsa had ever come to actually scolding us, though her tone spoke more of exhaustion than disapproval, and we both looked up at her sadly.

"I shall ring them immediately," she said.

"They aren't home," I told her.

Ilsa consulted her watch, holding it up very close to her eyes in order to make out the numbers because the watch was tiny, the face no larger than a dime. Once I had asked Ilsa why she did not get a bigger watch, one that she could simply glance at the way that other people did, but she said that that was precisely the reason—that one should never get into the habit of glancing at one's watch. "Please excuse me, my dears. I see that it is time to visit my apothecary," she said, and she stood and left the room.

"What is her apothecary?" I asked Martin, whispering, and he whispered back that he did not know but that perhaps she was referring to the bathroom.

We were quiet then, studying Ilsa's kitchen in a way that we had not been able to do when she was present. There was only one window, a single pane that faced a cement wall. This accounted for the dreariness, this and the fact that the room was tiny, three or even four times smaller than our kitchen. When I commented on this to Martin, he said, "I think that Ilsa's kitchen is the perfect size. You know what she always says—that she gets lost in our kitchen." But his tone was defensive, and I knew that he was disappointed as well.

"There's no island," I said suddenly. Our parents' kitchen had not one island but two, which Ilsa had given names. The one nearest the stove she called Jamaica and the other, Haiti, and when we helped her cook, she would hand us things, saying, "Ferry this cutting board over to Haiti," and "Tomatoes at the south end of Jamaica, please." Once, during a period when she had been enamored of religious dietary restrictions, she announced, "Dairy on Jamaica, my young sous chefs. Meat on Haiti," and we had cooked the entire meal according to her notions of kosher, though when it came time to eat, she had forgotten about the rules, stacking cheese and bacon on our hamburgers and pouring us each a large glass of milk.

From the other room, we heard a sound like maracas being rattled, which made me think of our birthdays because our parents always took us to Mexican Village, where a mariachi band came to our table and sang "Happy Birthday" in Spanish. We heard water running and then the parrot screaming obscenities again as Ilsa passed through the living room and back into the kitchen. She had put on a hat, one that we had not seen before, white with a bit of peacock feather glued to one side.

"This has been an absolutely splendid visit, but I must be getting the two of you home," she said. "Gather your things, my goslings." But we had come with nothing save the spices, which now sat in a pool of brown liquid, and so we had no things to gather.

When we arrived home that afternoon, our father was already there, waiting for us at the dining room table, where he sat with the tips of his hands pressed together forming a peak. He did not ask where we had been but instead told us to sit down because he needed to explain something to us, something about our mother, who would not be coming home that day. "You know that your mother works for your grandfather?" he began, and we nodded and waited. "Well, your grandfather has done something wrong. He's taken money from the bank."

"But it's his bank," I replied.

"Yes," said my father. "But the money is not his. It belongs to the people who use the bank, who put their money there so that it will be safe."

Again, we nodded, for we understood this about banks. In fact, we both had our own accounts at the bank, where we kept the money that we received for our birthdays. "He stole money?" I asked, for that was how it sounded, and I wanted to be sure.

"Well," said my father, "it's called embezzling." But when I looked up *embezzling* that evening, I discovered that our grandfather had indeed stolen money.

"And what about our mother?" Martin asked.

"It's complicated," said our father, "but they've arrested her also."

"Arrested?" I said, for there had been no talk of arresting before this.

"Yes," said my father, and then he began to cry.

We had never seen our father cry. He was, I learned that day, a silent crier. He laid his head on the table, his arms forming a nest around it, and we knew that he was crying only because his shoulders heaved up and down. I sat very still, not looking at him because I did not know how to think of him as anything but my father, instead focusing on the overhead light, waiting for it to click, which it generally did every thirty seconds or so. The sound was actually somewhere between a click and a scratch, easy to hear but apparently difficult to fix, for numerous electricians had been called in to do so and had failed. I had always complained mightily about the clicking, which prevented me from concentrating on my homework, but that day as I sat at the table with my weeping father and Martin, the light was silent, unexpectedly and overwhelmingly silent.

Then, without first consulting me with his eyes, our custom in matters relating to our parents, Martin slipped from his chair and stood next to my father, and, after a moment, placed a hand on my father's shoulder. In those days, Martin's hands were unusually plump, at odds with the rest of his body, and from where I sat, directly across from my father, Martin's hand looked like a fat, white bullfrog perched on my father's shoulder. My father's sobbing turned audible, a high-pitched whimper like a dog makes when left alone in a car, and then quickly flattened out and stopped.

"It will be okay," Martin said, rubbing my father's shoulder with his fat, white hand, and my father sat up and nodded several times in rapid succession, gulping as though he had been underwater.

But it would not be okay. After a very long trial, my mother went to jail, eight years with the possibility of parole after six. My grandfather was put on trial as well, but he died of a heart attack on the second day, leaving my mother to face the jury and crowded courtroom alone. Her lawyers wanted to blame everything on him, arguing that he was dead and thus unable to deny the charges or be punished, advice that my mother resisted until it became clear that she might be facing an even longer sentence. Martin and I learned all of this from the newspaper, which we were not supposed to read but did, and from the taunts hurled at us by children who used to be our friends but were no longer allowed to play with us because many of their parents had money in my grandfather's bank and even those who didn't felt that my mother had betrayed the entire community.

We missed her terribly in the beginning, my father most of all, though I believe that he grieved not at being separated from her but because the person she was, or that he had thought she was, no longer existed, which meant that he grieved almost as though she were dead. There was some speculation in the newspaper about my father, about what was referred to as his "possible complicity," but I remain convinced to this day that my father knew nothing about what had been going on at the bank, though whether it was true that it was all my grandfather's doing, that my mother had been nothing more than a loyal daughter as her lawyers claimed—this I will never know. Martin was of the opinion that it shouldn't matter, not to us, but I felt otherwise, particularly when he came home from school with scratches and bruises and black eyes that I knew were given to him because of her, though he always shrugged his shoulders when my father asked what had happened to him and, with a small smile, gave the same reply: "Such is the life of a fairy." My father did not know how to respond to words like *sissy* and *fairy,* nor to the matter-of-fact manner in which Martin uttered them, and so he said nothing, rubbing his ear vigorously for a moment and then turning away, as was his habit when presented with something that he would rather not hear.

Of course, as Ilsa walked us home from her cottage that day, we had no inkling of what lay ahead, no way of knowing that the familiar terrain of our childhoods would soon become a vast, unmarked landscape in which we would be left to wander, motherless and, it seemed to us at times, fatherless as well. Rather, as we walked along holding hands with Ilsa, our concerns were immediate. I fretted aloud that our parents would be angry, but Ilsa assured me that they were more likely to be worried, and though I did not like the idea of worrying them, it seemed far preferable to their anger. There was also the matter of Ilsa herself, Ilsa, who, even with her hat on, seemed unfamiliar, and so Martin and I worked desperately to interest her in the things that we saw around us, things that would have normally moved her to tears but which she now seemed hardly to notice. Across our path was a snail that had presumably been wooed out onto the sidewalk during the previous day's rain and crushed to bits by passersby. I stopped and pointed to it, waiting for her to cry out, "Death, be not proud!" and then to squeeze her eyes shut while allowing us to lead her safely past it, but she glanced at the crushed bits with no more interest than she would have shown a discarded candy wrapper.

As we neared our house, I could see my father's car in the driveway. "Can we visit you again, Ilsa?" I asked, turning to her.

"I am afraid that that will not be possible, children," she said. "You see, I will be setting off very soon—really any day now—on a long journey. I suspect that I may be gone for quite some time."

"Are you going to see the ocean?" I asked. At that time in my life I could not imagine anything more terrifying than the ocean, which I knew about only from maps and school and movies.

"Yes," she said after giving the question some thought. "As a matter of fact, I believe that I will see the ocean. Have you ever seen the ocean, children?"

Martin and I replied that we had not.

"But you must," she said gravely. "You absolutely must see the ocean."

"Why?" I asked, both frightened and encouraged by her tone. "Why must we?"

"Well," she said after a moment. "However can you expect to understand the bigness of the world if you do not see the ocean?"

"Is there no other way?" Martin asked.

"I suppose there are other ways," Ilsa conceded. "Though certainly the ocean is the most effective."

"But why must we understand the bigness of the world?" I asked.

We were in front of our house by then, and Ilsa stopped and looked at us. "My dear Martin and Veronica," she said in the high, quivery voice that we had been longing for. "I know it may sound frightening, yet I assure you that there have been times in my life when the bigness of the world was my only consolation."

Then, she gave us each a small kiss on the forehead, and we watched her go, her gait unsteady, like that of someone thinking too much about the simple act of walking, her white hat bobbing like a sail. At the corner she stopped and turned, and seeing us there still, called, "In you go, children. Your parents will be waiting," so that these were Ilsa's final words to us— ordinary and rushed and, as we would soon discover, untrue.

Bed Death

We met Mr. Mani because we paused on the footbridge that spanned Jalan Munshi Abdullah, a busy street near our hotel, for it was only from up there that the sign for his school, the unobtrusively named English Institute, could be seen. The school, which occupied the second floor of the decrepit building just below us, did not look promising, and when we trotted back down the steps to the street and went inside, it seemed even less so. Still, we presented our résumés to the young woman at the front desk, and she, not knowing what to do with them or us, summoned Mr. Mani from class.

Mr. Mani was a small Indian man in his sixties, no taller than either Julia or I, which put us immediately at ease, and when he smiled, he seemed at once boyish and ancient because he was missing his top front teeth. He did not speak Malaysian English, which we were still struggling to understand, but sounded in every way British, to the point that when he heard our American accents, he winced, which could have annoyed us but instead made us laugh. He studied our résumés at length before explaining, apologetically, that the school provided only enough work for him, though when we met him for dinner that evening, we learned that he rarely spent fewer than twelve hours a day at the school, teaching mornings and afternoons and then, at night, checking homework and attending to paperwork. We discovered also that the empty space created by his missing teeth accommodated perfectly the neck of a whiskey bottle, which spent more and more time there as the night wore on, and after he had consumed a fair amount, he revealed that he stayed late at the school also as a way of hiding from his wife, whom he referred to as "my Queen."

I do not think that it occurred to him, ever, that Julia and I were a couple, yet he spoke to us without the usual nonsense or innuendo that so often marks discourse between the sexes. He talked mainly about his marriage, which had been arranged, stating repeatedly that he did not question the matchmaker's thinking in putting together a poor but educated man from Kuala Lumpur and an illiterate woman from the rubber plantation. "After all, we have produced eleven children," he pointed out proudly, confessing that, given his long hours, he saw them only when they brought his meals or attended their weekly English lessons. His favorite was the fifth child, a girl by the name of Suseelah who loved Orwell as much as he did and loathed Dickens almost as much. In fact, he spoke of Dickens often, always with contempt, and I could not help but view it as a classic example of a man railing against his maker, for Mani was a character straight from Dickens, an affable, penniless fellow who bordered on being a caricature of himself.

When he had consumed the entire bottle of whiskey, he declared the evening complete and insisted on the minor gallantry of walking us back to our hotel, a seedy place that he promptly deemed "unsuitable for two ladies." At the door, he shook our hands sadly and said, as though the evening had been nothing more than an extended job interview, "My ladies, I am afraid that I cannot hire you."

"Thank you for meeting with us," I replied.

He turned to leave but stopped, saying, "I shall pass your résumés to my old friend Narayanasamy at Raffles College. If there are no objections, of course. The school is newly opened here in Malacca, though quite established in other areas of Malaysia, I assure you."

We thanked him for his kindness, but I am ashamed to admit that we dismissed his offer as drunken posturing so, of course, we were surprised to return to our hotel the next day to find a note from him informing us that Mr. Narayanasamy wished to meet us. We left early for the interview the following morning, half-expecting the directions that Mani had included to be faulty, which is how we came to be waiting in the overly air-conditioned office of Mr. Narayanasamy, briefcases on our laps, as he finished a heated telephone discussion regarding funds for a copy machine.

I leaned toward Julia. "What do you make of the bed?" I whispered.

"What bed?" she whispered back.

"What bed?" I repeated, indignation adding to my volume, for, simply put, Julia often overlooked the obvious.

"Welcome to Raffles College," Mr. Narayanasamy announced, putting down the phone and rising, hand extended, to greet us, inquiring in the next breath what had brought us to Malaysia and, more specifically, to his school. When I answered that what had brought us to his school was his friend Mr. Mani, he paused before replying, "Ah yes, Mani," the way that one would refer to laundry on the line several minutes after it has begun to rain. I knew then that I would not like this Mr. Narayanasamy. Still, we spent the next hour convincing him that we were indeed up to the task of teaching business communications, a subject we knew little about, for I was a writing teacher and Julia taught ESL, and as we stood to leave, he offered us the jobs.

In the process of making myself desirable and friendly, I forgot entirely about the bed, but as we passed through the main lobby, there it was again—enormous and pristine, housed behind glass like a museum exhibit—and Julia had the good grace to look sheepish. We stood before it in silence, believing that it would not do to be overheard discussing any aspect of our new place of employment, but finally Julia could not contain herself.

"It's huge," she said authoritatively, as though the bed were her find, an oddity that she was deigning to share with me but did not trust me to fully appreciate.

"Yes," I agreed. "I don't know how you missed it." Then, to press my point, I added, "Julia, sometimes I think you could get into bed at night and not notice that a car had been parked at the foot of it." I said this in an intentionally exasperated tone, a tone so exaggerated that I knew I could dismiss it as playful if need be, but Julia, pleased by our employment, merely laughed.

We settled quickly into a routine, teaching from eight in the morning until that same hour of the evening, with blocks free for eating and preparation. Business communications was tedious but not complicated, and we soon developed a system for teaching it, which we modified slightly for each of the three departments that we served: Marketing, Business, and Hospitality Management. The bed, we learned, belonged to the latter department, and we often saw its students huddled around it, notebooks open, as an instructor made and remade it, stopping to gesture at folds and even, with the aid of a meter stick, measuring the distance from bedspread to floor. Students visiting the college with their parents stopped to gaze at the bed as well, the entire family standing with a quiet air of expectation as though watching an empty cage at the zoo, and I came to realize that not only did these families consider it perfectly normal to have a bed on display, but they actually seemed impressed by it, impressed and reassured, as though the bed gave them a sense that the school was for real and not someplace where one did nothing but stare at books. Never did I see a student touch the bed, however, and when I asked one of the hospitality instructors why this was, she explained that what the students needed to know was theoretical, information that could be quantified via a multiple-choice exam—which meant there was no reason for them to touch it.

The hospitality management students were, ironically, the most timid of the lot; I was hard-pressed to imagine any of them behind the desk of an actual hotel, greeting guests and making them feel at home. "Do you even understand what *hospitality* means?" I blurted out one day, fed up with the way they sat in their stiff blue uniforms, red pocket kerchiefs peeking out with an almost obscene jauntiness, eyes turned downward whenever I asked a question. I turned and wrote *hospitality* across the board in large letters, and as I did, I heard behind me a low, scornful chuckle. I knew that it could be coming only from Malik, a corpulent young man who ignored the uniform policy and generally chose to wear purple, perhaps in keeping with the regal connotations of his name. Malik was an anomaly in the class— fat where the others were thin, the only Malay in a class full of Chinese, more often absent than present. He spent his days loitering around campus, attending classes sporadically, which was fine with me, for I had taken a thorough dislike to him and found it tiring to conceal the depth of my feelings. It bothered Julia greatly that I allowed myself to harbor such animosity toward a student, particularly one whom she saw as awkward and pathetic, one whose neediness, she claimed, was so wholly transparent that to respond to it as anything but neediness was to be purposely disingenuous. I mention this only so that one can see how it appeared from her perspective, for I believe (and have all along) that her position was the logical one, the one with which, in theory, I would have agreed had I never met Malik and discovered what it was like to be so utterly repelled by a student.

Already, I had been visited by his father, who was a *datuk*, a minor dignitary of the sort that made appearances at local events, speaking a few words to commemorate the occasion, generally after arriving late. He came unexpectedly during my lunch hour, and, to the horror of the colleague sent to find me, I insisted on finishing my noodles first. When I finally entered the room where Malik and the *datuk* waited, it was ripe with the smell of Malik, an oppressively musky odor that I suspected was caused by some sort of hormonal malfunction but that did nothing to make me better disposed toward him. His father was visibly annoyed at being made to wait, and I could see that this would only make things worse for Malik, which struck me as unfair but did not particularly bother me, for Malik had already caused me an inordinate amount of work and worry, and that also struck me as unfair.

Malik's father did not speak English, but not trusting his son to translate, he had brought along a translator, through whom I explained that Malik rarely attended class and never turned in homework but that I often saw him lounging around the cafeteria. When I spoke to him about his absences, he replied, with an annoying lilt to his voice, that he had not been feeling well. "Upset stomach," he would say coyly, patting his very large stomach as though it were a kitten he had not yet tired of. Once I sent another student to fetch him, but the boy returned alone. "He says that he is feeling faint," the boy reported, and the others looked at me hopefully, for the students enjoyed being surprised by my behavior, which they attributed to my being American. I sensed that Malik wanted me to find him and demand his presence, and so, unwilling to give him that pleasure, I did nothing.

Throughout the course of our exchange, the *datuk* and I made no eye contact, and when the meeting was finished, we stood, but even in parting, he did not acknowledge me, instead averting his eyes until I realized that he was waiting for me to leave first. I did, and as I closed the door behind me, I could hear him yelling and then a sound like an animal snuffling at a trough, which I suspected was Malik crying.

That night, as I passed through the dark lobby of the school, I was startled by what appeared to be a shape atop the bed, a shape not unlike that made by a supine body, albeit a very large one. I drew close to the glass, quite sure that once my eyes adjusted to the dim glow of the night lights, I would find nothing more than a hefty stack of linens awaiting the next day's lesson, but it was clearly a person, and, judging from the size, I knew that it could only be Malik. Slowly, the details of his face grew more pronounced, and I could not help but feel that lying there with his eyes closed, hands clasped high atop the mound of his stomach, he looked defenseless, almost benign. I had never been that close to him, so close that I could have reached out and touched his brow were it not for the glass between us. His lids began to flutter and his eyes rolled slowly open, casting about nervously until they settled on my face, recognition hardening them into two bits of coal that burned with unmitigated contempt.

The next morning, the bed looked as it always did, neatly made, ready for service. I mentioned the encounter to no one, certainly not Julia, who would have pursued one of her usual

melodramatic interpretations, bed as performance space or sac-
rificial altar, rather than simply a comfortable place to snooze.

Mr. Narayanasamy had warned that our work permits might
take a week, even two, suggesting that we "stay put" at our
hotel until they were issued. We agreed, though we had already
been living at our seedy hotel for two weeks by then, two long
weeks during which a man of indeterminate age wearing only
a pair of shorts lay upon a plastic chaise lounge in the hallway
just outside our door, groaning day and night, no doubt from
the pain caused by the gaping wound that ran from one of his
nipples to his navel. Although we never saw anyone attending
to him, we knew that somebody was because some days the
wound was concealed by an unskillfully applied bandage while
other days it was exposed, flies gathering at it like poor people
lined up along a river to bathe.

We had no idea what had happened to the man and did
not ask, primarily because nobody had even acknowledged
the man's presence to us, but the wound resembled a knife cut,
approximately eight inches long and jagged with a suggestion
of violence to it, though we understood that the shabbiness of
the hotel, combined with the fact that blood still seeped from
the wound, contributed to this effect. Since he was directly outside our door and prone to groaning, particularly at night, we
often found it difficult to sleep, but it was unthinkable that we
ask him to groan less, to keep his misery to himself. There was
also the issue of whether to greet him as we paused to lock or
unlock our door. Julia felt that we should, that a hello was in
order; otherwise, it was like treating him as though he were
invisible, dead in fact, but as I prefer to pass my own illnesses
without interference, I maintained that we should not ask him

to engage in unnecessary politenesses when he so obviously needed his energy for mending. Of course, this quickly became an argument not about the wounded man but about me, or, more specifically, about what Julia termed my stubborn disbelief in the world's ability to maintain a position at odds with my own, which I felt was overstating the case.

The day after we were hired, a Saturday, we walked out toward the sea along a road cramped with vehicles that blew sand and oily exhaust into our faces. We returned to our room filthy and went together into our little bathroom, which was equipped with a traditional *mandi,* a large, water-filled tank from which one scooped water for bathing. There, we stripped down, laughing and lathering ourselves and each other and then shrieking at the water's coolness, welcome but startling nonetheless. We felt amazingly clean afterward and lay on the bed, naked and wet, enjoying the flutter of the fan across our bodies, our hands touching.

We could hear the wounded man shifting repeatedly on his chaise lounge, the fact that he was moving so much suggesting that he felt stronger, perhaps even bored, and while the possibility of this cheered us greatly, for we had actually pondered what to do if we rose one morning to find him dead, there was something unsettling about the sound of his skin ripping away from the vinyl each time he moved. The thought began to creep into each of our heads that he was not feeling better at all but was instead flailing out in desperation against the narrowly defined, joyless space he now occupied. Furthermore, we worried that we had caused his agitation, that the sounds of pleasure we made as we bathed had led to his sudden despair. For the first time, we felt that the man was aware of us, even worse, that he had been aware of us all along, an intimacy that was too much to bear. It was ironic, for we had put up with so much—the sight of him, bloody and damaged, as we came and went, the groaning throughout the night—but somehow this, the feeling that our pleasure intensified his pain, this had overwhelmed us, and so we packed our bags, paused one last time over the wounded man, who was snoring lightly, and escaped down the street to the Kwee Hang Hotel, which was more expensive by far but did not involve a wounded man outside our door.

At the Kwee Hang Hotel, the long, sunny foyer was mopped twice daily, our toilet paper was monitored, and when we returned each night, the bathroom smelled pleasantly medicinal and the beds stood neatly made with sheets that bore the fresh smell of a dryer. The only thing that we had to complain about really was that the owner and his son sat for hours behind a desk at the end of this long, sunny foyer with their eyes glued to the television, across which ran the ticker tape information for the Malaysian stock exchange during the day and international exchanges during the night, but even this we could not really form a complaint around, for they kept the sound muted, day and night, making, only occasionally, some sort of quiet comment to each other, a low chuckle of pleasure or a disgusted *"ay-yoh"* when things presumably had not gone their way. Of course, it made no sense for us to be paying by the day an amount that, each month, added up to half our salaries. Even the old man and his son began to tell us as much. "Find an apartment and stop paying like tourists," they said, but week after week, our visas were delayed, a state of affairs that we protested in only the most cursory fashion, for we were content.

Still, one feature of the room did bother us (though to call it a feature is misleading, for *feature* implies something added to make life more pleasant for hotel guests, rather than less): there existed, on the inside of the wardrobe door, a crudely rendered drawing of two penises, both erect and facing each other as though, I could not help but think, they were about to duel. It had been made with a thick-tipped black marker, hastily, so that one of the penises had unevenly sized scrota and black slashes of hair while the other was symmetrical but hairless. Beneath the picture, in a more controlled hand, somebody—I assumed the artist—had written: "I am waiting every night on the footbridge." Since we generally opened only the left door and the drawing was on the right, we did not discover it for weeks, but once we had, we began to feel different about the room, which we now understood to have a history, a life that was separate from us, yet not entirely. It sounds naive to say that we had never considered this before, for it was a hotel after all, but until then, we had never stopped to imagine that things had been said and done in this room, upon these beds, prior to our arrival. Worse, I began to feel sheepish around the father and son, the drawing inserting itself into the conversation each time I spoke to them about something as ordinary as getting an extra towel or was warned that the stairs were wet.

We knew the referred-to footbridge, of course. From it, we had first spotted Mr. Mani's school, and we crossed it often as we made our way to and from our favorite food stalls. But once we had learned of its secret, we found ourselves increasingly drawn there, particularly at night, when a handful of men gathered and spread out across it, maintaining their posts as vigilantly and nervously as sentries. Each time we climbed the stairs, they turned toward us, their faces momentarily hopeful, hungry for something that we could not provide. Still, we felt comfortable there among men who regarded us with so little interest, and as we crossed, I sometimes glanced surreptitiously at a face and wondered what the man was thinking, wondered whether he had ever been in love.

Descending the steps of the footbridge one evening, we

noticed that the light in Mr. Mani's office was on and decided to pay him a visit, a long overdue visit, for although we had been teaching at the college some two months, we had not yet thanked Mr. Mani for securing us the positions. It was after eight, but the outer door was unlocked, and we went in calling his name. We found him reclining on an unmade cot that was wedged into one corner of his tiny office, whiskey bottle in hand.

"My American ladies," he announced, smiling his toothless smile and struggling like an overturned cockroach to sit up. "Kindly join me for a nightcap." He thrust the bottle toward us, tipping forward with the weight of it.

"Perhaps we should return another time," I said, but he looked hurt at the suggestion and, focusing deeply, stood and wobbled to his desk.

"Please, have a seat," he said, gesturing at the cot.

The room, I had noticed as we entered, possessed a rank odor, attributable, I thought, to its smallness and to the fact that its one window was closed. It was the sort of smell to which one adjusted quickly, unlike the overwhelming stench that rose up, surrounding us, as we settled on the cot, its dominant feature sourness, sour in the way of sheets that have been sweated in for nights on end and never washed, and beneath this, a second-ary stink, a unique blend that included but was not limited to the following: clove cigarettes, spices, whiskey, unwashed feet, urine, and moldy books. Next to me, Julia gagged, covering it with a cough, and I, holding my breath so that my voice came out nasally, said, "We've come to thank you for your help."

"I'm happy to be of service," said Mani, looking, in fact, about to cry.

"Mr. Mani, are you living here?" I asked.

"Yes," he replied mournfully. "My Queen has banned me from our dwelling. My clothes and the bed were delivered two months ago, shortly after the splendid evening the three of us spent together. I have not seen her since. Of course, she still sends my meals twice daily, but while I know that her hands prepared them, it is not the same."

"But why?" I asked.

He shrugged. "I cannot explain to you the mind of a woman," he said, as though Julia and I were not women, and then he took a small sip from his bottle. "Ladies, do you know the story of the British man and the snake? It is a famous Malaysian tale." When we shook our heads, he gathered himself up and said, "Then I shall tell you, but be warned: it is a story about love." I acknowledged this with a nod.

"A British man," he began, "lived on his tea plantation up in the highlands, all alone save for the servants who attended to his fairly simple needs. Each afternoon, he took a lengthy walk, disappearing with his hat and walking stick for hours, going where and doing what, no one knew. This remained his habit for many years.

"Eventually, he became engaged, but just two days before the wedding was to transpire, the man went out for his walk and did not return. A search party was formed. He was found the next morning, his legs protruding from the mouth of a large snake, both of them dead by the time that this strange union was discovered. The snake had to be hacked apart with machetes in order to extricate the man's body. Later, it was determined that the man had died of asphyxiation, which meant that the snake had attempted to swallow him while he was still alive."

"Should we be worried about snakes, Mr. Mani?" asked Julia, speaking for the first time. She was afraid of snakes, even more so because a pair of paramedics with whom we had chatted soon after arriving told us that they spent an inordinate amount of time removing snakes from houses.

"No, ladies, you are missing the point. I mean, yes, the snake's behavior is the point, but only because it is highly unusual. And so there is no way to explain it, as any Malaysian will tell you, except that the snake was in love with the man, and—"

"In love?" I interrupted.

"Yes," Mr. Mani replied firmly. "They were in love with each other, and that day the man had finally come clean—he had informed the snake of his impending marriage. But the snake could not bear the news, and so . . ." He shrugged, brought his hands together as though to pray, and then thrust them outward, away from each other, away from himself. "That is jealousy, you see. Everything destroyed."

"And you believe this also, Mr. Mani?" I asked, though I could see that he did.

Mr. Mani regarded us for a moment. "Well," he said at last, "with love, there are always two: there is the snake who devours, and there is the one who cooperates by placing his head inside the snake's mouth."

The next afternoon as we were leaving the school, Miss Kumar, who handled payroll, approached us. "I hear that you require an apartment," she whispered. "I know one. Cheap. Not too big. It belongs to my sister-in-law."

This, we knew, was Mr. Mani's doing, for as we had stood to leave the night before, he had requested our address and, upon learning that we still lived in a hotel, shook his head in horror. "It is not right, and it is not proper," he said repeatedly as I explained about the visas, and then, "I am surprised by my old friend Narayanasamy."

We recognized immediately the building that Miss Kumar stopped in front of: Nine-Story Building, which we had passed

numerous times, commenting on how much taller it was than
everything around it and how this made it seem awkward and
defenseless, like a young girl who had shot up much faster than
her classmates. We entered near the courtyard, a large asphalt
area around which rose the four sections that collectively made
up Nine-Story Building and which Miss Kumar herded us past,
saying, "Please, my sister-in-law is waiting." But she was not
waiting, and we stood outside the apartment for ten minutes
until she stepped off the elevator at a trot, speaking Tamil rapidly into a cell phone. She was, in every way, a hurried woman,
and when she stooped to unlock the door, knees bent primly,
phone wedged against her ear with an upraised shoulder,
and wiggled her fingers impatiently, we took on her sense of
urgency, which is to say that we found ourselves the tenants
of a dark, one-bedroom, squat-toilet apartment on the fourth
floor of Nine-Story Building, closer to the bottom than the top,
which was apparently considered desirable, for she mentioned
it repeatedly.

Our colleagues considered our move to Nine-Story Building strange, though perhaps no stranger than the fact that we
had continued to live in a hotel for months, and in the weeks
that followed, they inquired frequently about our new lodg-
ings. When we answered, "Everything is fine," they appeared
skeptical, and so we began complaining about the elevator,
which smelled of urine masked by curry and made noises suggesting that it was not up to the task of carrying passengers up
and down day after day. Soon we began using the stairs, which
we generally had to ourselves because the other tenants seemed
not to mind the elevator's strange noises, or minded more the
certainty of the exertion that the stairs required than the mere
possibilities suggested by the noises, and so we went back to
answering that everything was fine, dismissing our colleagues'

interest as yet another example of the unsolicited attention that we received in Malacca, where we seemed to be the only Westerners in residence.

In fact, as we walked around town, people whom we had never met called out, "Hello, Miss Raffles College," greeting us both in this same way. We were regarded as the American spinsters, teachers so devoted to our work that it had rendered us sexless, left us married to the school. We were thought of in this way because we were strict with healthy expectations—that students study and not cheat, that they arrive on time, that they not take on the disaffected pose that teenagers find so appealing—but also, I suspect, because we were women without men.

As spinsters, we were thought to possess a certain prudishness, a notion that was clearly behind the request that Mr. Narayanasamy made of us one day after summoning us to his office. "We have a grave situation requiring our expeditious attention," he began, gesturing grandly at the produce market visible from the window to the left of his desk. "That is the produce market," he said, assuming that American spinsters would be unfamiliar with such a dirty, chaotic place, though in fact we stopped there often to buy vegetables and practice our Malay because the vendors rarely tried to cheat us.

"I have just this morning received an upsetting visit from several of the vendors. It seems that two of our students have been observed holding hands and even"—he cleared his throat—"kissing." He looked at us apologetically, as though announcing that we would not be receiving raises, and we nodded because we knew the couple to whom he referred.

"You must speak to them," he declared, slapping his hand down on his desk.

"And tell them what?" Julia asked.

"Tell them that they must stop," he explained in a reasonable tone. "Tell them that they are discrediting the school, their families, and themselves."

"But they're adults," Julia said.

"Very well," said Mr. Narayanasamy, looking back and forth between the two of us. "Then I shall speak to them, though I too am busy. Still, it is my duty to attend to the duties for which others lack time." He reached up as though to tighten his tie, but the knot already sat snugly against his throat, and Julia and I departed, allowing our refusal to stand as an issue of time constraints.

"You let me do all the talking," said Julia several minutes later as we sat outside a café, waiting for our orange juice to arrive. We had become a bit obsessed with orange juice, for no matter how carefully we stressed that we did not want sugar, we had yet to receive juice that met this simple specification. "You made me seem like the unreasonable one."

I knew that Julia hated to appear unreasonable, and so I considered apologizing. "Care to bet on the sugar?" I said instead, hoping to redirect her ire, to remind her that I was an ally, at least when it came to sugar.

The waitress, a young Malay woman with a prominent black tooth, appeared balancing two very full glasses of orange juice on a tray. As she drew near, she seemed to lose speed, as though she sensed the depth of our thirst and was overwhelmed by the power she held to alleviate it, finally stopping altogether and resting the tray on the back of a nearby chair. As we watched, she picked up one of the glasses and took a sip before placing it back on the tray and continuing toward us. Smiling, she set the sipped-from glass in front of me, the untouched one in front of Julia.

"Excuse me," I said politely. "I believe you drank from my glass."

She smiled at me. "Is fine," she replied and departed gracefully.

"What did she mean by that?" I asked Julia. "Did she mean, 'Yes, I did drink from your glass and the fact that I did so is fine,' or did she simply mean that the juice is fine? As in, 'I took a sip of your juice just to make sure, and it's fine.'"

We studied the juices for a moment. I knew that Julia wanted to drink hers, and why shouldn't she? Nobody had sipped from her glass.

"Well," I said peevishly. "Go ahead."

"Maybe she was just smelling it," she suggested once she had taken two very long drinks.

"Smelling it?" I said.

"Yes, you know. Just sniffing it."

"You saw her drink from it."

"Yes, she definitely drank from it," she agreed, changing tack. "Though I don't see what the big deal is."

I considered the implications of this last statement—considered it, that is, within the context of our relationship. Julia and I had been together for two years, not a lifetime, granted, but it was, I believed, a *sufficient* length of time. She knew things about me: that I could not tolerate the smell of fish in the morning; that I felt suffocated at being told the details of other people's bodily functions; that I abhorred public nose picking, both the studied sort in which some of my students engaged and the fast poking at which I always seemed to catch people on buses or in line. Then, too, there was the matter of what she jokingly referred to as "the zones," which, simply put, are the areas of the body that I do not care to have touched or to see touched on others or, quite frankly, to even hear discussed. During my last checkup just before we left for Malaysia, my doctor nonchalantly pressed her hands to my abdomen, coming far too close to my navel, which, along with my neck, is a primary zone.

"Could you please not brush against my navel?" I had said, perhaps a bit sharply.

"Your navel?" she replied, pulling back as though I had accused her of biting.

"Yes," I said. "It unsettles me." I felt that *unsettles* was a perfectly appropriate word for the situation, precise enough in connotation to convey my displeasure, but cryptic enough to save me from feeling foolish, assuming that she had the good manners not to press the issue, which she did not.

"How strange," she replied, pausing to regard me. Then, her hands drawn to her own navel, she began to massage it. "The navel, you know, is the final remaining symbol of our connection to our mothers, a reminder of our past dependence." Her rubbing intensified, and I suspected that she might be newly pregnant.

"Please," I said stiffly. "I would prefer that you not touch your navel in my presence. In fact, I would prefer that we not even discuss navels."

When I arrived home that afternoon, I told Julia about the encounter, huffily, in a way that suggested that the doctor had been intentionally trying to goad me. She had been sympathetic, but that night at dinner, she had tentatively broached the subject again, her tone suggesting that she found my reaction perplexing, even perturbing, and though I concealed my dismay, I could not help but recall the early days of our relationship, when she had stroked my brow encouragingly as I related the story of the wood tick that had worked its way deep into my navel when I was eight.

"The big deal," I replied, speaking loudly, which Julia hates, "the big deal is that this is my juice." That night, as I lay in bed,

Julia asleep next to me, it occurred to me that I did not even know whether the juice had come with sugar or without.

The following Saturday, Julia and I encountered Malik on the footbridge. I was surprised to see him there, though not surprised at what his presence meant. He was wearing a pair of large white pants that flapped like sails in the evening breeze and, as usual, a purple shirt. As we passed him, he looked away, thus acknowledging my presence, and I, in deference to his wishes as well as bridge etiquette, said nothing.

"Poor fellow," Julia remarked as we descended the steps at the other end.

"It does not justify his behavior," I said vehemently, for I sensed something in her tone, particularly in her use of the word *fellow,* which made Malik seem hapless, free of guile.

The next morning, Sunday, we were awakened early by the sounds of screaming, and when we dressed quickly and stepped out of our apartment, we found our neighbors gathered on the walkway outside, pressed against the railing that curved around the courtyard, like theater patrons looking down from their box seats. As we wiggled our way in next to them, we saw that all around Nine-Story Building, the tenants stood in similar rows, everyone peering downward, at where a body lay in the court-yard below, facedown, arms out, like a doll flung aside by a bored child.

"But this is becoming too much," complained our neighbor Prahkash. "Why must they always come here to do themselves in? I pay the rent, not they. We should begin charging admission." He spit over the rail, and I watched the drop fall and disappear.

The next day, we read in the newspaper that the victim was a Chinese man in his late forties who had just returned from a gambling trip to Australia, where he had lost the equivalent of fifty thousand U.S. dollars, a sum of money that it had taken his family five years to save. They were preparing to start a business, a karaoke restaurant, and the man, impatient to begin, had flown to Sydney, lost everything at the blackjack tables, and returned to Malaysia broke, taking a taxi from the airport in Kuala Lumpur back to Malacca. He was dropped at the night market, where he drank a cup of coffee at one of the stalls, leaving his suitcase behind when he departed. After seeing the man's picture in the paper the next day, the stall owner had announced that he had the man's suitcase, the suitcase that had, presumably, been used to tote the fifty thousand dollars on its one-way journey. The story of the abandoned suitcase had appeared as a separate article, next to a picture of the stall owner holding it aloft.

"Did you see the suitcase in the newspaper?" a neighbor inquired several days later as Julia and I passed her in the hall.

"Yes. The poor man," I replied sourly. "Misplaced his suitcase as well."

She paused and then, not unkindly, said, "Ours is the only building tall enough. It can't be helped, you see." She was trying to prepare me, letting me know that this was not an anomaly, but perhaps I looked puzzled or in need of further convincing, for she said it again, with the same air of resignation that tenants used to discuss the smell of urine in the elevator: ours was the only building tall enough—she paused—tall enough to ensure success. That was the word she used—*success*—from which I understood that somebody who jumped and lived would also have to suffer the humiliation of failure.

Julia said nothing during this exchange, but after we closed our door, she turned to me angrily and said, "Why do you have to act that way?"

"What way?" I asked, feigning innocence.

"Like you're the only one who cares what happened to that man. Like she's a jerk for even talking about him."

"She was not talking about him," I replied. "She was talking about his suitcase."

"People are never just talking about a suitcase," Julia said quietly.

That night, she did not come into our bedroom to sleep, which was fine with me, as I found sleeping alone preferable in the tropical heat, though I had not mentioned this to Julia because it seemed imprudent to discuss anything related to our bed at that particular moment. There is a term that lesbians use—*bed death*—to describe what had already begun happening long before Julia took the bigger step of physically removing herself from our bed. In fact, at the risk of sounding confessional, a tendency that I despise, I'll admit that we had not actually touched in any meaningful way since the afternoon that we bathed together at the seedy hotel. That this kind of thing occurred with enough frequency among lesbians to have acquired its own terminology in no way made me feel better. If anything, it made me feel worse, for I dislike contributing in any way to the affirmation of stereotypes.

Then, on the second Friday after she stopped sleeping in our bed, an arrangement that had continued without discussion, I was returning from Mahkota Parade with groceries when I ran into three students. "We saw Miss Julia at the bus station," announced Paul, an amiable boy with a slightly misshapen head. This happened often, people reporting to us on the other's activities and even our own, as though we might have forgotten that we had eaten barbecued eel at a stall near the water the night before.

"Oh?" I replied, striving for a nonchalant *oh* rather than one that indicated surprise or begged for elaboration.

"Is she going back?" Paul asked, by which he meant leaving.

"Yes," I said without hesitation, knowing it to be true, for, as Paul spoke, I had the sense that I was simply being reminded of something that had already happened.

Her clothing and computer were gone, but so too were the smaller, everyday pieces of her life: the earplugs she kept beneath her pillow, the biography of Indira Gandhi that she was halfway through, the photo of her great-grandmother Ragnilde with her long hair puddled on the floor. In fact, their absence hurt more, for it suggested a plan, a methodical progression toward that moment when she boarded the bus with her carefully packed bags, leaving nothing behind— not even, it turned out, a note, which meant that she had left without any sort of goodbye, that she had considered the silence that reigned between us those last few weeks a sufficient coda. I sat on the bed and tried to determine the exact moment her decision had been made, when she had thought to herself, "Enough," but I could not, for it seemed to me a bit like trying to pinpoint the exact sip with which one had become drunk.

Eventually—hours later I suppose, for it had grown dark outside—I realized that I was hungry and, with no desire to cook the food that I had purchased for the two of us that afternoon, decided to visit our favorite stall, where we had often whiled away the cool evenings eating noodles and potato leaves and, occasionally, a few orders of dim sum. I knew, also, that the owner would ask about Julia's absence and that this would afford me the opportunity to begin adjusting to the question and perfecting a response.

I locked our apartment door, but as I turned toward the stairwell out of habit, I felt a heaviness in my legs and considered taking the elevator. If Julia had been there, she would have said, "We are *not* taking the elevator," and I would have felt obligated to make a small stand in favor of it, but Julia was not there, which meant that the decision was mine: if I took the stairs, it would be as though Julia still held sway, but if I took the elevator, it would seem too deliberate, a reaction against her, particularly as I hated the elevator as much as she. As I stood debating in the poorly lit doorway of the stairwell, there came from farther up the stairs a heavy thudding sound. I imagined some large, hungry beast making its way down the steps toward me, for boundaries between inside and out did not always exist in Malaysia, and I shrank back, prepared to flee.

A moment later, Malik appeared, lumbering onto the landing where I stood. My first, naive reaction was to wonder whom he had been visiting there in Nine-Story Building, and my next, to marvel that he, whose body literally reeked of lethargy, had chosen the stairs. He paused on the landing, catching his breath in wet, heaving gasps, and then turned, looking back over his shoulder like a hunted creature. His face was streaked with tears and snot and displayed neither the coyness nor the mocking obsequiousness that I had come to expect; even his jowls, those quivering, disdainful jowls, sagged more than usual. In that instant, of course, I understood what had brought Malik to Nine-Story Building, the realization crashing down on me with all the weight of Malik himself. From my hiding place, I looked on as he removed a large, dirty handkerchief from his pocket and cleaned his face. Then, keeping a distance between us, I followed him down the four flights of stairs and out onto the busy night street. Julia would have insisted on something more, but Julia was no longer there, and so I watched Malik shuffle off down the sidewalk before I turned in the opposite direction, joining the flow of people exhausted from being out in the world all day who were finally heading home to their beds.

Talking Fowl with My Father

I. TURKEY: A CIRCULAR ARGUMENT

My father wants to know what I had for lunch today. I haven't called in months, but this is what interests him.

"I had a turkey sandwich," I say.

"Turkey," he says with clear disgust. Last year, my father's doctor gave him a list of safe foods, foods recommended for someone in my father's condition. Turkey was high on the list. My father has never liked turkey, except at Thanksgiving, and only then because it comes with all sorts of things that he does like—fatty skin swaddled in strips of bacon, mashed potatoes, gravy, rolls and butter, ham (yes, ham). My father has always managed to treat turkey as the annoying but harmless relative who shows up once a year on the holiday, but now, now turkey has become my father's enemy.

Of course, he has numerous reasons for not liking turkey, first among them being that he likes beef. And while this might not seem like a reason, it is what my father tells me whenever I ask him why he doesn't like turkey.

"Because I like beef," he says.

"It's not an either/or question," I say. "It's like salt and pepper. You can like both of them. Now, if turkey and beef are sitting in a room alone and someone says that you can pick only one thing from the room, okay. Then, it's true—you can have turkey or you can have beef. But this isn't like that." Geraldine and I just spent our tenth anniversary in Greece, two blissful weeks walking where Plato and Socrates once walked, both of us nearly in tears at the thought of it, and here I am, one month later, having this conversation.

Reason number two: because it is on his list.

Reason number three: because my baby brother, whom he considers henpecked, eats turkey in some guise or other for dinner every night, or so my father claims. The one time that Geraldine and I visited my brother and his wife at their overly childproofed house in a suburb of the Twin Cities, the four of us and their five children ate lunch together (turkey sloppy joes, for the record) while discussing the pros and cons of my brother's retirement plan. As he spoke, he stared at Geraldine as though he couldn't quite figure out who she was or how she had come to be sitting at his wood veneer table. His wife, whom I was meeting for the first and what would turn out to be the only time, said very little during the meal, but when I reached for the water pitcher, she noticed my raggedy fingernails and broke her silence to announce bitterly that my brother chewed not just his fingernails but his toenails as well, addressing her complaint specifically to me, as though this were some sort of Lindquist family conspiracy for which I was equally answerable.

Geraldine and I flew back to San Francisco that evening, and when I called my father several weeks later to tell him that we had made it home safely, the first thing he wanted to know was what my sister-in-law had served for lunch. "Sloppy joes," I told him, and there was a short pause of disappointment before my father, who has never cooked anything in his life, replied triumphantly, "I'll bet they were turkey. You know, all she gives him is turkey."

It is worth noting that the two parts of my father's argument regarding the state of my brother's diet and marriage are interchangeable, that both can (and do) function as Conclusion or Premise, depending on what we are arguing about—whether my father is trying to convince me that my brother does eat turkey every day or that he is, indeed, henpecked.

Argument A: *My brother is henpecked because he eats turkey every day.*

In this argument, my father is demonstrating that my brother is henpecked, and so the daily eating of turkey becomes his first (and only) premise, one that he nonetheless shores up amply: "Turkey breasts, burgers, chili, lasagna. Everything's turkey with her."

Argument B: *Because my brother is henpecked, he eats turkey every day.*

Occasionally, one of us (usually me but sometimes my sister) will be foolish enough to suggest that our brother does not eat turkey every single day. My father, in this case, cites as proof the fact that my brother is henpecked, his argument succinct and unshakable: "Of course he does. She doesn't even let him wipe his own ass."

II. BROASTED CHICKEN: A STUDY IN SEMANTICS

"The café in Fentonville has two broasted-chicken specials," my father begins the conversation, not bothering with more standard pleasantries. "Mashed potatoes, a roll with butter, gravy, some kind of vegetable or other." It is as though he is reading love poetry over the phone, his voice greedy and helpless.

I try to recall what broasted chicken is, how it differs from roasted chicken, what the addition of the *b* actually means, but the word has been dropped into the conversation with such ease that I know I cannot ask him to explain. "Broasted chicken," he would reply automatically, the words so familiar to him that they are their own definition. Then, after the slightest pause, he would say it again, "Broasted chicken," asserting the words in a way that means both "You never visit" and "What kind of world do you live in?" It is true that I visit infrequently, once every three or four years, just as it is true that I live in a world devoid of broasted chicken, which is not to say that there are no broasted chickens in San Francisco. Of course there are. There would have to be.

Sometimes, when I have not called my father in a particularly long time, he will begin the conversation by announcing, "A lot has changed." Then, he will proceed to fill me in on events that happened years ago as a way of making clear my neglectfulness. "Your sister got married," he will say, though my sister has been married for seven years and has two boys, odd little fellows who refuse to speak to me on the telephone because they are busy cutting. Each boy has his own cutting box, a cigar box in which he keeps a pair of blunt-ended scissors and his most recent clippings, advertisements for cereal and batteries as well as carefully snipped photos of dead ducks and elk from his father's hunting magazines. When I ask to speak to them, my sister holds out the receiver, and I hear Trevor, who just turned six, saying, "Tell her to call when we're not cutting."

"All they do is cut," my father complains. My sister has told me that they are afraid of my father, afraid of his largeness, of the way that his feet seem poured into his shoes, the flesh straining against the laces so that they can no longer be tied. They are afraid of the way that he falls asleep talking and then awakens with a start a moment later, screaming, "What?" when they have said nothing, because anger has become his most immediate response.

"I doubt you'd even recognize this place," my father says at other times, referring to Morton, the town where I grew up, the town where he has always lived, except for a brief period just after high school when the army borrowed him. This was in 1945, at the very end of the war, which was over before he got any farther away than Florida, but something about this experience put him off the world, unnerved him so much that he forgot about college and went immediately back to Morton, picking up where he had left off, helping my grandfather run his hardware store and eventually taking it over himself. He continued to read, preferring characters to actual people, and maintained an extensive library, which he housed in our basement, choosing the only room that was windowless, as though having so many books were something best kept secret. Still, the world outside worked its way in, entering through small fissures in the house's foundation that grew larger over time, filling our basement with water. Spring was particularly insidious, for as the snow outside slowly melted, the water level rose within, gradually, as though a tap had been turned on somewhere within the bowels of the house, a tap that none of us could locate, left open to a small but unstoppable trickle.

For many years, it was our job—my siblings' and mine—to mop up the standing water, but as we got older, we procrastinated a bit more each time until finally our parents grew tired of our laziness, tired of their own nagging, and laid down thick carpeting throughout the entire basement, a cheap, urine-colored shag that they said would act as a giant sponge, and in this way, our basement was turned over to the mold. Throughout my childhood, I liked my father's library better than any other room in the house, liked the moldy smell of books that hung in the air and clung to my clothing. In fact, I considered this the natural odor of books and wondered, each time I checked out a book from the school library, what they had done wrong that caused their books to smell as they did—of paper and ink and the sweatiness of children's hands.

My father proceeds to give me an oral tour of Morton over the phone, block by block, resident by resident, as though proving my absence to me. "We've got Amish now," he tells me. "Dan Klimek's got them working out at the cardboard plant he put in just east of town." But when I ask who Dan Klimek is, my father uses the voice that he would use to explain broasted chicken to me if I were foolish enough to ask. "Dan Klimek. Danny Klimek. Of course you know Danny Klimek," he says, his voice startled and angry, the syllables like waves beating frantically against the shore. This is a metaphor that would make no sense to my father, for he has lived his life surrounded by lakes and ponds, placid bodies of water whose waves do not beat or pound or crash but rather lap gently at the shore, a steady, soothing sound like that of a cat drinking milk.

Somehow, almost unintentionally, I became a teacher, a profession of which my father greatly disapproves, considering it a waste of my talents and, on some level, suspect. "Teachers and preachers," he is fond of saying, "never pay their bills." For several years I taught high school English, which is how I met Geraldine, but eventually I grew tired of counting my successes in such meager ways, and so I quit and began instead to teach English to adults, to foreigners who need me and thus nod patiently when I require that they answer "How are you?" with "Well," even though out in the real world people are quick to correct them, explaining, "You need to say *good*. *Well* just sounds like you're kind of depressed."

I begin class each Monday morning with a vocabulary quiz,

testing them on words that we have encountered over the semester and compiled into a list, adding to it daily and occasionally winnowing it down, letting drop those words and expressions that might have meant something to them back home, where they were pilots and geneticists and science teachers, but contribute nothing to their lives here. They are not lazy people, my students, but on Monday mornings, overwhelmed by the week ahead after a weekend spent delivering pizzas and cleaning houses, they become lazy. They become lazy, and in their laziness, they write things like *"Threaten* is to make a threat" and "A *shoplifter* is someone who shoplifts," knowing, of course, that I will mark their answers wrong, that I will write in the margins next to them: "A word cannot be used to define itself."

III. THE PHEASANT AS OVERT SYMBOL

My father wants to FedEx me a pheasant.

"A pheasant?" I say. "I doubt that FedEx delivers poultry."

"Pheasants aren't poultry," he corrects me. "English teachers should know such things. They're fowl, but they are not poultry. Poultry is domestic. I shot this bird myself out near the pond on Lekander's farm."

For the last year, according to my sister, my father has been using a broom as a cane, bristles up, leaning heavily as he goes from bedroom to kitchen, from kitchen to bathroom. I am fairly sure that this is the first broom he has ever held in his life. This is the same man, after all, whose mother washed his hair for him until he was forty, which is when he married my mother and she took over the task.

"When?" I ask, keeping my voice casual. "When did you shoot it?"

"How would I know when I shot it?" he replies impatiently.

"Well, when was the last time that you hunted?" I ask, feigning ignorance. I know the answer to this, know that he has not hunted in five years because my brother-in-law, Mike, who used to take my father hunting, stopped hunting five years ago after his brother, while looking up and tracking a flock of mallards with his eyes, tripped over a rock and discharged his gun into Mike's buttocks. The doctors were able to extricate all of the shot, but for weeks sitting had been uncomfortable if not downright painful, which meant that Mike had also had to endure the embarrassment of explaining to his clients why he suddenly preferred to stand during sales calls.

Mike is a fertilizer salesman in Fargo, North Dakota, a description that, here in San Francisco, sounds like the setup for a joke; but in Fargo, where he and my sister really do live and where he really does sell fertilizer, having a sister-in-law who lives in San Francisco with her girlfriend is considered just as funny. I like my brother-in-law, whom I have met only twice, both times during visits that Geraldine and I made to Fargo. The first time, we shook hands and he said that I was like a plague of locusts, visiting once every seven years. I laughed because it was funny and sort of true, wondering whether the allusion was inspired by religion or profession. I suspected the latter: locust plagues struck me as the sort of thing that a fertilizer salesman from North Dakota would know about.

"Locusts are actually the only invertebrates considered kosher," said Geraldine, addressing both of us, though she and Mike had not yet been introduced.

"Really?" I said, and then, "Mike, this is Geraldine." They nodded at each other in a decidedly Midwestern way, though Geraldine is anything but Midwestern.

"Yes, not all species of course," she continued, her tone turning cautionary. "Actually, I believe that only the Yemeni Jews still know how to determine which species are kosher."

"Are you Jewish?" Mike asked Geraldine, who, despite the deceptive first name, is Jewish, though Jewish strictly in the "isn't it interesting that locusts are kosher?" sense.

"Yes," she replied. "Culturally speaking." Mike nodded deeply as though this were a distinction of relevance in Fargo, North Dakota.

Later that afternoon, as we sat playing with the boys, my sister turned to Geraldine and said, "I hear you're Jewish."

"News travels fast," I said.

"Jewish?" said Mike's mother, who was also visiting for the day, though in her case, from just sixty miles away, a town called Florence, which is where Mike grew up. Florence, North Dakota, my sister had informed me, was even smaller than Morton, about a third the size, which put the population at around seventy people, two of whom were sitting here in front of me. There was something vaguely impressive about this.

"You know about the Holocaust?" Mike's mother said. I could see that Geraldine was bothered by this question, and she remained so even later when I explained to her what I knew to be the truth: it wasn't that Mike's mother believed Geraldine might actually be unaware of the Holocaust, but rather that she was establishing her own awareness, broaching the subject the way that we are taught to where I come from—by turning knowledge into a question. Of course, only I could tell that Geraldine was annoyed, and when she answered, her voice was gentle, reassuring. Yes, she told Mike's mother, she did know about the Holocaust, and Mike's mother nodded, pressing the back of her fork tines against the crumbs of her rhubarb cake. "It was a terrible thing," she said.

* * *

The next time Geraldine and I visited my sister and brother-in-law, we flew into Minneapolis and drove west along I-94 to Fargo, stopping in Morton to pick up my father, who alternated between ignoring Geraldine completely and ceremoniously reciting things for us in Swedish—poems and songs and jokes, which he made no attempt to translate, though he did chuckle to let us know when something was funny. My father is entirely Swedish, a fact that gives him enormous pleasure. We, his children, are *mixed* because my mother was half-Norwegian. "The Norwegians have always been arrogant," my father reminded us frequently when we were young, a comment that he generally made out of the blue. Once, sighing heavily, he had added, "In my day, we buried the Norwegians and Swedes in separate cemeteries." ("You see," Geraldine said, laughing, when I related this to her. "There's no hope for the world. Even the Swedes and Norwegians can't get along.")

He had spoken Swedish as a boy, forgotten it, and then relearned it almost fifty years later from a retired Swedish professor who settled on one of the lakes near Morton and occasionally came into my father's hardware store to buy things that my father considered "odd," by which he meant odd for a man to buy—the little skewers that are set into the ends of hot corncobs, Mason jars, plastic sunflowers that spin frantically in the wind. Once, early on, the professor had come in wearing a button that said "N.O.W.," and my father had asked him, "Now what?" I was in graduate school at the time, living far away in Colorado, and when my father related this story to me, I could tell, even over the phone, that he was disappointed I did not laugh. I wanted to, but I felt that it was dangerous to encourage my father in such ways.

"It's a club of some sort," my father told me. "A club for women."

"Anyone can join," I said. "It's the National Organization for Women."

"Yes," my father said. "For women."

"He's not married," he continued a moment later. "Never has been." I understood my father's point, the suspicion that surrounded men and women of a certain age who had never married. My father had remained single until forty, and sometimes I thought that he had married my mother simply to escape being the object of gossip and speculation. In fact, I was hard-pressed to discover any other reason, for my parents had been ill suited for each other, a state of affairs foreshadowed on their first date, when my father lent my mother a book to read so that they would have something to discuss on their second. My mother had returned the book to him unread, claiming that she could tell from the cover, which was blue, that the book was not going to be about anything.

My father had shown me the book once, a heavy tome called *Gus the Great*. He had read it and *The Great Gatsby* one after the other and, for this reason (and perhaps because both titles included *Great*), always thought of them together, though he had much preferred the former. When I asked him what *Gus the Great* was about, he said that it had to do with the circus. "The circus?" I replied. I had never known my father to have any interest in the circus. "Yes, but that's not what it's about," he said. "Not really. Anyway, it's much funnier than that Gatsby book." Later, when I finally read *Gatsby,* I was puzzled by this comment, for there was no way to think that Fitzgerald had been attempting humor, but I eventually realized that my father was simply saying something about himself, about what he had needed in his life at that time.

* * *

Ten years ago, I spent a week with my father shortly after my mother died. Geraldine and I had just met a few months earlier, and we spoke daily by phone. This was stressful, for it forced me to juggle two conflicting emotions: the elation I felt when I picked up the telephone and heard her voice, and the guilt I felt at not hiding it better. Furthermore, we were firmly in the getting-to-know-each-other stage, yet I never felt truly like myself in my parents' house, where my past self still lingered oppressively. I worried about this at night as I lay in my old bed, the top half of a bunk bed on which I used to pile everything that was important to me, books mainly, a few photos, and the beginnings of a stamp collection that never got off the ground. I had not mentioned Geraldine to my father, thinking that it hardly seemed an appropriate time to do so, but he was nosy about such things, nosy in a stoic, Minnesotan sort of way, which meant that he would never come right out and ask who called each evening at eight but instead took matters into his own hands. On the fifth night, he retired earlier than usual, and when the phone rang, he picked up his bedroom extension quickly.

"For you," he announced in a loud, flat voice that carried easily down the hallway, and when I picked up, I could sense him there—hostile but, I could not help thinking, perhaps secretly wanting to understand this thing that made no sense to him, and so, for just an instant, I considered letting him listen.

"Yes?" I said brusquely, greeting Geraldine the way I would a telemarketer.

There was a pause. In a low, confused voice, she asked, "Are you okay?" and I saw at once the folly of thinking that I could inhabit both lives at once.

"Dad, I've got it," I said sternly, and I heard the double click of him hanging up as it traveled across the line and through the house.

My parents were both pack rats—had become even more so during my mother's illness—and I felt it my duty, during that visit, to establish some order. The first morning, wishing to take stock of the worst of it, I ventured down into the basement, where I had not been in many years. The carpet was brittle, almost crunchy, under my feet, and when I touched the paneling that ran the length of the hallway, my hand came away chalky with mold. So overwhelmed were my other senses, even taste, that my hearing felt dull by contrast. As the mold spores settled in my lungs, I began to breathe heavily, wheezing as I made my way through the rooms counting sofas (or davenports, as we had always called them). I found five, then opened the door of my father's library onto a sixth, a slippery horsehair settee that blocked the entrance so that I had to climb over it to get in. The two bottom shelves held books bloated with water. I removed one of them, the illustrated *Rip Van Winkle* that I had liked as a child, its cover now warped and wavy, the pages stuck permanently together, rendering its contents inaccessible.

From there, I entered the main room, which had once contained the house's infrastructure: my father's workshop, the laundry area, a wood-burning stove, and three freezers. Only the freezers still hummed with purpose. Here, another smell hung in the air, vying with the mustiness, a distinctly porkish odor, the source of which it took me several minutes to locate: beside one of the freezers sat a green plastic bushel basket filled with lard, its white, fatty surface embedded with dead insects and dust. Still, compared with everything else, the lard seemed manageable, and I decided to begin with it, to lobby for its disposal that night at dinner, when my father's mood would surely be elevated by the presence of food.

Dinner, however, got off to a bad start. "Dinner," I called down the hallway at six thirty. Several minutes passed, and I called again before walking down to my father's bedroom, where I found him propped up on his bed reading the newspaper.

"Didn't you hear me calling you for dinner?" I asked.

"I heard," he said, not looking up. "But in this house, we eat dinner at noon. If you want me to come for supper, you'll need to say so."

There was a long, silent standoff between us. "Fine," I said at last. "Supper is served." My father got up and followed me down the hallway to the table. He sat down, and I set his plate in front of him. "Shouldn't we throw out that lard?" I said. "That big tub that's just sitting there in the basement?"

"Leave it," he said. "I might make soap."

"Really? And when, exactly, did you start making soap?"

"I said I might make it, but I can't if you go around throwing out the lard."

"Fine," I said after only the slightest pause. "How about the toasters then?"

On a shelf near his worktable I had found nineteen of them, the two-slicers from early in my parents' marriage pushed behind the family-size four-slicers, every toaster from my childhood and then some, the potential for sixty-eight simultaneous slices of toast (I had counted) gathered in a state of disrepair.

"What about them?"

"Well," I said. "They're toasters. When they break, you throw them out."

"In my time, we fixed things. We didn't just toss them on the trash heap."

"Well, they aren't fixed. They're broken, and they've been broken for more than thirty years, some of them. Listen," I said then. "I've arranged for a truck to come tomorrow to haul away the sofas—*davenports*—before they become even more infested with mice than they already are."

"Mice need a place to live," he replied fiercely, though I had never known him to be anything less than absolute in his treatment of mice.

"Yes, they do," I agreed. "And tomorrow they'll be living at the dump with the davenports."

"They closed that dump years ago." He studied his food. "What is this anyway?"

"Fajitas," I said. "It's everything that you like—beef, peppers, onions."

"Everything I like is to have it fried up in a pan with some Crisco and salt. Not this," he said. We both knew that I had prepared it this way, grilled under the broiler, letting the grease collect in the pan so that it could be discarded, because the doctor had told him that he needed less fat in his diet—less fat, less salt, less food.

"That's not how I cook," I said.

"Well, this is not how I eat," he said, and he picked the plate up and turned it upside down on the table.

When the two men arrived the next day to haul away the sofas, my father waited until they had carried the fourth one up from the basement and jimmied it around the corner at the top of the stairs before he came out and instructed them to put every single davenport back exactly where they had found it. They did, of course, without even looking my way.

That afternoon as my father napped in front of the television, I went through all three freezers, throwing out anything that looked suspect, peas and string beans and berries that had taken on the desiccated look of long-frozen food. There were rings and rings of potato sausage, which the entire family had always been involved in making but only my parents had liked; my siblings and I could never overcome the memory of making it, the bushel baskets of potatoes that it took us the entire day to peel, the long night of grinding the blackened potatoes together with pork and venison and onions, of stuffing this into pig intestines, and then, at dawn, when we were feeling nauseated from lack of sleep, the stench of leftover meat being fried up for our breakfast.

I filled five garbage bags, which I dragged outside and lifted into the garbage cans lined up behind the house. There were eight of them, eight garbage cans for a man who did not even discard empty pill bottles. Then, because I felt I had earned a break, I walked into town, ducking my head or lifting my hand back at people as they drove by, at these strangers for whom waving was a reflex. My father would have known every one of them, of course, though my father would never have taken a walk along the highway like that because it would have caused people to talk, and more than anything, my father did not want people speculating about his business.

Years before, when his doctor had first begun to mention diet and exercise, before my father decided to stand firm against anything that might benefit his health, he went through a brief period of highly anomalous behavior—namely, following his doctor's advice. For almost two months, he and my mother drove back into town each night after dark and locked themselves inside their store, where, for forty-five minutes, they walked. They went up and down the same aisles where they spent their days, past gopher traps and sprinklers and all kinds of joinery, my father in the lead, my mother several steps behind. After my mother accidentally let this secret slip and I asked why, why, when they could be out looking at lakes and trees and fields of corn, they preferred to walk indoors, she said, "You know your father doesn't want people knowing his business."

I walked for five hours that day, walked until I no longer felt mold each time I breathed in, and when I returned, my father said, "What did you do? Walk all over the county?" He was still in front of the television, and he spoke in a cranky way that implied that he had spent the entire afternoon sitting right there, waiting for me to return, but the next morning when I got up early to cart the garbage cans down to the road for pickup, they were all empty. While I had been out walking around letting people know my business, my father had undone all of my work, returning everything to the freezers. That was day three. We spent the last four days of my stay in idle silence.

Ten years have passed since that visit, but it's right there between us—the unspoken betrayal—when I ask my father how long ago he shot the pheasant that he now wants to FedEx me. Finally, I say what I mean—"That pheasant must be at least five years old"—and he hangs up on me; I, ever my father's daughter, wait until the next evening to call back, and when I do, though I let the phone ring thirty, and then forty, times, there is no answer.

This, I suppose, is the moment when other children pause to consider broken hips, burst hearts, a sudden, irrevocable loosening of the mind. "He's in the bathroom," calls Geraldine from the study, her voice overly reassuring, for she too knows his pattern: startled by the first ring, setting aside his book on the second, picking up, always, on the third, answering, "Yut," as though the ringing were a question. "Dad?" I always reply, this, too, a question, and then, before we begin talking, he tells me which phone he is on, kitchen or bedroom, because he wants me to be able to picture him—where he is sitting, what he is seeing—as our voices float back and forth across the distance.

Tonight, the rings adding up in my ear, I imagine him, broom in hand, descending those sixteen treacherous steps, both feet resting briefly on each one until he stands surrounded by a lifetime's worth of broken toasters and davenports, a roomful of books nearby, their words trapped between waterlogged pages. The freezers are open, all three of them, lids tilted up like coffin covers, and he pauses in their white glow, trying to take it all in: this wealth before him, this carpet dissolving beneath his feet.

The Day You Were Born

When Annabel comes home from school on Tuesday, her father is back, standing at the corner of Indian School and University, across the street from where the bus drops her and the other children from her apartment complex. When the light finally changes, the two of them cross hurriedly toward each other, and so their reunion takes place in the middle of the street, her father twirling her around several times and then releasing her abruptly in order to present his middle finger to an old woman in a Volvo station wagon who has beeped tentatively to let them know that the light has gone red.

"So, are you surprised?" her father asks as they pass through the front doors of the complex, and because his tone is light and he is holding her hand and yanking her arm about in a happy, frenetic way that does not match their steps, she responds honestly, "Yes," without pausing to think through the possible implications of his question or her answer.

"Why are you surprised?" he asks, stopping suddenly and squeezing her hand hard to underscore the question. "Did you think I wasn't coming back?" The pressure on her hand increases. "Did your mother say something?" She looks down then.

"Look at me, Annabel," he says, and she does.

"She said you were in the hospital and the doctors didn't know when you would come home," she tells him, which is

69

more or less the truth, the *less* part of it being that her mother actually told her, just two days earlier in fact, that the doctors were not sure that he would ever be able to come home. "I'm so happy you're home," she adds, because she is and because she does not want to talk to him about her mother.

They stand outside their apartment door for several minutes as her father searches through his pockets for his key until Annabel suggests that they use her key, which she takes from around her neck and hands to him. His hand trembles slightly as he fumbles to insert it in the lock, and Annabel looks away, breathes in deeply, and concentrates on thinking absolutely nothing. This works, for when she turns back, her father has the door open and is gesturing, with a gentleman's low bow and flourish, for her to enter.

"So, are you ready for a snack?" he asks, his tone light again, and when she nods, he says, "What are you in the mood for?"

"Anything," she tells him, and she goes into her room to change, knowing that when she comes out, her father will have made something awful, something like sardines and melted marshmallows on saltine crackers.

"How much do you love your dad?" he'll ask, motioning with his head for her to be seated, and though she always tries to think of new ways to answer this question, she never comes up with anything but the same old responses—*a whole lot, very much, tons.*

"Enough to eat sardines with marshmallows?" he'll say, setting the plate in front of her. And she does—*does* love him that much, *does* eat it, polishes off the entire plate, in fact, of whatever he puts before her while he sits watching her chew and swallow and demonstrate her love in a way that she does not know how to do with words.

"That's my girl," he'll say when she's finished, words that

prove to her that it was worth everything—the awful taste and the feel of the food sitting in her stomach like a stone or tumbling about like clothes in a washer. Sometimes, the nausea overwhelms her and she excuses herself, slips into the bathroom, where she leans way down into the toilet bowl, her face nearly touching the water, and vomits as quietly as possible.

Today, when she comes out in her after-school clothes and they go through the usual routine, what her father sets before her is a plate of celery sticks, three of them, arranged like canoes, overflowing with mayonnaise and topped generously with chocolate sprinkles. Her father, of course, knows that she hates mayonnaise more than anything, that she finds even the smell of it unbearable. It occurs to her then that her father is still angry, and so she eats with extra diligence, her father watching as usual, and when she is finished, she looks up at him hopefully. "That's a girl," he says, but Annabel understands that there is a difference, a very big one, between "a girl" and "my girl."

"Did your mother tell you about these?" he asks matter-of-factly, pulling back the cuffs of his shirt and laying his thin, white arms out on the table between them, elbows turned down, wrists facing up. Her mother had not told her, of course, had said only that her father was tired and needed a rest, and Annabel sits looking at his wrists, feeling the mayonnaise inside of her like something living, something that wants out, but she will not allow it, not today.

"Touch them," her father says, his voice gentle but urgent. "It's okay. I want you to. You won't hurt me."

Already the cuts have risen up in angry welts around the stitches, which she studies carefully, thinking about the fact that they were put there by someone she does not even know, a stranger who held her father's wrists and created these precise, black marks. There are nine of them, she notes, four on the right wrist, five on the left, and as she places a small finger against each of them, one by one, she closes her eyes and tries to imagine that they are something else, the stitching on a baseball, for example. She loves baseball, not the sport in its entirety but playing catch, which she and her father do together regularly in the park. Her father throws the ball so hard that her hand stings each time she catches it, which she usually does, and sometimes her palm aches for days afterward, though she would never tell her father this. Still, even with her eyes closed, she cannot really pretend that she is touching a baseball because her father's skin is warm and soft and she can feel his pulse, a slight, rhythmic quivering that means that he is still hers.

Later, when her mother comes home, Annabel hears the two of them arguing, her mother saying, "What is wrong with you? She's a child, Max. A child." Annabel is only nine, but she already understands about her mother, knows, for example, that her mother would be angry to learn that Annabel and her father spent the afternoon inspecting his wrists, and so Annabel would never think to tell her this. She cannot help but wonder how it is that her father, who is an adult after all, does not understand such things.

The next day when she arrives home from school, her father is sitting barebacked on the sofa. She knows what this means, that the maggots have returned and are writhing just beneath his skin, making him twitchy and unable to sit still, just as she knows that even the merest brush of cloth against his skin riles the maggots even more. He has explained all of this to her many times, but she cannot actually imagine how such a thing feels, though she knows that it must be awful. His neck is bothered most by the maggots, and when he is forced to put on a shirt—in order to greet her mother or to go outdoors—he shrugs his shoulders repeatedly and tugs incessantly at the neckline until it dips, like a very relaxed cowl, to his belly button.

"The maggots?" she asks quietly, standing next to the sofa with her book bag still strapped to her back.

"Yes," he answers wearily.

"Are they bad?"

"It's all I can think about," he tells her. "Your mother doesn't understand, of course. Do you know what she tells me? She tells me to just not think about it." He laughs when he says this, in a way that invites her to join in, to find humor in her mother's insensitivity. He has told her this before, many times, explaining that it is because her mother grew up in Minnesota, where they prize something called stoicism.

"What is *stoicism*?" she had asked him once.

"Well," he had said, thinking for a moment. "It's like this. Let's say that your mother and I are out taking a walk and I get a pebble in my shoe. What would I do?"

"Take it out," she had suggested, her voice rising faintly at the end so that her words occupied the space between statement and question, but her father had ignored her uncertainty.

"That's right," he said. "Of course. I would take it out. Any normal person would. Now, what would your mother do?"

To be honest, she did not know what her mother would do, but she felt that it would disappoint her father were she to admit this, and so, because she understood the direction in which he was nudging her, she said, "Leave it."

"Right again. Because your mother *likes* to suffer, Annabel. She *likes* to feel that pebble in her shoe. And then, at the end of the walk, do you know what your mother would do?" He had become more excited, warming to his explanation, not really expecting her to answer. "She would tell me about the pebble. She would say, 'Max, I've had this pebble in my shoe the whole time we've been walking, and it's really starting to hurt.'" When he said this, his voice changed, becoming higher like her mother's voice and drawing out the *o*'s as he did when he teased her mother about being from Minnesota. "She would expect me to feel sorry for her, but I wouldn't, of course. I'd tell her, 'Well, sit down and take the damn thing out.' And you know what she'd say then? She'd say, 'Oh, never mind, Max. It's okay. We're almost home anyway.'"

He had paused then, eyes closed, clasping his hands in front of him as her grandparents did when they prayed before eating, but Annabel knew that her father was not praying. He did not believe in it. After a moment, his breathing slowed, and he opened his eyes and said, "You see, Annabel, your mother needs that pebble. She wouldn't know what to do without it. You can see that, can't you, Annabel?" His tone was fierce, beseeching her, his face glowing red, the way it used to when he came in from gardening, back when they had a garden, back when they had a house.

She had nodded, though she'd never seen pebbles in her mother's shoes, had not even heard her mother mention pebbles. "You need to be on your guard, honey. Okay?" he said. "Because if your mother has her way, you'll be walking around with a pebble in your shoe, too." He breathed in deeply through his nostrils, as though the air were very fresh and only now could he enjoy it.

On Saturdays, Annabel and her mother visit her grandparents. Her father does not go along, even though they are his parents, because he says that they stare at him. During these visits, her grandfather and grandmother both sit in their recliners, which have been placed up on cinder blocks so that when they stand, they do not have to hoist themselves upward in a way that would strain their hips. She and her mother sit on a floral sofa across from them, and Annabel feels self-conscious because there is a picture of Jesus hanging right above her, which means that when her grandparents look at her, they are seeing Jesus as well. They generally talk about uninteresting topics such as what songs were performed on *Lawrence Welk* during the week's reruns and how many times they saw the retired barber who lives across the street mowing his lawn. Once, he mowed his lawn three times during a single week, and they reported this to Annabel and her mother with a great deal of indignation.

"Doesn't the man have anything better to do with his time?" her grandfather had asked again and again, shaking his head.

"Maybe he misses cutting," her mother said, which was a joke, but Annabel's grandparents do not acknowledge jokes.

Her grandparents are very pale because they do not go outside and have not for many years. In their garage sits her grandfather's car, which has not been driven in six years. Every other week, she and her mother go out and start the car to keep the battery in good condition, just in case. A couple of times, she and her mother went to the gas station and filled a large red can with gasoline, which they poured into her grandfather's car.

"Why don't we just take the car to the gas station?" she asked her mother. "Wouldn't it be easier?"

"Your grandfather does not want the car moved," her mother explained.

"Why?"

"Because something might happen to it. We might get into an accident, and then he wouldn't have the car if he needed it."

First, her mother rolls open the garage door, even though they will not be going anywhere. They climb in, and her mother pulls the seat forward so that she can reach the pedals. She is always careful to push it back again when they are finished, in deference to Annabel's grandfather, who is very tall. Then, the two of them sit in the idling vehicle, staring straight ahead at the rakes that hang from the walls of the garage in neat, orderly rows.

"Why do they need so many rakes?" she asked her mother once, after she had counted and discovered that there were twelve of them. Then, she repeated the question, but this time she said, "Why do they need a dozen rakes?" She was six and had just learned in school that *twelve* was also called *a dozen,* and she thought about this often, wondering why there were two words for the number twelve. It seemed unnecessary, unnecessary and odd, for if a number were going to be given two names, the number ten seemed more deserving.

Her mother laughed at her question.

"What's funny?" Annabel asked.

"Oh, it's just that you don't usually use *dozen* for things like rakes," her mother said, but when Annabel asked why, her mother replied, "Well, you usually just say *a dozen* for eggs, or doughnuts, or things like that." When Annabel later asked her father why you couldn't say "a dozen rakes," she expected one of his usual explanations, which were generally long and left nothing out, but instead he replied angrily, "Of course you can. Who told you that? Your mother? Listen to me, Annabel. You can say 'a dozen rakes' to me anytime you want. Okay?"

As she and her mother sit in her grandfather's car on the Saturday after her father's return from the hospital, her mother says, "Don't mention your father's wrists to your grandparents." She and her mother have not discussed her father's wrists either, but Annabel does not see any reason to point this out to her mother. "Okay," she says, though she never *mentions* anything to her grandparents and her mother knows this.

Her mother looks at her watch and says, "Fifteen minutes. That should do it. Let's go back in and make your grandparents a little something."

They always make the same thing, a hot drink mix that her grandparents call Russian tea. The mix consists primarily of Tang, which Annabel dislikes, and cloves. It is her job to carry the china cups filled with the brownish orange liquid out to her grandparents, both of whom bring the hot tea immediately up to their mouths and hold it there, as though the cups were receptacles, or conductors, for their words. It is only then—as they sit with their mouths hidden and their eyes partially concealed by the steam fogging their glasses—that they turn their attention to more interesting topics, namely her father.

"How is he?" one of them generally asks her mother at this point, as though they believe that a pronoun in place of his name will keep Annabel from knowing that it is her father to whom they are referring.

"He's fine," her mother always replies sharply, inclining her head toward Annabel, who pretends not to be listening, hoping, futilely, that they might be persuaded to say more. Instead, they all sip their Russian tea and gaze at the photograph of her father that hangs on the wall near the television, a picture in which her father, wearing a green bolo tie, looks cheerful and handsome and not a bit like the twitchy, shirtless man they have come to know.

Today, however, there is no mention of her father, and Annabel wonders whether they have forgotten to ask or whether this omission is something intentional, something that they planned beforehand. She actually hopes that it is the latter because the idea that her father has simply been forgotten, particularly in the midst of such tedium, is too much for her to bear. She turns toward her father's photograph, but it is gone, which means that the entire time that she and her mother have been sitting here, listening to her grandparents talk about the barber and his mowing, it was already gone—gone, and she had not even noticed.

Most Saturday nights after Annabel and her mother return from her grandparents' house, she and her father follow the same routine: her father helps her get ready for bed, and once she is settled beneath her Raggedy Ann quilt, he asks her to describe the visit to his parents. He listens quietly to her report, and when she finishes, he says, "Just remember, Annabel, that these are the people who made your father sleep on the cot."

"Yes," she always replies. "I remember."

"Good girl," he says as though they are finished with the matter, but then he tells her the story of the cot again anyway, because he likes to remind himself of it, particularly as she is snuggled against him in her very own comfortable bed in her very own room.

"Your grandparents," he always begins, "had produced seven children by the time I made my appearance. Imagine, Annabel, four boys, three girls, and the two of them living in a tiny, three-bedroom house." During the introduction, his tone is always noncommittal, as though the story just might unfold in a way that allows for sympathy toward these nine people, his family, crammed together like peas even before his arrival.

"Well," he continues, "I was put in your grandparents' room to sleep, in a crib wobbly from overuse." And there it is, the hardening in his voice at the words *wobbly from overuse*.

At the age of two, her father had gone from sleeping in this crib to sleeping in the hallway outside his parents' bedroom, on a cot that was folded up and rolled behind the door of his sisters' bedroom each morning. The hallway, he told her so that she could picture it because her grandparents had long ago left that house, was like the backbone of a capital *E,* and the three bedrooms, which jutted out to the left, were its arms.

"It's not even that I minded the cot," he always told Annabel at this point, after he had impressed upon her the image of this small boy, him, isolated from every other member of his family. "It was comfortable enough." No, what he had minded, he said, was the fact that when his parents unfolded the cot and set it up for him each night, they always placed it as far to the right as possible so that it stood just at the edge of the staircase that connected the upstairs sleeping area with the main floor—despite the fact that there was no railing separating the upstairs, and thus him, from the empty space of the stairwell.

Sometimes, he told her, his arm hung down off the cot in his sleep so that his hand brushed his father's head as his father climbed the stairs for bed. "I would wake to that feeling, the brush of my father's hair against my fingertips, and for a moment, I had no idea where I was. You see, already I thought of sleep as a period of isolation, and that was so ingrained in me, Annabel, that even half-awake, I found the feel of another person disorienting." Then, he would reach out to stroke her head or caress her earlobe before he went on.

"It was like sleeping on the edge of a cliff. On any given night, I could have rolled right instead of left, and that would have been it. I would have gone right over the edge." This is where her father's story always ended, with the understanding that had he been a different sort of boy—less vigilant, less aware—he would have simply rolled over the edge and been gone.

* * *

This Saturday, when she and her mother return from her grandparents' house, her father is not there. She and her mother eat dinner together quietly, and when her mother puts her to bed because her father is not there to do it, her mother perches awkwardly on the edge of the bed and says, "I told him to leave, Annabel. It was just getting to be too much. I hope that some-day you will understand this, maybe when you're older." Her mother goes out of the room quickly, forgetting to leave the hallway light on as her father always does because he under-stands about the dark.

The next day, Sunday, the telephone rings again and again, and when the answering machine picks up because her mother has told her that she is not to answer it, there is her father, sing-ing a song or telling them about something unimportant—a snapped shoelace, the way his orange juice tasted that morn-ing because he forgot and brushed his teeth before he drank it—as though he is right there in the room with them. By eve-ning, however, he has begun pleading with her mother. "Think about Annabel," he says. "Have you asked her what she wants?" Before they go to bed, her mother erases the entire tape, and then she unplugs the answering machine.

When Annabel opens the door to the apartment on Mon-day, letting herself in with the key that she carries around her neck, the telephone is ringing, and she cannot help but feel for a moment that the apartment does not belong to her because the ringing was there before her. She knows that she should not answer it because her mother has instructed her not to, but after several rings, she picks it up, justifying this course of action by telling herself that it could be her mother calling to make sure that she has arrived home safely. However, once she has already committed herself by lifting the receiver, she realizes that if it is her mother calling, she is only doing so to test Annabel.

"How's my girl?" says her father, whispering as he used to when she was young and having bad dreams in the middle of the night.

"Hi," she says in response, surveying the apartment nervously because she cannot fully shake the feeling that her mother is there somewhere, sitting off to the side, listening.

"Did you get my messages yesterday?" he asks.

"Yes."

"I miss you."

"I miss you," she answers, whispering now also.

"Listen," he says then. "I need your help. I need you to write down some things. You know, things that your mother says about me, things that we could use if we had to." She doesn't answer, and then he says, "Annabel, she doesn't want me to see you or even talk to you. It doesn't make sense. It's not as though this is the first time. She acts like this is the first time, but it's not, so why now, Annabel? Do you understand? Because I don't. I surely don't." There is a very long silence.

"The day you were born," he declares suddenly, no longer whispering. "That was the first time. I bet you didn't know that, did you? It was the day you were born. Your mother made me promise that I would never tell you that, but what's the purpose of these secrets? I mean really, Annabel, what *is* the purpose?" He is speaking slowly now, forming these last four words with great care.

"I don't know," she says.

"It was because I loved you so much, even before you were born, and I could feel how much you loved me. That's why I did it. Do you know that, Annabel?" He pauses, as though waiting for her to reply. "At night, when your mother was asleep with you between us, I would put my hand on her stomach, on you, and I could feel you telling me that, Annabel. I could feel you saying that you loved me. That already you loved me more than anyone had ever loved me or ever would."

She thinks that her father might be crying, but she isn't sure, and for a while neither of them says anything. "So you see," he says finally, his words tapering off as though he is falling asleep. "It doesn't make sense." Annabel waits, but her father doesn't speak again, and after several minutes, she hangs the telephone up, gently, not wanting to wake him.

When her mother gets home, she seems distracted, but she goes through the usual set of questions: *Did you have a snack? Did you do your homework? What sounds good for dinner?* Annabel answers these *No, Sort of,* and *I don't know,* and when her mother adds a new one, "Did your father call?" Annabel pauses for just a moment, and then, very calmly, says, "No." Her mother looks so relieved that Annabel understands, with sudden clarity, that lying is not always a bad thing, not when it so obviously means that she can help them both; later, she even hears her mother humming as she makes fried ham, which is Annabel's favorite.

The next day when Annabel arrives home from school, the phone is ringing again, but she knows what she needs to do, and she sits on the sofa listening to it, her hands tucked beneath her thighs. Eventually, she gets up and sets the table, two places instead of three, so that everything will seem right when her mother gets home. When the ringing finally stops nearly two hours later, she feels its absence like a sharp, sudden pain, but she understands now how it is: that this pain, this pain is how much she loves him.

Nobody Walks to the Mennonites

The two American women read in their guidebook that there were Mennonites not far from town, so on the second morning they set out to find them. The women were staying perhaps a quarter of a mile outside of town in a bungalow, a round structure with cinder block walls, one of several grouped together along a footpath behind the main office. At some point, perhaps when bungalows were in greater demand, a flimsy wall had been erected down the middle of each, slicing it into two separate, though by no means soundproof, units. Now, however, the entire place stood empty, the grass along the footpath left uncut so that mosquitoes swarmed above it, attacking the women's bare legs as they walked to and from their bungalow.

When they first entered the office from the road and inquired whether there were vacancies, the man behind the counter nodded his head, looking almost ashamed, and said, "Sure, we got rooms. Just go ahead and take your pick." He was an older man, quite black with grizzled hair, and he wore only a pair of shorts and a necklace from which hung some sort of animal's tooth. Because they did not want him to feel more defeated than he already seemed, they did not comment on the lack of other guests, though they were, in fact, elated.

The guidebook had warned that the town itself could get noisy at night—too many bars—and since neither of them had much tolerance for unabashed revelry, the sort that people tend to engage in while vacationing in someone else's country, they had heeded the book's suggestion to stay just outside the limits of the town proper. They had to walk into town to eat, of course, but it was nice, if not a bit disorienting, coming home in the dark like that. They simply followed the lane that led out of town, sliding their feet along the gravel rather than lifting them up and taking actual steps, which would have required far more trust than the two women felt able to invest at that point, either in this country or in themselves. Still, they liked the walk, particularly the final stretch with the field on the left that contained a dozen cows whose silent, sturdy presence comforted them.

In all regards, the women (Sarah and Sara, who, because they were both visual people, did not think of themselves as having the same name) found this town vastly superior to Belize City, from which they had just escaped, after spending only one night there in a hotel above a bar where their room had throbbed with a steady bass throughout most of the night. In the room next to them was a very young Japanese couple who had spent the last three years trying to see the world, "the whole world," the young man had informed them, so that they could return to Japan and begin working and not feel as though they had missed something. They had gone through Asia first, and then into Africa and Europe, and now they were working their way up from South America. But Belize City, they told the two American women in careful English, was the very worst place they had ever been, "so dirty and"—this after pausing to weigh all of the English words at their disposal—"evil," and Sara and Sarah, who had just spent the last four hours walking around Belize City, agreed, though they kept their opinion to themselves, as was their tendency when talking to fellow tourists.

Their plan had been to take a taxi from the Belize City airport to a pleasant bed-and-breakfast that their guidebook highly recommended (it was run by an American), but instead the taxi driver had taken them straight into the dirty, crowded heart of the city and dumped them in front of the hotel. "Cheap," he told them. "Cheap and very near." He did not say very near what, but it appeared to be very near every trash heap and vice the city had to offer. Still, they were tired of sitting, so they got out of the taxi, paid the driver, and checked into the hotel, where there was not actually a room ready for them. Instead, they had nervously entrusted their suitcases to the proprietor, who assured them that he would move the bags himself into the first available room.

Then, though the guidebook had recommended *not* doing so, they walked down along the empty pier, stopping eventually for drinks at a small café attached to the side of a house. The sign out front claimed that the café was open, but when they followed the arrow around the house to the side door marked "Café," they found themselves in an empty, poorly lit room with several tables and a dartboard. They sat down anyway because neither woman was ready to face the street again, where they felt conspicuous and vulnerable to all of the dangers that the guidebook had warned of: drive-by shootings, gangs, drugs, purse snatchers, con artists, and ass grabbers, though they were not sure whether the book had actually mentioned the last of these or whether they were simply allowing their imaginations to get the better of them. The room was cloyingly hot and musty, and at one point Sara, who had grown up in Minnesota and was fond of explaining to people that the state actually contained almost one hundred thousand bodies of water, commented that the room reminded her of a lake cabin.

"It's the smell," Sarah replied, "the smell and the paneling."

"No," Sara said firmly. "That's not it. There's just something about it, something I can't quite put my finger on, but it's not that obvious."

"That's exactly what it is," Sarah told her. "You just think that because I'm from Iowa, I don't know anything about lake cabins." She spoke almost sneeringly, and Sara looked startled, for the two of them rarely argued. They were quiet then, and after several more minutes, a door near the back of the room creaked open, and they sensed that they were being watched.

"Yes?" Sarah said sharply, turning toward the door. There was no answer, but they heard a dog growl, and she called out again. "Yes? Are you open?"

Finally, a child's voice—they could not tell whether it was a boy or a girl—announced: "My mother went to the store. Please wait." Then the door slammed shut, and they heard several locks fall into place.

Neither woman had an immediate reaction—to go or to stay—and so they stayed, but Sarah, who was the more impatient one, soon stood, walked to the window, and studied her watch. When she returned to the table, she said quietly, "We've been here nearly half an hour now," and Sara understood that this was her way of suggesting that they leave. It occurred to them, however, that the room had become cooler, that, in fact, they were both shivering slightly, which meant that someone, presumably the child, had turned on the air conditioner. It was settled yet again: they could not leave. Instead, they spent the next fifteen minutes looking forward to the rest of their trip, to the moment when they would leave Belize City behind, and eventually they heard the locks being undone and the door from the house opening again.

A small woman carrying a tray approached the table, and as she got closer, they saw that she was Chinese. "High tea?" she asked softly, and because they could see that she had already prepared something, they did not have the heart to say that they just wanted sodas.

"Yes," they both said and then nodded vigorously. The woman set a small plate in front of each of them, placed a pot of tea in the middle of the table, and set about arranging cups and saucers, cloth napkins, and various pieces of cutlery. When she was done, she gestured gracefully toward the table, an invitation to begin eating, and hurried away. Each plate contained a slice of white bread spread thickly with rancid butter and topped with chocolate sprinkles. To the side were cucumber slices, spilled out like coins.

They ate everything, of course, because they couldn't bear the thought of the woman staring sadly at their scraps, and Sara, who always carried the money, wedged a dollar bill under her saucer after settling the bill. They both nodded politely at the woman, who was hovering near the dartboard, and left, their eyelids fluttering rapidly against the sudden brightness outside. They had thought they would find a taxi, but there were none, and so they walked quickly back in the direction of the hotel, their fanny packs slung low across their buttocks like shields.

They returned to the hotel to find that their bags had indeed been taken up to their room as promised, though they realized, as the proprietor led them up a rickety, winding set of stairs and down a narrow hallway, that the hotel was, in fact, nothing more than three rooms wedged between the first-floor bar and the third floor, where the proprietor and his family lived. They stopped in front of a particleboard door, and the proprietor handed them a key attached to a plastic coffee mug. "Your room, ladies," he mumbled and hurried off without showing them the interior.

There were no windows or fans in the room; the only suggestion of circulation came from an open transom above the door, which did nothing to alleviate the heat or the smell of raw sewage that hung in the air, an odor that wafted up from the toilet. They tried flushing it again and again, but the toilet had no lid that could be closed to block the smell, which rose up from the pipes and filled the room. The final insult, for that's how it seemed to the women at this point, was that the toilet stood shamelessly out in the open, within touching distance of the bed and without even a curtain that could be drawn around it when it was in use; in fact, it was almost as though the room had been designed to showcase the toilet, for it sat atop a platform, which one had to ascend like royalty. Still, and this was always a consolation, the room had been quite cheap.

Sara and Sarah knew how to *pass time,* an expression that they used often and without self-consciousness, considering it an important skill whether one liked to travel or not. At home, where portability was not a concern, Sarah was teaching herself the art of papermaking, and both women enjoyed gardening; also, while they understood that recycling was technically not a hobby, they liked to devote time to that as well. When they traveled, the two passed time by reading, though they also carried a deck of cards with which to play cribbage. Thus, they spent the early evening hours in Belize City in their hotel room playing round after round of cribbage, keeping score on a pad of paper because they both agreed that a cribbage board was unnecessary. Next, turning their books alternately toward the light from the transom and the weak glow offered by the bedside lamp, they read, Sara from a Belizean novel titled *Beka Lamb* and Sarah from the guidebook. It was then that the Japanese couple had knocked furtively at their door and asked whether they could possibly change some American currency into Belizean dollars. They didn't have enough for a bus, the young man explained, and they couldn't bear the thought of waiting around in the morning until the banks opened. As he said this, the young woman began to sob, and so they had given the couple half of their money, changing it at the bank rate even though they had just purchased it at the higher airport rate that afternoon. After the couple left, bowing slightly and thanking them repeatedly, they returned to their books.

At ten o'clock, they turned off the lamp, though there was nothing they could do about the light coming through the transom or the throbbing music from the bar downstairs. Sarah engaged in a relaxation method that involved focusing on each part of her body and encouraging it to ignore the noise while Sara simply covered her head with the pillow. Eventually, they fell asleep. At some point during the night, however, the music stopped abruptly, and they both awakened to a soft lapping sound inside their room, though neither could be sure afterward which had woken them—the sudden cessation of one sound or the quiet proximity of another. They turned the light on quickly, without even speaking, to discover a mangy, sore-infested street cat crouched on the toilet seat drinking from the bowl. It fixed them with a slow, dazed look, and then it leapt from the toilet seat, clawed its way frantically up the wooden door of their room, and hoisted itself out through the open transom.

So, of course, after Belize City, they slept inordinately well that first night in the bungalow. The second night, however, as they lay in bed reading, they heard a group of people, Americans also, coming down the path that led to their bungalow. The group paused for a moment, looking for a key, and the women realized that these people were going to be inhabiting the other half of the bungalow, sleeping on the other side of the flimsy dividing wall. It became difficult to read then, for the newcomers—a family they suspected—were celebrating, their voices loud and merry with everyone talking at once, interrupting one another without giving offense and laughing in unison like people who had shared years of finding the same things funny. There were the sounds of bottles being opened, and periodically someone said, "I'm ready for another, Shel," an announcement that was followed by the clink of glass hitting glass as another drink was poured. They were discussing something that they all seemed to find extremely amusing, something that had happened on the Cayes just a day or two earlier, so the incident was still fresh in their minds. In the middle of the story came the very loud, unmistakable sound of someone passing gas, and two or three voices said at once, with practiced indignation, "Dad!," which confirmed what they had initially suspected, that it was a family on the other side. Neither woman could understand this, a family still taking vacations together as adults, actually finding it restful to be in one another's company.

The sounds of drinking continued as the story from the Cayes was related again and again so that eventually they were able to piece together the gist of it, which involved this man— Dad—and his inability to climb back into the boat after a morning of snorkeling along the coral reef off the Cayes. The boat had been ladderless, and he had been unable to summon the strength to pull himself up and over the side, so finally the captain and several of their fellow snorkelers had lowered themselves back into the water and hoisted him over the rail and onto the deck. Each time they retold the story, Dad chuckled along good-naturedly, as though it did not bother him to be the butt of the new family joke.

The night went on like this, moving further and further back in time to include past family vacations, stories accompanied by more drinking and gas passing and groaning. The women stopped trying to read and instead just lay there in their twin beds listening, and when they occasionally communicated, they did so in whispers because it would have seemed odd to make their presence known then, so long after the family had arrived. Finally they shut off their light, but the flimsy wall stopped short of the thatched roof, so the light from the family's room shone into theirs. Both women found this strangely comforting.

Still, they did not sleep, and Sarah, who was in the bed on the right, was reminded suddenly of a moment from her childhood. During her last week of sixth grade, she had come down with the measles, and her parents had confined her to her bedroom for nearly two weeks, where she had lain with the door shut and the lights off in order to protect her eyes from permanent damage. At one point—she did not know how many days it was into her quarantine—she had woken from a deep afternoon sleep to find that her siblings were home from school. She could hear them at the kitchen table discussing their days, and she had mentally taken roll, listening for each sibling's voice to offer up some anecdote or casual insight regarding a teacher, only to realize that the whole family was present save for her and her father, who was at work. The light from the kitchen had crept in under her door, and it had soothed her at first because she had spent so much time in the dark. But then she had started to think about how rare it was—her family gathering together like this—and she could not help but conclude that it was her absence, her guaranteed absence, that made it possible. She had lain there for quite a while, listening to them laugh, until at some point she slept again. She had slowly become well, the spots had disappeared, but she was never able to shake that feeling that they were happier, more complete, without her. Later, before she became an adult, when she was still a sporadically pensive teenager, she had arrived at a theory that somehow made her feel better, useful even. She had decided that each family has a member whose absence rounds out the family far more than his or her presence ever could. The theory had continued to be a source of pride for her over the years, though, oddly, she had forgotten, until now, the incident that had sparked its formation.

She rolled toward Sara in the dark and whispered, "Sara?" and when Sara turned toward her, she said, "Remember my theory?"

"What theory?" Sara asked, but Sarah didn't answer.

The family talked far into the night until finally someone said, "My God, it's nearly three," and within moments they had cleared the glasses, and a chorus of voices called out, "Good night, Dad. Sleep well." A male voice, one that had been heard infrequently during the night, said, somewhat awkwardly, "Remember, Dad, we're just one bungalow over . . . if you need anything." Then the door opened and closed.

"Which way?" asked Shel, the evening's bartender, from outside their window. "I can't see a thing."

Another woman said, "Well, he seems fine," but she lowered her voice to do so. Nobody responded, and finally one of the men said, "Let's get some sleep." And then they were gone.

In the other half of the bungalow, there was silence at first, and then they heard the man go into the bathroom. The water ran for a minute or two, followed by the sound of urine streaming ferociously into the toilet bowl. He flushed, left the bathroom, undressed, and fell heavily into bed. When he shut off his lamp, at last, the darkness seemed abrupt to them, final. The three of them lay in the dark bungalow like that for a while, the two women feeling oddly like intruders. Then a low wailing rose up, and the women briefly imagined that an animal had become trapped in the thatch of the roof. After a few seconds, the wailing evened out into a deep, bitter sobbing, and then, of course, they realized that it was not a trapped animal at all, that it was the man, Dad, and they both turned instinctively in their separate beds onto their sides and away from each other.

The next morning they ate rice for breakfast at a Chinese restaurant that was not yet open for the day. When they went in and asked the old woman washing glasses behind the bar whether there was rice to be had, she nodded for them to sit down. Then she continued washing glasses for several more minutes while they sat at a table discussing whether she had misunderstood their request. Just when they were about to leave, the door opened and a young *mestiza* came in quietly, though she had about her the look of someone who had previously been hurrying. She nodded to the old Chinese woman, and the old Chinese woman nodded back at her and then toward them, placed the glass that she had been drying carefully back on a shelf beneath the bar, and walked, with a slight limp, toward the kitchen.

The young *mestiza* turned toward them and said in Spanish, without first stopping to inquire whether they spoke Spanish, "I am always late." She said it with an air of resignation, as though commenting on some unalterable quality like thinning hair. "And *la chinita,* she rises earlier and earlier each morning." She sighed and then, switching to wobbly English, asked what they wished to drink. They paused for a moment, for they had not given thought to anything more than food.

"Beer?" she suggested, and they both looked shocked.

"But it is far too early for beer," said Sarah in Spanish.

The woman seemed puzzled. "For tourists, it is not too early, I think."

They were annoyed to be called tourists but did not say so. Instead, they both ordered coffees, black and without sugar, though when the young woman returned with the coffees, both contained sugar. They said nothing, sipping from their cups as she hovered nearby. Finally, Sara asked her in Spanish for chopsticks, and she again appeared puzzled but went off behind the bar and returned with toothpicks, which were also called *palillos*. She set the toothpicks down in the middle of their table and then stood back to watch what they would do with them. They could have laughed and explained the misunderstanding, pretending to eat with chopsticks to demonstrate what they had really wanted, but neither of them had the energy for it, so instead they reached for the toothpicks and sat with them in their mouths until the rice arrived.

The old woman had prepared fried rice for them with plenty of tidbits, which they suspected were scraps left from the night before, chicken and beef that had been ordered and picked at by other diners, and though in theory they were impressed by this degree of resourcefulness, in fact they found their stomachs turning. Both women took up the forks that they had been given and worked through the rice carefully, as though they had lost something of great importance amid the grains. In this way, everything that was not rice was removed and added to a pile on the side of each woman's plate, perhaps, they hoped, to be recycled one more time.

As they finished eating, the door opened again, and a dapper black man in a pressed linen suit came in and proceeded at a trot to a table not far from them. Before he sat, he removed his Panama hat and tipped it in their direction, and they could see then that he was much older than his quick step had suggested. "Top of the morning, ladies," he said, setting the hat on a chair and seating himself beside it. The old woman hobbled out from the kitchen and over to his table, and he repeated the greeting to her, using her name, which was Mrs. Chu. Mrs. Chu returned the greeting, speaking with a strong Chinese accent.

"How's the honey?" he asked, and she nodded vigorously.

"Ah yes, honey still have. Thank you," she told him. Then, uncharacteristically they thought (though they had only just met her), Mrs. Chu giggled and a blush of sorts spread across her cheeks.

The dapper man leaned back in his chair so that he could see both Sara and Sarah before he spoke. "Perhaps you ladies would be interested to know that I am a beekeeper," he said.

They both nodded politely. "Beekeeping. Now that must be a fascinating profession," observed Sara.

He nodded solemnly. "Yes. Indeed it is. You may not be at all surprised to learn that my father before me also kept bees. In fact, everything I know, I learned from that man. Say," he said after a moment, "how many times do you suppose I've been stung over the years? Go ahead—wager a guess."

After a moment, Sarah suggested a hundred and five times and Sara agreed that that sounded like a reasonable number. The old man chuckled and brought his hands together in front of his face, forming a large circle through which he peered at them. "Ladies, would you believe it," he said dramatically. "The answer is zero. Those bees just don't fancy me. But I'll tell you this, and nobody would deny it. I raise the best honey around." He paused thoughtfully before reconfirming Sara's earlier observation: "Yes," he said, "a fascinating profession."

There was an uncomfortable silence then, though uncomfortable only for the two women, who felt that the conversation ball had been bounced back to them and that they were simply sitting with it. Finally, to fill the silence, Sarah said, to nobody in particular, "The bee." She stretched the word out thoughtfully, as though she planned to offer insight, but the old Chinese woman misunderstood her, thinking that she was requesting *the bill*. In turn, she called out sharply to the *mestiza,* who rushed in with a large, colorful bird perched on one shoulder and presented them with a slip of paper bearing the price of their breakfast, two Belizean dollars and fifty cents.

"Excuse me, but do you know how far it is to the Mennonites?" Sarah asked politely in Spanish as she handed her the money for the bill.

"The Mennonites," the *mestiza* answered in English. "They are very far. Maybe you go thirty kilometers, maybe you go more. The Mennonites are far from us."

"The Mennonites?" the dapper black man said, breaking in on their conversation. "The Mennonites are not far. I would say precisely twelve kilometers, give or take a few. Which route do you plan to take?"

"The shortest," they answered in unison. "We're walking," Sarah explained.

"Walking!" the beekeeper exclaimed in horror. "Nobody walks to the Mennonites. And the Mennonites, for their part, do not walk to us."

"Well, we're walking," said Sarah again, "so if you would be kind enough to point us in the right direction, we would be grateful."

"Come," said the beekeeper, struggling to his feet. They stood also and waited as he placed his Panama hat precisely atop his head, and then they followed him from the restaurant.

"Do you see this road?" the beekeeper asked, but the sun was strong already, and they both had trouble seeing after the darkness of the restaurant. Finally, when Sarah's eyes had adjusted sufficiently, she found that he was pointing straight down at the very road that they were standing on, which was also the road that led to their bungalow.

"Yes," she told him. "I do see this road."

"Very well." He went on to explain that they should follow this road out of town. "You will pass some bungalows," he said, and they nodded. "You must continue past the bungalows for approximately one more kilometer. On your right, you will see a river. Leave the road and walk down to the edge of the river. Stand by the edge in full view of the other side, and soon somebody from the other side will come for you in a boat and ferry you across. You should give him fifty cents apiece. When you reach the other side, you will see another road, and you should continue along that road. There will be people to guide you." They thanked him and started on their way, though they were skeptical about the river crossing. In fact, everything unfolded as the beekeeper predicted, and when they each handed the boatman fifty cents, he tipped his straw hat at them and extended his oar for them to hold on to as they stepped from the boat onto a cluster of damp rocks and from there to the shore.

They walked all morning, but the longer they walked toward the Mennonites, the farther away from the Mennonites they were, or at least that was how it seemed, for as they stopped at the various houses and huts along the road to inquire about the distance, the numbers tossed out grew steadily larger. At one hut, the woman opened her refrigerator and took out two sodas, which she offered to them. They drank them, but when they prepared to leave, she told them that they owed her two dollars for "the refreshments." They gave her the money and didn't mind really because they had been thirsty and they knew that she needed to make a living. Then, after they had paid her, as they were waving goodbye, she said, quite matter-of-factly, "You will never reach the Mennonites," and for some reason, this, they minded.

Several times during the day, they sat down along the side of the road, generally under a tree, to drink from their water bottles, and each time, a passing vehicle stopped and the driver offered them a ride. Finally, they were afraid even to pause because they found it difficult to reject the offers again and again. At one point, several schoolchildren approached them, giggling, and asked for water, so they gave the children a bottle that was half full and told them to keep it, though they both knew that they were acting less out of generosity than a shared fear of germs. Finally, after they had been walking for more than six hours, they decided that they had no choice—they would accept the next ride, which turned out to come from a very large, blond man in overalls accompanied by two equally blond, similarly dressed teenage boys all crammed together in the cab of an old pickup truck. The man in overalls nodded toward the back, and they climbed in and squatted as though preparing to urinate.

"Mennonites!" Sarah mouthed excitedly.

"Yes, but now what do we do? We can't very well tell them that we're on our way to see them."

The Mennonites did not ask where they were going, however. Instead, the large, blond man drove and the two teenagers rocked gently in the seat next to him. They had driven several miles when, coming over a hill, the women found the landscape startlingly different. Scattered at intervals were farm houses, large and white and sturdy, with barns off to the side and a silo, sometimes even two, attached to the barns. And everywhere they looked there was corn, rows and rows of it. Best of all, the smell of worked soil hung thickly in the air.

"It just feels so weird," said Sara after they had both studied the scenery for a moment. "It's just like Minnesota. It even smells like Minnesota."

"Or Iowa," said Sarah without a hint of annoyance. Rather, she sounded relieved, and Sara, hearing this in her voice, looked over at her quickly. They smiled, and Sara began to sing then, giddily, a song rushing to her from her childhood: "Ho, ho, ho. Happy are we. Anderson and Henderson and Lundstrom and me."

The truck turned into a driveway and continued for several yards toward the house before the driver pressed gently on the brakes, put the truck in reverse, and backed toward the road, stopping at the point where the driveway and the road met. Still, nobody in the cab spoke to them or even turned around to acknowledge them, and the women stood up uncertainly, clutching the sides of the truck lest it begin to move again. When they had dropped to the ground, they waved *thank you,* and the truck crept forward again toward the house.

Now that they were at the Mennonites, they did not know what to do. The day was warm, and the swaying of the truck had left them both drowsy, their legs rubbery. They stood for a time in the road, taking in the corn, and then they turned and began to walk back in the direction from which they had just come. They had not gone far when they heard behind them the whir of bicycles approaching, and so they moved to the side of the road, out of the way. The first bicycle passed quickly, astride it a boy of perhaps twelve pedaling furiously, one leg of his overalls bunched up around his white thigh to keep it from being sucked into the bicycle chain. As he went by, he turned and smiled at them, but it was not a friendly smile; in fact, it was decidedly unfriendly, as though the boy knew why they had come, and they felt ashamed of themselves then for thinking of the Mennonites as a destination.

As Sara looked down, the second bicycle slowly passed on her right, and she felt a hand on her breast, squeezing hard. It took her a second to understand what had happened, as though she were translating from a language that she had just begun to make sense of. Sarah, who was a half step behind her, saw the boy's hand come out and knew instinctively what he was about to do, and she kicked at him, too late. Next, she screamed at the boy, at both boys, who stood on the pedals of their bicycles, heads turned back toward the women to witness their response. Finally, she picked up rocks and began hurling them at the boys, but they were too far away for the rocks to do anything but provoke laughter. The boys pedaled furiously up a hill, and when they crested it, they stopped briefly to wave at the women, and then they were gone.

"Bastards," Sarah screamed, and then, because there was nothing more that she could do, she turned back toward Sara, who was hiccuping sobs, and they stood awkwardly together by the side of the road, all around them the dark earth that had made them think of home. Sarah studied the handprint, thinking how young the boy had looked to have such large hands and how dark, like the soil, the mark was, emblazoned across the white of the shirt. The hand was directly over Sara's breast, appeared to be cupping it, in fact, rising and falling with it as she breathed.

Upon Completion of Baldness

My girlfriend returned from Hong Kong bald, thoroughly bald, the bumps and veins of her skull rising up in relief, as neat and stark as the stitching on a baseball. When we embraced, I noted that her scalp had a sickly yellowish cast to it, the influence of the airport's fluorescent lights apparently, for once we were home, the yellowness had vanished, leaving nothing but white. It may surprise you to know that I did not address her baldness immediately, right there in the airport, but I did not. Rather, we stepped free of our embrace and then rode the escalator down a level to retrieve her suitcase, though I will admit to standing a step above her as we descended in order to survey the very top of her head, the crown, which appeared freer of veins than the rest of her head and brought to mind a bird's belly.

"How was Hong Kong?" I asked as we waited for the conveyor belt to start up and produce her suitcase.

"Tiring," she said with a small, exhausted smile meant to confirm her reply.

Then we stood in silence for several minutes, waiting for her bag to appear, which it did, bright orange and easy to spot. The closest I come to experiencing a sense of wonder in regard to the world and its workings is at the moment that I catch sight of a familiar piece of luggage, last seen thousands of miles away, chugging up the conveyor belt from the bowels of the airport.

I simply do not expect it. Perhaps this seems overly pessimistic, for something must be done with those scores of bags so carefully collected and tagged on the other end. They cannot all simply disappear into nothingness. True. However, I fully expect the other travelers' bags to arrive; it is only the appearance of my own that provokes awe. Furthermore, for the sake of full disclosure, I will reveal that only once has my luggage actually gone astray, and not during one of my more complicated international flights but after the shortest hop imaginable—fifty minutes, Denver to Albuquerque, Albuquerque being home.

When we walked from the car to the house, the chilly desert air seemed to startle her as though, in that moment, she realized that there was a price to be paid for having no hair, and while I still said nothing, I was happy to see her suffer just a bit. She unpacked immediately, unusual for her, while I sat on the bed and watched, focusing on her hands, which dipped in and out of the suitcase, bearing all of the familiar clothing with which she had departed just a week ago, several pairs of black dress pants and lots of orange—blouses, sweaters, a scarf. Somehow she can combine black and orange and not come off looking as though she's dressed for Halloween, but with her nude head bobbing atop her shoulders like a pumpkin, it occurred to me that things might be different now. And still I said nothing, for I hadn't decided yet what it was that I felt—anger, sorrow, embarrassment, perhaps all three.

"Here," she said, handing me a plastic bag containing what appeared to be individually wrapped squares of candy, but when I unwrapped a cube and set it on my tongue, it was definitely not candy. I sucked on it a moment and then bit down.

"Bouillon?" I inquired politely. She laughed, and it sounded the same, rich and frothy, but when I glanced up, her head was bald, and she stopped.

"Dried tuna with wasabi," she said, and we fell silent.

We brushed our teeth together, both of us vying for the sink, a common occurrence, but when the mint of the tooth-paste mixed with the residual taste of dried tuna and wasabi, I nudged her quickly out of the way and leaned over the bowl, gagging. When I glanced up in the mirror, she was there behind me, perhaps looking concerned, though I cannot be sure of that. I do know that with the toothbrush protruding from her mouth, her baldness seemed almost mechanical, as though her head were nothing more than a giant socket, a home for various parts. Later, when we were in bed, I opened my eyes, expecting to see her head illuminated, a full moon rising over her pillow, but there was nothing, only the faint throttle of her breathing.

We had spoken just once while she was away, the day after she arrived in Hong Kong, a brief conversation that seems, in retrospect, to have focused solely on our neighbors, the retired wrestling coach and his wife, who had not yet removed their Christmas lights although it was past Saint Patrick's Day and moving swiftly toward Easter. "Shall I speak to them about it?" I had asked, but she sounded distracted, which at the time I attributed to jet lag. Could it be, I now wondered, that she was already bald, even then? That as I was speaking to her about such trivial matters as Christmas lights, she was pressing the telephone to her bald head fifteen hours ahead of me in Hong Kong? Thus, the first discernible emotion related to her bald-ness: anger. Or perhaps annoyance. Yes, simple annoyance, for it would not do to overstate the matter.

I lay there listening to her sinuses rattle for a good hour before I got out of bed and, in an attempt to understand the situation—her motivations, my reticence—began to write this all down, to record the details as they occurred to me and then to study what I had written, to analyze it in much the same way that I would a text, the analyzing of texts being both my forte and my livelihood. I suspect that most people would be happier if they could manage their relationships in this way, applying their professional training toward making sense of their personal lives as well, though I am obviously in a better position to do so than, say, a plumber or somebody who handles money for a living.

I must confess that, in recording these simple facts, I immediately encountered a snag: in the first sentence, I wrote "my girlfriend," but only after elaborate hesitation, realizing that I had no fixed designation for her other than her name, which is Felicity, an overtly, almost aggressively, symbolic name that I have nevertheless learned to use without smirking. I briefly considered *lover,* but felt that the term put a disproportionate emphasis, inaccurately I might add, on one particular aspect of our relationship. As for *partner* and *significant other,* nothing need be said. Thus it was that I chose the unequivocally precise (albeit bland) designation *girlfriend,* though not without experiencing the aforementioned hesitation, for simply put, *girlfriend* sounds juvenile and might mislead one about our ages, which I will now describe as fortyish.

As I wrote, I could not help but dwell, with some frustration, on certain matters that I had hoped to discuss with Felicity before we returned to school the next day, but she had chosen to arrive home bald instead, preempting discussion. There was the ongoing situation with Mr. Matthers, who, like us, was in his first year of employment at the school, a private high school, technically without a religious bent, though there are shades of such everywhere these days. Felicity had laughed when I told her, early on, that it would behoove us (yes, I used *behoove*) to pay attention to the stir that he was already causing; the three of us were hired together, I pointed out sternly, and thus were associated with one another in the minds of our colleagues, but she said that it *behooved* us (mocking me, no doubt) to pay attention to ourselves.

At that point, there had been only the vague reports that Mr. Matthers was teaching with both hands held in the air, not fully extended like in a holdup, but partially, with his hands sprouting out just above his shoulders. I began to hear more specifically about this strange behavior from my students, many of whom were in his science classes. One day, while my tenth graders worked at their desks diagramming sentences, which, for the record, I still consider a worthy endeavor, I crept down the hall and around the corner to Mr. Matthers's room. He was wearing a tan lab coat with *Let's Bake Bread* stenciled across the front, standing before the class with his heels together and his toes pointed out at a ninety-degree angle, in what we were taught was the appropriate stance for reciting the Pledge of Allegiance or acknowledging "The Star-Spangled Banner" when I was young. And yes, his hands were aloft, not gesturing or even keeping rhythm with what he was saying but simply floating, perfectly still, as though he had thrown them up in a moment of surprise and forgotten them there.

However, that night at dinner, when I informed Felicity that I had gone down to Mr. Matthers's classroom and witnessed his strange behavior firsthand, she remained dismissive. "Maybe it's part of a science experiment," she suggested, chewing as she spoke.

"A science experiment," I replied incredulously, though I paused to swallow first. "The students say that he teaches the entire class like that. How could it possibly be part of a science experiment?"

"Well, perhaps Mr. Matthers is experiencing problems with his circulation. Perhaps he is simply following the advice of a doctor," she had suggested next.

"Perhaps," I replied. "But wouldn't he explain this to the students if that were the case?"

"Perhaps Mr. Matthers is of the opinion that his duty to the students is to explain science," she replied, getting in the final "perhaps," though I knew that she did not care for Mr. Matthers either.

That had been our last discussion of the matter, but during her week away, a second problem had arisen with Mr. Matthers, one that I wanted to apprise her of before she returned to school. I couldn't very well rouse her from a deep, jet-lagged sleep to do so, but the next morning, once we were in the car, I turned to her and said, "Mr. Matthers has been up to his old tricks." She was still bald, of course—not that you would imagine otherwise.

Our commute took approximately twenty-five minutes, enough time to have discussed both Mr. Matthers and the *other* situation had Felicity been amenable to a discussion, which she was not on that particular morning. There were signs. Some mornings, she turned toward the window and rested her forehead against the glass, "appreciating its coolness," she said. Other days, she hummed, a habit she'd had as long as I'd known her. In both cases, I knew not to make any conversational overtures. I do consider it worth mentioning that she did not hum when she was alone, at least not to my knowledge. Rather, the humming was a purely public gesture, a means by which she kept others at a distance. I had pointed this out to her—the impoliteness of it—because that is the sort of thing that one wants to know, but she just laughed.

"Don't be silly," she said. "Humming is a joyful sound, an expression of tranquillity and ease." What does one say to that?

Ten minutes into our commute, she had still offered none of the positive indicators that meant she welcomed conversation.

She had not turned toward me with her left arm flung up along my seat back, fingertips extended invitingly. Nor had she called me *DriverDriver,* which was her nickname for me, borrowed from our friend Sandy, an accounts analyst who was often perplexed by the workings of the human mind. Aware of her shortcoming, Sandy administered personality assessment tests to all of her employees and then interacted with each according to the guidelines prescribed for his or her personality type. When she asked Felicity and me to take one of these tests as well, to help her be a "better friend" as she put it, we of course obliged. I tested into the *driver* camp for both primary and secondary traits, thus the nickname.

Drivers are the control freaks, the ones who cannot let anything slide, though the nickname was meant as a joke, of course, a play on the fact that I literally never let anyone else drive. I've tried, but I get panicky the minute anyone else is behind the wheel. It's the speed, I suspect, for I feel the same way when a plane surges forward on takeoff, moving faster and faster down the runway with no possibility of turning back: my heart rate accelerates, and I am struck by an overwhelming desire to scream, "Stop the plane!" I can imagine few things more mortifying, and the fear of embarrassing myself in this way somehow only exacerbates my panic. Still, I have found that I can calm myself in the middle of these attacks by focusing on something small and unchanging, a meaningless line of text from the airline catalog or the knuckles of my hands.

"Mr. Matthers is up to his old tricks," I repeated, for though Felicity had not extended any of her conversation invitations, neither was she humming or resting her forehead against the window.

"What has he done now? Taken to overseeing the labs with his legs bowed?" she replied, in a voice suggesting that she really did not care to know. Still, she had asked, and that was enough of an opening, particularly if I ignored the latter half of her question.

"Well," I said, perhaps too eagerly. "Remember how you commented just last week that Mrs. Chavez is really starting to show?" Mrs. Chavez, who, like Felicity, is a math teacher, announced just after the Christmas holiday that she was pregnant.

"I do."

"Well, Mr. Matthers has taken to asking her, every time he sees her, in fact, whether she has ever experienced a miscarriage. On Thursday, four or five of us were in the lounge, and we all heard him. We knew about it already, of course, because Mrs. Chavez had mentioned it to several of us." This made it sound as though I were one of the people that Mrs. Chavez confided in, though that was not the case. "Then, Ms. Gutierrez scolded him right there in front of everyone. She told him that it wasn't proper to ask any woman, but especially a pregnant one, whether she'd ever had a miscarriage."

"And has he stopped?" Felicity asked, showing more interest than I expected.

"Well, I haven't heard of anything else, but I left right at the bell on Friday. I had the show, you know."

The show, because I realize that I haven't explained about the shows yet, was a cat show in Los Angeles, for which I left immediately after school on Friday, returning Sunday afternoon in time to grade a set of mediocre essays before picking Felicity up from the airport. Felicity and I are both highly skilled cat judges and, as such, find our services requested at cat shows all over the world. When we were hired at the school, the principal, who is a cat lover as well (though of the mixed-breed, pound-affiliated variety), was quite accommodating about our obligations. In turn, as a gesture of goodwill, we put forth that, except in cases of emergency, we would not accept judging duties that resulted in our being absent from work at the same time. Thus, Felicity agreed to do the Hong Kong show while I stayed behind, holding up our end of the bargain, teaching while she was off, as it turned out, having her head shaved.

By this time, we were pulling into the school parking lot, so Felicity was preoccupied, taking it all in after a week away, her head pivoting in tight, frenetic movements, like a sparrow's, which might have been the way she always moved her head, though, in the past, her hair was there to soften things. We got out of the car, walked across the parking lot and through the front doors, our paths diverging immediately—mathematics left, English right.

And so, I did not tell her about the other incident, the one that had nothing to do with Mr. Matthers at all. It happened on Friday, during third period, with the tenth graders, of whom I am rather fond. I had started them on Salinger, despite the fact that another English teacher, whose name I shall not disclose, had suggested that Salinger, with all his "New Yorkiness," had little to "say" to a group of students who had grown up here in New Mexico.

"I believe that Salinger has something to *say* to all tenth graders," I had replied, perhaps overearnestly. "I myself was once a tenth grader growing up in Minnesota, and I found that he had plenty to say." I do not buy into this idea that one learns more from literature that is familiar; in fact, it seems only logical that one would learn most from subject matter that one has not already mastered through the daily grind of one's existence, which is what I shall tell my colleague the next time she bothers me about Salinger.

I arrived in the classroom just as the bell was ringing, for I had paused briefly outside Mr. Matthers's room on my way back from the teachers' lounge, which is where I generally spend second period, my free hour. When I entered the classroom, the students were unusually still, already in their seats and seemingly engrossed in their Salingers. I felt a momentary thrill at being proven correct, but I had not turned to my right as I entered, so I did not yet know what was there, written in large letters on the blackboard.

"Good morning, class," said I, then waited while they responded in kind, for one of the things that we had been working on was the forgotten art of basic, cross-generational politeness. They always had plenty to say to one another, but on the first day of class, they had stared blankly at me when I greeted them, and so I had related the story of my sixth-grade teacher, Mrs. Kjelmer, who required us to line up at the end of each day and pass by her on our way out of the room, pausing to shake her hand and thank her for some specific contribution that she had made to our educations that day. I am fairly sure that we did not find this odd or extreme, but my students had stared at me in horror as I recounted the tale, a few of them even gasping, as though each day had ended with the beheading of a student rather than this basic gesture of appreciation.

Having acknowledged their return greeting with an inclination of my head, I turned around toward the board, and there, in an awkward teenage scrawl, was their summary of my relationship with Felicity:

MISS LUNDSTROM & MISS SHAPIRO
ARE LEZZIE LOVERS!!

My immediate reaction, as you might expect, was akin to my feelings upon takeoff—that is, I felt remarkably close to crying out, "Stop the plane!" Instead, I did what a speech teacher long ago had advised, which was always to act in opposition to what one's nerves dictated. Thus, instead of mumbling and stammering my way through a demand to know whose work this was on the board, I turned back toward the class and asked, in a very precise, audible tone, whether anyone could recall my position on the ampersand.

There they sat with their mouths drifting open like a choir fading out after a sustained high note, and so I took several steps backward toward the board and pointed, with a surprisingly steady finger, at the offending ampersand. "This symbol, as you may recall, is called the ampersand. Like all symbols used to replace perfectly good words, it is, in my opinion, a symbol primarily of laziness and should be tolerated only on signs or in computer programming." With the side of my hand, I deftly swiped at the ampersand, then picked up a piece of chalk and neatly wrote the word *and* in its place.

"Well," I said, turning again to the class. "Who would like to go next?"

They were familiar with this exercise, of course, for each time I handed back a set of essays, I selected five particularly poor sentences from among them, which I copied onto the blackboard. Then we worked our way through them, one at a time, making corrections and revisions. Nonetheless, I was surprised when Keith, a short boy with a purple smattering of acne, raised his hand.

"Keith," I said.

"The exclamation points?" he asked.

"What about them?" I prodded.

"Do you really need two of them?" The students understood how I felt about the exclamation point, the impact of which I illustrated early on by passing around a print of Edvard Munch's *The Scream*.

"Good," I said. "Though I think that begs the question, Do we really need even one?" I held the chalk out and Keith came dutifully to the front of the room, erased the exclamation marks, and inserted a simple period in their place.

"Well, I suppose that naturally brings us to the excessiveness of all uppercase lettering, does it not?" I said, the students nodding as I rewrote the statement in lowercase, retaining the essential capital letters, of course.

We turned our attention to word choice then, with Clara S., as she always signed her name, suggesting that *lezzie* seemed "informal—or something."

"Hmm," I replied. "Yes, I suppose that a case could be made for informal. Does anyone else have any thoughts on the word *lezzie?*"

"It's spelled wrong?" suggested Beth, an exceedingly poor speller who walked with a strange, gliding motion, as though she were skiing.

"I know," cried Manuel, who was the sort to answer only those questions that the other students had already, and unsuccessfully, attempted. "It's prejudicial." He sat back with his long arms crossed triumphantly, a gesture that did nothing to endear him to the other students.

"What would you suggest?" I asked.

"Lesbian?" Manuel replied after a careful pause, having the good grace to uncross his arms as he spoke. Still, the other students became quiet, unsure perhaps where *lesbian* stood on the "prejudicial" scale, but I was saved the need to make a reassuring response by Tina, a shy girl, partial to plaid, who asked, "Isn't that redundant? I mean, you know they're lesbians because they're both women and they're lovers." Had I been in a different frame of mind, I might have turned the discussion to her seemingly unconscious reference to me and Felicity in the third person, though hadn't I been urging the students all year to please, oh please, just distance themselves a bit from the text?

"Nice work, Tina," I said, and she blushed deeply, in keeping with the type of personality that is attentive to redundancy.

The critique session took nearly half an hour, at the end of which the students slumped in their seats, looking dazed and exhausted. On the board was our final revision: *Ms. Lundstrom and Ms. Shapiro are lovers.* Of course, we had changed "Miss" to "Ms." in both cases, for, as I pointed out to them, Ms. Shapiro and I were not schoolgirls, nor was this the 1950s.

Felicity and I were introduced six years ago by a mutual friend whom I shall call Sally. Sally and I had, once upon a time, been English majors together, but she had gone on to accept a position, temporary she assured me at the time, with a company that replaced windshield glass. The company, however, was not accustomed to having employees who could put an estimate into proper letter format or utilize the semicolon, and soon she had been promoted to regional manager. There was a long period after college during which Sally and I were not in contact, but when I moved to the Twin Cities, I called her and we met for lunch. She looked nearly the same, although puffier and with a penchant for purple, and when she asked what I had been doing for the last fifteen years, I blurted out this parallel list of accomplishments: I had earned a master's degree, done some teaching, and established that I was a lesbian.

Sally was new to the idea of knowing lesbians and admitted to being somewhat nervous, though she seemed unable to articulate the source of her nervousness. I have found that, when presented with this revelation, many people take a careful step back, keeping their mouths shut for fear of saying something wrong, but I have always found myself more charmed by those of Sally's nature, those who barrel right in, unaware that a list of right-and-wrong-things-to-say even exists. Thus, while Sally confessed to a certain nervousness, it was certainly, and refreshingly I might add, nothing that compelled her to err on the side of caution. She telephoned not long after our lunch meeting to announce that she had just met another lesbian, suggesting, with much enthusiasm, that I might wish to meet her new acquaintance, a customer named Felicity whose windshield had been shot out by a neighbor who resented people parking on the street in front of his house.

"And why might I want to meet somebody with such a ridiculous name?" I asked.

Sally paused, for I don't think that it had occurred to her that her suggestion might be met with anything but equal, possibly greater, zeal. "You're of the same ilk," she said at last.

Assuming that by *ilk* she meant a shared orientation, I replied that her "lowest common denominator" approach to matchmaking was a bit insulting.

"But you're both lesbians," she insisted indignantly.

"That," I explained, trying to be gentler, "is the 'lowest common denominator' to which I refer. It is a necessary factor, true, but it hardly qualifies as, well, ilkiness." In her defense, she did not know the special attachment I had to the word *ilk*.

Sally, however, was of a persistent nature, and so, several weeks later, when she and I again met for lunch, Felicity was there as well, though I learned afterward that she had been no more apprised of this meeting than I. At the time, I was putting the finishing touches on my dissertation, which dealt with the practicalities of teaching grammar and writing to older-than-average students. I had discovered, for example, that in a class made up largely of women in their fifties, coordinate and subordinate clauses made sudden sense for them when likened to marriages, the former a marriage in which the two parties were equals, the latter a marriage in which one party was dependent on the other for meaning. In my dissertation, I had neglected to mention, as a corollary to this discovery, that many of the women steadfastly purged their writing of all subordinate clauses following this lesson, suddenly seeing something shameful in each *if* and *because*.

I arrived for lunch that day bearing a list of problematic sentences from my dissertation, hoping to review them with Sally in order to ensure that my meaning, as I intended it, was patently clear, even to the less engaged reader. I saw no reason to alter my plans simply because Felicity was present. In turn, she felt that it was perfectly acceptable to interrupt me and my troubling sentences almost immediately with the following observation: "You have no control over what the reader thinks; you do realize that, I would hope. It doesn't matter *what* you intended."

I'd had my fill of critical theory by that time, so I certainly did not need to be eating lunch with some amateur reader-response critic, but when I suggested, coyly, that perhaps she had been reading too much Stanley Fish, she stared back at me blankly. "I don't believe that I am familiar with Mr. Fish's work," she replied, overly politely I felt. "I'm simply making a point about the way that people communicate. This conversation is a perfect example," she added, pointing her fork at me severely and, I might add, not unbecomingly. "I'm *saying* one thing, but you *think* I'm talking about something else entirely, about some Fish fellow, whom I've never even heard of."

I will admit that her use of *whom* left me undone, even with that preposition dangling unattractively at the end, but then I'm afraid that I've always been attracted to such things, the ability to differentiate between subject and object forms, a refusal to use *if* when the situation requires *whether*.

"This," she was saying, "is what makes mathematics so appealing. The number one is simply that—one. Everyone who sees it thinks the same thing." She looked smugly at me across the table.

"Yes," I replied. "But numbers are just as much symbols as words are." I had nowhere to go from there, but I babbled on. "This," I said, pounding the table, "is a table, the actual, tangible thing, not to be confused with the word. The same can be said for your number *one,* I am afraid." I sketched out the number in the air between us.

Of course I was ashamed of myself, using basic Plato to impress this woman, though, to her credit, she did not look impressed. There was a moment of stiff silence, which compelled me to continue. "To quote one of my students, 'Why is a sheep a sheep and not a rock?'" I said lamely, a bit of irrelevant nonsense to end the discussion, but to my great pleasure, she laughed. Sally, in case you were wondering, was still present, sitting there eating her Cobb salad and, I was to find out later, listening to us argue and regretting the fact that she had ever thought us *ilkstresses* (my word, of course, not the windshield-fixing Sally's).

Over the next few days, Felicity and I did not discuss her baldness or the incident with the chalkboard or even the ongoing escapades of Mr. Matthers, who had just posted several signs in the teachers' lounge announcing that he was interested in acquiring used Tupperware, the word *used* underlined thrice. She made a point of emphasizing her busyness and her jet lag, and before we knew it, it was Friday and I was off again, this time to a cat show in Scottsdale, and when I returned on Sunday evening, taking a taxi from the airport as we had planned, Felicity was gone. I'm sure that to the average, discerning reader, this comes as no surprise, and so I am embarrassed to admit that I never saw it coming.

She left a short letter, of course, in which she explained that she had moved into a studio apartment downtown and purchased a used car, drawing entirely on her "own funds," she was careful to note. The car, she wrote, had belonged to one of the teachers at the school, but she did not refer to this teacher by name, an omission that struck me as a total denial of the degree to which our lives were intertwined. She acknowledged this interconnectedness only at the very end when she wrote that it was her desire that we not "advertise" the change in our relationship at work, that she did realize there would be speculation and gossip, particularly after she filed her new address with the school secretary, but that she hoped we could "absent ourselves from such conversations and treat each other with the politeness and friendly rivalry accorded colleagues."

I was most bothered by the reference to her "own funds," for I was not aware of any funds other than the meager sum of money that resided in our joint checking account, though the mystery of these funds resolved itself soon enough. I made a quick sweep of the house, noting that she had taken all of her books, an easily accomplished task for we had never merged our collections, but left those that we had acquired together. Appliances and kitchen items also remained, though when I counted the cutlery and dinnerware, both of which we had purchased in sets of twelve, I found that each set now consisted of eleven pieces—a consolation, for had there been two of each missing, it would have suggested a situation that I lacked the emotional wherewithal to face.

One of my suitcases was gone, but I forgave her this, for I had taken her suitcase with me to Scottsdale, the suitcase that we always fought over because it was light and maneuverable and orange—easy to spot on the luggage carousel. I fetched it from where I had parked it just inside the door and, not one to let sorrow sideline the moment's practical requirements, began to unpack—placing clothes in the hamper, hanging my toothbrush in its usual slot, though both were now available, and transferring the set of essays that I had graded on the plane into my briefcase.

Inside the suitcase's small, inner compartment, which overzealousness required that I check even though I had not used it, I discovered a piece of paper folded carelessly in half. It bore a pinhole near the top, and several Chinese characters marched down one side, so I knew immediately that it had been left behind after Felicity's less-methodical style of unpacking, carried out exactly one week earlier upon her return from Hong Kong. The rest of the text, which was in English, read thusly:

NOTICE

Kindly to all hotel guests.

A Hong Kong film company has need of the following:

1. Several women (Caucasian) to serve as extras. Roles require British Victorian maidens, but as there is no speaking requirement, Americans and Australians are acceptable. Costumes provided. No stipend, but scene involves eating. Real food provided.
2. Caucasian woman, any age, for horror film. No speaking, but must be willing to shave head on camera. Upon

completion of baldness, a fee of $2500 (U.S.) will be paid in cash.

Interested parties should please inquire from Mr. Simon Woo, front desk, for contact particulars. Thank you.

I read the notice twice, the English teacher in me making mental corrections, before tucking it away inside my desk, in the notebook containing this account, and though I tried to sleep then, I could not. Finally, I rose, retrieved this notebook, and proceeded to read back over my text thus far, but gone were my student days when everything seemed clearer in the middle of the night. I did realize, in looking back over what I had written, that I had said nothing of Felicity's hair, beyond noting its absence. For the record, it was blond, though not purely so, but I dislike expressions such as *dirty blond* and *dishwater blond*. Perhaps what I most admired about her hair, purely from an aesthetic point of view, were the two patches of white that grew in little tufts on either side of her head, directly at her temples. A beautician told her once that these white patches were caused by the use of forceps during childbirth, which I liked to think was the case, suggesting as it did that her stubbornness-bordering-on-truculence had been there all along, making its debut in her unwillingness to cooperate with her own birth, and while the beautician had seemed confident in her theory, she had also maintained with equal assurance that she herself had been born with the ability to understand both German and Chinese, so you can understand my reluctance to put full faith in her explanation.

When I parked in the school lot the next morning, I looked around at the other cars, wondering which was the used car that Felicity had purchased with her own funds, the source of which

I had identified but did not wish to dwell upon. She and I did not cross paths that morning, which was not surprising, for, as I have already indicated, math and English occupied different sides of the school. I made it through my first class and chose to spend my free period in my classroom rather than in the teachers' lounge, so I was there, sitting at my desk, when my tenth graders arrived, Salingers in hand. It was impossible, of course, that they knew anything of our breakup, but I could not shake the feeling that they sensed something, for they struck me as oddly muted that morning, restrained, like caricatures of what they believed perfect students to be.

I handed back their essays, the ones that I had graded on the airplane in a state of oblivion as my bald girlfriend was transporting her few possessions, via her new used car, to her studio downtown, but when I turned toward the blackboard to copy out the five worst sentences from their papers, something struck me, perhaps the memory of the last sentence that we had revised, pushing and prodding it into some sort of straightforward, grammatically sound ideal: *Ms. Lundstrom and Ms. Shapiro are lovers.* In any case, as I stood there at the board, chalk in hand, set to record their most recent transgressions, I began to sob. I did so quietly, of course, but eventually they understood that something was amiss, and I felt them become perfectly still behind me. For several minutes, I stared at a particular spot on the blackboard, at what appeared to be the remains of a letter *b,* composing myself, and then I turned to face my tenth graders, wholly unprepared for the looks of sheer terror and helplessness that sat upon their faces. We stayed as we were, facing one another, I in front of the blackboard and they, sitting erect in their seats, eyes focused uniformly downward, with the exception of Tina, my timid, plaid-wearing redundancy expert, who sat in the back row regarding me closely and nodding.

"Class," I said at last, "please forgive me. I am not in the habit of indulging in such outbursts." At hearing me sound reasonably like myself, they tilted their faces upward again, relief settling collectively upon them; I recalled, in that instant, the vulnerability of youth. I would like to say that this put me fully in charge of my emotions and that the remainder of the class passed without incident, but that was not the case. Rather, as the tears began to flow once more down my face, I blurted out—in an attempt to explain myself and perhaps offer reassurance—these words: "Ms. Shapiro is bald."

And Down We Went

I. THE LAST TIME

I have been defecated on three times in my life, literally crapped on, that is, for I am not the sort to go around characterizing any victimization I might feel in such vulgar metaphorical terms. In each case, the offending party was a bird, the incidents occurring on three different continents over the course of thirty-five years, the third and most recent incident occurring on a quiet street in Kuala Lumpur, Malaysia, as Georgia and I stood beneath the eaves of an antique textile shop waiting for it to open. We had first visited the shop two days earlier and were not particularly looking forward to seeing the owner again, for, like a certain type of gay man everywhere, even Malaysia it turned out, he could not take lesbians seriously and responded to our questions regarding *songket* and *ikat* with a barely concealed smirk. At one point, he wrapped a shawl around my shoulders and stepped back, declaring, "Ideal for the streets of Manhattan," though I was not from New York and had said nothing to suggest otherwise. "And more reasonably priced than other pieces in the collection," he added, tucking his hands behind his back as if to suggest that he was at my service.

The shop was late in opening that morning, though lateness was something we had come to expect in the year that we had been teaching in Malaysia. There was even an expression that Malaysians used—*rubber time*—to sum up their general feelings about time, which they saw as something that could be stretched and pulled, even snapped, as the occasion required. I was familiar with lateness from my years in New Mexico, but I could not adjust to the rubber analogy, perhaps because I had been living so long in the desert, a place where rubber turned quickly brittle, bags of unused rubber bands crumbling in my desk drawer. Thus, when my Malaysian students, tethered to their invisible rubber bands of time, arrived late for class day after day, my patience grew brittle. "Tardiness sends a nonverbal message," I reasoned with them, employing the language of business communications, which is what I had been hired to teach them, after all, but they stared back at me with looks that implied that business communications was a subject best left to theory.

Eventually, I began locking them out, but they simply gathered in the hallway, waiting patiently for me to relent. I always did, for I knew that they were sorry—not sorry that they had been late but sorry that their lateness upset me, which were two different things. But as I unlocked the door one morning, prepared to listen to the usual excuses about the rain and late buses and uncooperative scooters, I saw myself as they must: a middle-aged woman who lectured them day after day regarding a notion whose value she seemed to measure in inverse proportion to the blatant disregard attached to it by others, who pounded the doorjamb, her neck growing blotchy, as they looked on quietly, their shuffling feet the only suggestion of protest. When, I wondered, had this woman begun to view tardiness as a symbol of moral decay, a personal attack being perpetrated against her daily? And when had I become her?

I spent the first eighteen years of my life in rural Minnesota, attending school with farm children who often arrived late for some reason or other—because milking had taken longer than usual or a calf had become sick. There were times, too, at the beginning and end of the year, when they missed entire days, a state of affairs toward which most teachers in our school were tolerant. The exception was third grade: that year, as the farm children slouched in exhausted and disoriented, excuse notes in hand, Mrs. Carlstrom, our teacher, stopped whatever we were doing to assess each note, and then, picking up her chalk once again, addressed the recently arrived child, saying, "Mr. Otto, how nice that you could fit us into your busy schedule," after which she chuckled dryly. We were afraid of Mrs. Carlstrom for a variety of reasons: because she talked like this, using our surnames and speaking as though we were adults who made our own decisions about time and attendance and our educations in general, and because, unlike our other teachers, she did not alter her tone or diction level when she addressed us, not even her notion of humor, which was tied closely to the first two and which none of us understood.

My parents owned the only eating establishment in town, the Trout Café, and were thus acquainted with Mrs. Carlstrom, who occasionally came in after school and drank several cups of coffee while grading our homework, a process that often involved little more than drawing an angry red line diagonally across a page, which meant that the work was, as she put it, unacceptable. My father told me once that she had a "caustic wit," which, he said, was something that most people did not appreciate. I did not know this word, *caustic,* and, until I bothered to look it up, mistakenly assumed it had something to do with *cause,* though what I thought it caused, I cannot say—shame and uneasiness, I suppose, judging from my classmates' reactions. When I finally did check its meaning, I found that *caustic wit* had actually to do with bitterness and that bitterness (this also from the dictionary, for I was too young to have learned these things in any other way) had much to do with disappointment.

During that year in Malaysia, I realized that I had had enough of teaching, which I had been doing for fifteen years with a fair amount of success and, it must be said, an increasing sense of bitterness. We both felt this way, I think, Georgia to the lesser degree and I to the much greater, though we spoke of it only in small, petty complaints. The day that my classroom epiphany occurred was my forty-fourth birthday, no milestone event but significant nonetheless, for that was Mrs. Carlstrom's age when I was her pupil. We had been in Malaysia for six months by then, but I had told no one at the college that it was my birthday, certainly not my students, who would have stared at me awkwardly, wondering what they were to do with the information. However, when we awoke that morning, Georgia made no mention of it either, though we had celebrated the occasion together fourteen times. Throughout the day, when we met in the hallway at school or sat together in the cramped teachers' room, I looked for signs that she was pretending, perhaps to heighten the pleasure of a planned surprise, but as the day wore on, surpriseless, I knew that she truly had forgotten, and I consoled myself by blaming the tropics, which did not provide the usual seasonal markers—turning leaves and shortening days—that keep us attuned to weeks and months and the passing of time.

Late that afternoon, as we sat together grading papers at our only table, Georgia threw down her pen with a startled look and blurted out, "Happy birthday."

"Thank you," I answered cordially.

She looked around wildly for a moment, as though she had misplaced something of importance. "I thought that we might go out for noodles," she said at last, and though this was something we did at least twice a week, I replied, "That sounds nice."

That night, after we had eaten our noodles and raised our Tiger beers in a toast, after we were back home and in bed, lying far apart in the darkness (presumably because of the heat) and speaking of trivial matters, I found myself overcome with desire, a yearning so strong that it was like a presence there in the bed between us, something separate from me, outside my control. In the early days of our relationship, we had often lain awake all night, not making love but talking, as though only by forfeiting sleep could we tell each other all of the things we wanted to say. Of course, we had sex also, but sex was secondary, an act that we engaged in at dawn, when the sky began to lighten, making us too shy for words. In fact, sex for us then was like the cigarette that other people smoke *after* sex, a way to separate into two discrete beings. I do not recall now when our days started to fill with events deemed unworthy of discussion, but they did, and as silence or, even worse, inconsequential chatter followed us to bed, sex took on a cathartic role, becoming a constant toward which we could turn to find any number of things—pleasure, comfort, and even reconciliation.

The desire I felt that night was not sexual, however—that is, I knew that the simple act of sex would do nothing to alleviate it. Rather, what I felt was nothing less than a desperate need to pass the long hours of the night telling Georgia about my day: how, as I unlocked the classroom door that morning and faced my tardy students, I had watched myself as though watching a stranger, noting the way that the students regarded me, with a mixture of pity and awe and resentment, and how all of this had left me feeling deeply disoriented and alone. I saw then that my desire was not a presence between us but a void, a deep pit that we both turned instinctively away from, rolling toward our opposite sides of the bed, Georgia snorting as she often did just before falling into a quiet, motionless sleep.

In Malaysia at that time, the mid-nineties, everyone was engaged in the making of money, and though Georgia and I had never fared well at this, largely due to lack of trying, we allowed ourselves to be wooed by the ease with which students and colleagues alike engaged in various sorts of entrepreneurial maneuvering, doing so without any of the soul-searching or shame that often accompanied such things back home. We lived in Malacca, an old port city known for its antique shops, which we took to perusing on the weekends. It was there that we met Jackson, a portly Chinese man several years our junior who owned a shop specializing in sea salvage, pottery mainly, scavenged from sunken trading ships along the coast. Jackson was an expert in any number of things, and as we spent more and more time in his shop, he became like a mentor to us, teaching us practical skills, such as how to determine what tools had been used in a chest's construction and whether a textile had been stitched by hand; most important, Jackson treated our new-found interest in business as something normal, even desirable.

One Saturday, as we drank tea in the back of Jackson's shop, a partially enclosed courtyard overgrown with lush tropical plants, a man came back to where we sat and opened a suitcase on the table in front of us. Inside, beneath a stack of sweaters and trousers, unlikely tropical wear, lay twelve lumpy socks, which he picked up by the toes one at a time, letting the contents of each spill into his hand. "Fossilized red coral," Jackson explained as we held the carvings, which were smooth and surprisingly cool. "From Tibet."

Then, lulled not just by the tactile sensation but also by the soothing staccato of Chinese as Jackson and the man bargained, disagreeing and then—their tones unchanged—agreeing, I felt, for the first time in weeks, fully relaxed. And though this was indeed pleasant, the significance of that afternoon lay in what happened next. After the man departed, we admired Jackson's purchases while he proudly recounted the details of his bargaining, in doing so referring repeatedly to this man with whom we had just been sitting as *the smuggler*. He did so casually, as though smugglers were a daily part of life, not just his own but ours as well. How to explain the overwhelming gratitude I felt at that moment, the sheer giddiness at being treated like somebody accustomed to the company of smugglers?

And so, shortly thereafter, during a two-week visit to Java, Georgia and I decided to become proprietresses, traders in Asian furniture and antiques, announcing our decision via a letter that we sent to family and friends back home and receiving, in return, letters of surprise and, in the case of Georgia's grandmother, disapproval at what she disdainfully termed our "foray into commerce." I soon began waking up most nights in a panic, unable to imagine the shift from a professional life that revolved around instructing others in the rules of grammar, interactions I regarded as pure, to one in which conversations about furniture would dominate—conversations, moreover, that would be aimed at nudging my audience toward the purchase of a piece of said furniture: a teak daybed, a dowry chest, or, my favorite, a *dingklik*.

A *dingklik* is a primitive bench, innocuous in and of itself,

though the word, which was like two dueling interjections—
Ding! Klik!—delighted me with its exotic dissonance. Later, I
fretted that it was my pleasure in speaking the word that had led
us to purchase seven of them, along with fifty-three other pieces
of furniture, during our visit to Java, for the trip, our first period
of sustained relaxation in several years, had done what such
things often do: it had acted as a referendum on our lives, allowing us the opportunity to assess our situation, to find it lacking,
and, through the purchase of a container of furniture that represented our combined life savings, to, in effect, vote for change.

Georgia had cheated on me. The high school in Albuquerque where she taught had arranged an overnight camping
retreat in an attempt to get the faculty to bond, a goal that they
had apparently achieved, for when she returned the next day,
Georgia immediately confessed that she had been placed with
a much younger colleague in what she referred to ridiculously
as a "tent-cabin" and that, during the night, they had spoken
openly and intimately about many things. "Something happened," she whispered, and then she began to sob.

"She's twenty-six," I said. "You were twenty when she was
born. You could be friends with her mother." I did not say that
she could *be* her mother because I found such a statement too
dramatic. Nor do I know why I chose to make the discussion
about age, as though it were the woman's age that I objected
to, as though I would have been perfectly happy had Georgia
cheated on me in a "tent-cabin" with a woman in her forties.
Beyond this, we had decided not to discuss the details, or, in
fairness, I should say that I had decided this for us, and in order
to make my wishes perfectly clear, I ended what was to be our
only discussion of the topic with the most flippant comment that
I could muster on such short notice. "A younger woman," I said.
"Since when did we begin engaging in heterosexual clichés?"

After several weeks of moping around the house, Georgia suggested that we needed "a challenge" and broached the idea of going overseas. I understood that she was making a gesture, and so we went, abandoning established lives involving jobs and friends and a house, choosing Malaysia for no other reason than that it seemed an ignored country, the one that tourists leapt over as they passed from Thailand to Indonesia. The move, however, had solved nothing, and so we had taken this more dramatic step, binding ourselves to each other by using every cent we had to buy *dingkliks* and *palungans* and *gereboks,* to buy a whole new vocabulary in order to avoid the ordinary words that one uses to discuss such an ordinary event as cheating.

This was how we came to be standing on the steps of Gerard Tung's antique textile shop that morning, waiting for it to open. As we waited, a bird in the eaves above us, knowing nothing of the events that had brought us there, defecated down the front of my blouse and, for good measure, onto my skirt. The bird's waste hit with the force of a water balloon, giving the impression of an intentional blow rather than what it was, a by-product of nature that I had unwittingly placed myself in the path of. In fact, I believe that it was this—the randomness coupled with the utter absence of malice—that triggered my highly uncharacteristic response: under the strain of attempting to suppress my tears, my chin began to quiver, dimpling like a golf ball.

Georgia fumbled around in her backpack. "Don't cry," she said.

There are, I have learned, numerous ways to make this statement. There is the *Don't cry* that is issued as a demonstration of solidarity and sympathy and that is succeeded, most often, by the words *or you'll get me started*. There is the more detached and perhaps reflective *Don't cry,* one suggesting that the situation, and often life in general, does not merit tears, a tone that I generally find both reassuring and persuasive. Then there is the *Don't cry* that is pure threat, that warns, *Do not start because I am not in a position to think about you or your needs, and if you do start, you will see this and most surely be disappointed.*

This last one was the "Don't cry" that came from Georgia's mouth the morning that I was defecated upon for the third time in my life. By the time that Gerard Tung appeared with his key and his attitude, I was sitting on the step outside his textile store, crying and swiping at the eggy mess on my skirt.

"Where is your friend today?" he asked, making no mention of my state.

"My friend?" I replied, though it was none of his business. "My friend is gone."

II. THE PENULTIMATE

The second time occurred when I was twenty-nine, in Madrid, where the woman who was to become my lover (yes, Georgia) had not yet become my lover, despite the fact that we had moved to Spain in order to bring such a thing to fruition, a motivation that neither of us had acknowledged, not even to ourselves. We had met some months earlier in Albuquerque, but our courtship had seemed impossible there, for neither of us could bear the thought of others watching it unfold, offering comments that would make us more self-conscious, particularly given our mutual tendency toward shyness, mine of the Midwestern sort, a reticence that was like a dog holding fast to a bone, Georgia's an easily misread shyness that manifested itself in a steady stream of words.

When we met, Georgia was dating Lisa, a perfectly nice woman who took her lesbianism seriously, despite having not informed her parents of its existence. This she blamed on the fact that she was Korean. "When I visit my parents, I am still expected to greet my father at the door when he returns from work each night," she told us one evening over beers, by way of explaining just how difficult it would be to tell them.

"But you don't even speak Korean," Georgia observed, for the sake of understanding as well as arguing, which were two equally compelling tendencies in her personality, though I knew that her point lay in the latter camp.

"Exactly," replied Lisa. "So how could I tell them?"

Lisa was in medical school, and though I liked her and enjoyed our weekly tennis matches, cordial yet competitive affairs, I referred to her, disparagingly, as the Medic because I could not get over the fact that she did not like poetry and thought nothing of blurting out, "I don't get poetry at all," by which she meant that she not only didn't understand it but even questioned its value.

Late one Sunday afternoon, as the three of us sat in the yard in front of Georgia's apartment, a tiny place above what had once been a carriage house, the talk turned to poetry, as it often did when Georgia and I were together. Lisa reached, by reflex, for her medical book and began to read about digestive disorders while Georgia and I attempted to piece together "The Burial of the Dead" from memory. Eventually, she retrieved her *Complete Works of T. S. Eliot* and read the piece aloud.

"Try to guess my favorite line," I teased in the poem's afterglow, sure, in fact, that she could not, for in a poem filled with April's cruelty and Madame Sosostris, I was drawn to a seemingly innocuous line about sledding. Georgia thought for a moment and then, without consulting the text, recited, "'Marie, Marie, hold on tight. And down we went,'" speaking quietly, her voice capturing the wistfulness that I too sensed in these lines.

"Yes," I replied, but only after demonstrating a lengthy interest in the patch of grass directly beneath my crossed legs. "Yes, that's it."

The confidence with which she had recited these lines quickly gave way to nervousness, the sort that hangs in the air like a scent, and the Medic, looking up from her digestive disorders, sniffed delicately like a cat, then closed her book with a loud clap. "Well, should we start cooking?" she asked, for the three of us had planned to make dinner together. I knew, however, that I could not enter Georgia's narrow attic apartment and stand cooking with them in its tiny kitchen, the ceiling slanting crazily down around us, and so I made an awkward excuse and left, but as I let myself out at the gate, I felt inexplicably giddy, as though exiting a lecture that had presented a familiar topic in an entirely new, and unexpected, light.

"Don't leave Eliot outside," I called happily back to them, gesturing at the book, which lay side by side with the Medic's textbook, indistinguishable from afar, unlikely twins keeping company in the grass.

Just weeks earlier, I had finished my master's degree in literature and taken to walking for much of the day, a purposeless endeavor that provided something I had missed during my years of poring over literary theory—a straightforward sense of progress. Georgia, who was on sabbatical from teaching high school, often joined me for the morning stint before heading off to her bartending job at the American Legion. Most mornings, she greeted me in her pajamas, apologizing profusely as she tamped down her curls and dressed, but the morning after our Eliot exchange, she was waiting fully dressed and exploded out the door, frantic, like a dog that has not been exercised in days. We were both fast walkers but particularly so that morning, our conversation, by contrast, stalling frequently, for many of our usual topics seemed suddenly unworthy of words. As we waited for the green light at the corner of Mountain and Twelfth Street, our attention safely fixed on a woman pushing a stroller across the intersection toward us, I blurted out my intention to go abroad, an intention that was being formed even as I opened my mouth to describe it. The stroller, choosing this moment to collapse, doubled in on the sleeping baby, who awoke and made his displeasure known, and we rushed out to carry the stroller to safety, the mother trotting behind us with the shrieking infant.

"Where will you go?" Georgia asked quietly as we worked at resurrecting the contraption.

"Hungary," I replied, an answer reflecting less a personal interest than a need to seem in possession of a considered response.

"I'll go with you," Georgia said, her voice rising uncertainly. "If you want." She added, "It could be fun," and then, finally, "We broke up last night."

Three weeks later, we were in Spain, Hungary having proven an unexpectedly complicated destination. However, once we were there, alone in a cheaply furnished apartment with too many bedrooms and massive furniture that shed its veneer in large strips, which we dutifully glued back in place, we did not know what to do next, for we simply did not know how to take the final steps toward each other. Thus, we found ourselves easily frustrated by nearly everything: the country, the language, but, most of all, each other.

Spain exhausted us: people stayed up all night drinking and smoking, and then, judging from the evidence in the streets, vomiting and shedding shoes as they made their ways home, all of this performed loudly, of course, for Spaniards seemed inordinately loud, a state of affairs that we both found unnerving, perhaps because we held something so fragile between us. There were other things that we disliked. Vegetables were always overcooked in restaurants. Also, when we shook our rugs from our balcony, Juan Carlos, who lived below us, came up and scolded us, and when we pointed out that the old ladies all shook their rugs from their balconies, he told us that *we,* and not the old ladies, lived above *him,* and so we were forced to lug our rugs down three flights to the street, where, as we stood shaking them, the old ladies came by and ridiculed us to boot.

I did not like the old ladies in Spain, who laughed openly at my pronunciation and thought nothing of pushing me aside in the market and calling out "I am" when the butcher asked who was next or of screaming out the names of the fruits and vegetables I was trying to procure quietly by pointing. Furthermore, they insisted on going out for bread in their robes each morning and then gathering at the corner beneath our apartment to chat, speaking to one another so loudly that I thought, the first time, that someone was being attacked, until I stepped out onto the balcony and saw only them beneath me, clutching *pistolas* of warm bread to their breasts, their overweight lapdogs guarding their ankles.

One morning, I carried our dirty rugs down to the street, where four men in blue jumpsuits stood on the sidewalk around a large hole that had been dug to expose our building's gas line, staring into it as they sipped cognac that had been delivered from the bar on the corner. It was ten thirty in the morning, a suitable hour for a drink apparently, for I had been watching this same cycle of events for nearly two weeks—two weeks, I should add, during which we had no gas for cooking or hot showers. The mailman arrived then and was invited to join them, which he did, eagerly claiming a cognac and edging up to the hole.

It disappointed me to see him so easily distracted from the rigor of his day, for one of the things I most liked about Spain was that mail was delivered not once, but twice, daily. Just the evening before, I had come home to find proof of this second round of deliveries, a letter from my father consisting of one sentence written on the back of a used café receipt. "Thought you'd be interested," it said, a reference to the attached clipping from the local paper describing the details of Mrs. Carlstrom's recent death.

It was in a similar fashion, two years earlier, that I had learned of the massive stroke that left her paralyzed and unable to speak, though there was speculation that her condition had worsened during the forty hours she lay on her kitchen floor, waiting for her husband, a truck driver, to return home and find her. "He's parked her in Lakeview," my father wrote at the end of that epistle, referring to the nursing home in Glenville, a place I knew well, for when I was ten, I made monthly visits there to a man whom the Girl Scouts had chosen to be my foster grandfather, though he was only thirty-two, younger even than my parents, and lived there because he was mentally retarded and had nowhere else to go. I brought him cookies, usually cinnamon logs. These he ate in a single sitting, always offering me one, which I refused because the smell of the place—urine and ointment and what I assumed to be aging flesh—made me gag. In fact, sitting perched on a chair beside him, I felt like an older sister charged with watching him eat, which he did loudly and messily. Though I did not do so, I had an overwhelming desire to scold him, to point to the wet crumbs scattered across his face and shirt, knowing that he would make an effort at reform, for, even though I was a child (or perhaps *because* I was a child), I could see that docility was expected from the residents, which is why I could not imagine Mrs. Carlstrom there—until it occurred to me that the stroke had imposed a docility all its own.

Thus, two years had passed, during which time I thought of her infrequently, if at all. According to the article, she had been visited daily by her husband, whom the staff described as "a quiet, overly devoted man." Indeed, he had given up trucking in order to sit beside her in silence, she unable to speak and he, presumably, not wont to, a routine that had continued day after day until he arrived one afternoon for his daily visit, placed a pistol directly above her left ear, and shot her as she sat propped up in her bed. The staff had gathered in the hallway, too afraid to enter the room where Mr. Carlstrom sat holding his wife's hand, the pistol resting atop the mound of her stomach. When the sheriff, a man with whom Mr. Carlstrom sometimes hunted, arrived, Mr. Carlstrom let go of her hand so that he could be handcuffed.

"I did it because I loved her," he was quoted as saying, a statement about which much had been made, by the community and, therefore, by the press, who devoted the remainder of the article to comments reflecting what was termed *community grief*: "He's nothing but a cold-blooded murderer," Alice, thirty-eight, of Glenville, had said, while a local pastor warned, "To say that this was done out of love is blasphemy." I showed the article to Georgia, my voice tight as I read aloud these statements from people who had been his neighbors and friends, people whom I knew I might recognize by sight or surname.

"They're in shock," she offered.

"You don't know that," I replied angrily. "You're from New York. You don't know the first thing about these people." Which implied that I did. We went off to our separate rooms, and in the morning when I awoke, Georgia had already gone out.

I knew that some sort of gesture was needed, an action that would be viewed as conciliatory, and so I had decided to clean the apartment, which is how I came to be standing on the sidewalk with the rugs, watching the men in blue jumpsuits drink cognac and nod at the gas line. Determined that their idleness not dictate my own, I dumped my bundle of rugs to the ground, chose one, and began shaking it mightily so that it snapped like a sail in the wind and filled the air with dust.

"*¡Olé!*" cried out one of the men while the others laughed and cheered me on.

"Don't you have work?" I asked in awkward Spanish, glaring at the hole.

"Ah," said the mailman. "You must be the American." He set down his cognac, dipped into his mailbag, and produced two letters, which I stepped toward him to receive. As I did so, however, extending my hand eagerly, I felt something hit my wrist, a warm, gentle splat, and I held it up for inspection. There it was, no bigger than a squirt of toothpaste, a small white glob drizzled with specks of black, so stunningly simple in appearance that it struck me as something that might be presented, atop an oversized dinner plate and with much fanfare, at a restaurant featuring haute cuisine.

"Asshole birds," said the mailman, shaking his head sadly, and the others joined in, loudly and creatively cursing the birds perched on the balcony above us.

I, though, was in no mood for sympathy, certainly not that tendered by a group of men who had been mocking me moments earlier and who, moreover, were the reason I had not enjoyed a hot shower in weeks. My anger, of course, was much broader, including in its scope any number of things: the fact that across the ocean, in the place where I had grown up, an old man sat in jail awaiting trial for what I deemed the ultimate act of love (because, at that age and fresh from years spent in the study of literature, I believed that sacrifice always implied love); that for this act he had already been judged harshly by those around him; and that I myself, despite my years of bookish devotion to such matters, had absolutely no idea how to engage in the pursuit of love.

"Chica," said one of the men, awkwardly (and loudly). "Don't cry." And I realized only then that I was.

He bent down and picked up a cognac, which he handed to me. "To the asshole birds that shit on us," he said cheerfully, waving his glass in the air as the others joined in. I clinked my glass against theirs and we drank, drank with the relish that comes from toasting adversity.

Dear Mr. Carlstrom [I wrote later that morning],

Twenty years ago, your wife was my teacher. From her, I learned, among other things, the correct use of the apostrophe. I am currently living in Spain, a country technically without apostrophes, though this does not prevent people from using them everywhere. Yesterday, for example, I saw a sign that read "Billiard's" and another offering "English language book's." I could not help but think of Mrs. Carlstrom, who would have inquired indignantly, "Of what, may I ask, are these billiards and books in possession?" I am teaching English to businessmen here, and though I am not suited for this particular audience, I believe that I may be suited for the profession itself.

There was something generally deceitful about the letter, which implied that Mrs. Carlstrom had somehow influenced my decision to become a teacher. She had not, nor had she taught me the correct usage of the apostrophe, although she had tried on several occasions, always unsuccessfully. Still, I felt that the letter contained the spirit of what I wanted to say, which was that she had, in some way, *marked* my childhood, and so I mailed it, addressing it simply, "Mr. Carlstrom, Glenville, MN, USA." As I walked home from the post office, I stopped to purchase a propane camping stove, and that evening I prepared a soup consisting of what we had on hand: ten shriveled carrots, a few potatoes, and frozen shrimp that turned mealy long before Georgia arrived home.

Still, she seemed pleased by the soup, and as we ate, tearing off chunks of bread and dipping them into the orange stew, I told her about my day, concluding nervously, "I feel that nothing has gone right here—for us, I mean."

Georgia chewed and swallowed a shrimp, gulping noisily as it went down. "The Medic broke up with me," she said.

"Oh," I replied, my face becoming hot.

"I mean," she quickly clarified, "she broke up with me because of that line from Eliot." She lifted her wineglass and bit noisily at the rim, troubled by having made what amounted to a declaration.

"Oh," I said again, this *oh* of a much different tenor. We both took a few swallows of wine, hoping to rinse away the carrots that clung to our teeth, though when we kissed, they were still there, small bits of orange that our tongues dislodged.

III. THE VERY FIRST

The first time happened long ago when I was a young girl growing up in that small town in Minnesota with no idea whatsoever that one day I might find myself in love or that the object of my affection might be a woman (moreover, a woman who would someday cheat on me) or that I might find myself a teacher living in such places as Spain and Malaysia, places vastly different from the world that I then knew, but, as it turned out, places where birds would defecate on me nonetheless.

That day, my third-grade class was making its way to the home of Mr. Nyquist, a very old man whose hobby was tumbling agates. Each Halloween, he dropped two or three of them into our bags instead of candy, so we all had examples of his work at home, which meant that as an outing, seeing Mr. Nyquist's agates held little appeal. He lived only a block and a half from the school, but we were still each assigned a walking buddy, a classmate with whom we were to hold hands and match steps. I was paired with Jaymy Korkowski, a skinny boy with legs far longer than mine. I recall that I expected his hand to be dry and cool in keeping with the thin, chalky look of him but that instead it was wet with perspiration, a fat boy's hand.

As we passed under an elm tree just half a block from the school, something hit my shoulder with the impact of a lightly packed snowball and, without letting go of Jaymy's hand, I stopped to inspect it. Each year on Mother's Day, I was made to present to my paternal grandmother, who did not like me, a box of chocolates from which I always managed to choose the most disgusting one, a chocolate filled with a yellowish, phlegm-like substance that bore an amazing resemblance to the glob that rested atop my shoulder that morning. When Jaymy Korkowski saw it, he dropped my hand, sat down hard on the sidewalk, and began to cry, great, wet, gasping sobs that shook his entire body. Of my thirty-three classmates, he was the one about whom I knew the least, and so I had nothing to draw upon in making sense of his reaction. I leaned down, taking in the full smell of him, which was not unpleasant, the dominant odor that of manure and beneath it, something sweeter, carrots perhaps.

"It's just bird poop," I said, though he cried even harder at being provided with this information.

By then, we had fallen well behind the other fifteen pairs, fifteen for there were two students missing that day, both of them farmers' children, no doubt kept home when it was learned that we would be wasting a precious portion of the day admiring rocks when they could be out in the fields removing them. Mrs. Carlstrom soon noticed our absence and brought the class to a halt. Then, while they waited, watched over by Mrs. Preebe, the portly assistant librarian who had been brought along in anticipation of just such an event, Mrs. Carlstrom marched back to us. By the time she arrived, however, Jaymy Korkowski was on his feet, fully recovered, and so her attention was directed toward my shoulder.

"You'll live," she said in the gravelly monotone that she used for explaining division and congratulating us on our birthdays; then, Jaymy Korkowski in tow, she turned and walked back to the others, leaving me behind.

Mrs. Carlstrom was, as I have already noted, nothing like our other teachers, who addressed us in high, cooing voices and seemed perpetually in awe of even our most minor accomplishments. Moreover, they all lived in town and often came into our café with their families, using their regular voices with my parents and slipping into the cooing voices whenever I appeared. I knew what foods they liked and had even seen several of them with ketchup dabbed colorfully on their faces. They were familiar, knowable. Only Mrs. Carlstrom lived elsewhere, eight miles away in Glenville, where my father had grown up and which, on warm Sunday evenings, we visited, driving slowly up and down its streets while he pointed to various houses, explaining who had lived there when he was a boy and who lived there now and how this transition had come about. One evening, he surprised us by looping out of town to show us a run-down trailer park, stopping in front of a lopsided trailer with an overturned wooden crate for steps. Three dogs stood in the dirt yard, eyeing us from behind a chicken wire fence.

"Do you know who lives there?" my father asked of me specifically, and from the backseat I said that I did not.

"That is your teacher's house," my father announced.

"Mrs. Carlstrom?" I said skeptically, unable to reconcile her with such a place.

"She's not much of a teacher," my father pointed out almost apologetically. "But that's generally the way it is with smart folks." As he spoke, he gestured in the general direction of her yard, so I did not know whether he meant that this—the dirt and crate steps and barking dogs—was the way it was with smart people or that she was not much of a teacher because she was smart. Until then, I had not even known that she was smart, though I did know that she was not much of a teacher: if we did not understand some aspect of the lesson, she did not offer examples that might help us better understand what was involved but instead repeated exactly what she had said the first time around, as though there were only one way to convey the information and this was it.

The elm tree from which the bird took aim at me that morning stood in front of the McHendrys' house, which I soon found myself inside along with Mrs. Preebe, whom Mrs. Carlstrom had sent back to deal with me while the others forged on with the field trip. We were shown into the bathroom, where Mrs. Preebe scrubbed my shirt while Mrs. McHendry, who possessed the frenetic energy displayed by certain types of very thin people, stood in the doorway regarding us through a haze of cigarette smoke, for these were the days when smokers simply smoked, without rules involved, by which I mean that they did not avoid certain rooms or take into consideration the presence of children.

The McHendrys owned one of two grocery stores in town, the one that we called the Market as opposed to the other, the V Store, as in *Variety,* which is what they provided—not just food but an assortment of school supplies and clothing as well as an entire section intriguingly entitled Notions. The McHendrys, by contrast, offered a butcher shop, where you could point to a block of pimento loaf, for example, and watch as Mr. McHendry sliced it right there in front of you. He would pinch the first slice between a folded sheet of wax paper and thrust it across the counter for your inspection. "Thinner?" he would ask, in a voice that implied that this was the ideal thickness but that he was giving you the option to ignorantly choose otherwise.

Years later, long after I had left that town, I would learn from my father that on a May day, the first warm day of spring, Mr. McHendry walked out of the Market, leaving behind the few dollars that he had taken in that morning, locked the front door, and took the key next door to the bank, where he handed it over to the bank president, the only person in town who knew exactly how poor business had been for years, and then went home to the house with the elm tree. From this house, according to my father, he did not emerge for nearly a decade. People considered his behavior extreme, some even suggesting that he was not well, and on the other end of the phone line, I could hear the sound of my father tapping his own head, clarifying the nature of this presumed illness. I, however, found his behavior perfectly logical: he had once divided his world between the Market and home, and this was the half left to him. I never wondered why he had given up, for I knew that people did, only why he had chosen that particular day to do so, why, after months of snow and ice, months during which he had gotten out of bed and carried on against the dearth of customers, the encroaching bills, the oppressive proximity of the bank, why he had awakened that morning to the promise of warmth and found it all too much to bear. Only later did I begin to understand the way that a simple gesture of sympathy or solidarity, even, it seemed, one of a meteorological nature, could crumble one's resolve far more quickly than adversity itself.

On the morning that I was defecated on for the first time in my life, a part of me wanted desperately to believe that Jaymy Korkowski was sobbing on my behalf, that his tears were shed over the small injustice I had suffered, though something, sheer stubbornness perhaps, kept me from doing so. I have since come to understand that this—the need to imagine our pain worthy of another's anguish, our circumstances capable of invoking sacrifice or even despair in another human being—is a basic human need, one felt even more deeply as we confront our own shortcomings in meeting this need for others.

In the weeks that followed, I committed myself wholeheartedly to learning about Jaymy Korkowski, hoping to make sense of his response, but in the end, I learned only this: that when Jaymy Korkowski was a baby, his father had caught his leg in a bear trap and it had been amputated right above the knee, an interesting but irrelevant bit of trivia, for I was a logical child who knew better than to complete a puzzle out of just two pieces. I have since come to believe that what caused his tears that morning was not something large at all—some deeply ingrained character trait or lasting trauma—but rather a small thing, some soon-forgotten incident that had taken place earlier that morning, coloring his mood for the day: his father had yelled at him, perhaps, for an error made during milking or he had been bullied by the Pipo boys on the school bus. This, after all, is the way our lives unfold.

What this means, of course, is that on a different day, one free of bullies or milking errors, Jaymy Korkowski and I might have joined hands and walked, and as we did, a bird, the same bird if you like, might have defecated on me, but because this was a different morning, Jaymy Korkowski instead might have begun to laugh at my misfortune, to laugh so hard that he wet himself; or, to laugh so hard that I began to cry; or, laughed so hard that I, a shy, tentative, untrusting child, found the sound of it contagious, and we fell together to the curb, shrieking wildly so that Mrs. Carlstrom, who was smart and caustic and a terrible teacher (for some things should not change), called to us to pull ourselves together, to rise and rejoin the group. In this unfolding of events, Jaymy Korkowski and I would go on to become best friends, for what else can two people do who have together laughed at adversity and defied authority? From his mouth would emerge the words that would allow me to understand a boy who cried at the sight of bird shit—though, of course, this boy, the boy offering such revelations, is not, and never can be, the boy who was moved to tears. For, at each turn, the people we hold close elude us, living their other lives, the lives that we can never know.

Idyllic Little Bali

Calvin goes first, telling them about the time he was in Florida and decided to attend a Beach Boys concert, not really knowing anything about the Beach Boys except that they played music for basking in the sun to, which, Calvin being from Michigan, might explain why he knew so little about them. He hitched a ride up to Fort Lauderdale, which is where the concert was being held, with a guy in a convertible who dropped him off right at the stadium, and it wasn't until the band came on stage hours later that he realized the convertible guy, the guy with whom he'd scored the ride, was actually one of the Beach Boys, the drummer, whose name he couldn't recall.

This is exactly how Calvin tells the story, his clauses like tired acrobats, and though the others at the table have known Calvin only a day, they are disappointed. Joe goes next, then Martin, and after them, Noreen and Sylvie begin a long story about their first date, on which they went to a run-down bar on the west side of Albuquerque, the kind of place, Sylvie explains, where Hispanic butch-femme couples show up in wedding gear on Saturday nights to hold their receptions, the butches playing pool in their tuxedos, the femmes taking over the bathrooms, where, in a never-ending cycle, they fix their makeup and cry with happiness.

"So," Sylvie says in a voice thick with drama. "There we are

149

on our first date, and Noreen invites this woman, Deb, to play pool with us."

Noreen cuts in, explaining that this Deb woman had actually struck up a conversation with *her* while Sylvie was off in the bathroom. She describes Deb as a massive-thighed Amazon who raised horses and engaged in competitive weight lifting, details that, in her mind, make clear that Deb had posed no threat to their date. She even tells them how Deb, who was wearing shorts, had said, "Go ahead. Feel it," flexing her very large thigh for Noreen, and how she, Noreen, had of course refused.

"I didn't even know her," she reports earnestly. "So why would I feel her thigh?" She actually seems to be soliciting their input, though it is not clear whether she is seeking plausible reasons that she (or anyone in that position) might have opted to feel the thigh or their approval for not having done so.

"It's irrelevant anyway," announces Sylvie, but Noreen doesn't reply because she is thinking about Deb's thigh, about the way that Deb had first extended her foot delicately, like someone testing the water in a pool, but then had ground her toes hard into the floor, making the leg muscles leap to the surface. There is absolutely nothing sexual about the memory. On the contrary, the thigh had been far too large, too freakish, for her to find it appealing. Noreen had felt the way she did the first time that she saw the penis of an aroused farm animal, fascinated and repulsed, actually unable to look away, but with no sense that what she was seeing had anything to do with her.

"She gave me the creeps. Immediately," continues Sylvie, by way of letting these relative strangers know that her instincts are keener than Noreen's. "But Noreen invited her to play pool with us, so what could I say? Then, halfway through the game, this really blond, granola-y type walks in and sits down at the bar. She's watching us play, so finally I go over and invite her to join the next game, and it turns out that she's Australian." She pauses as though she has revealed something significant.

"Olivia Newton-John?" suggests Calvin dryly, and the others laugh because, boring Beach Boys story aside, Calvin is funny.

"What?" says Sylvie nervously, bewildered by the laughter but still joining in, assuming that if others are laughing, then something must be funny. Perhaps because they have spent so much time around strangers on this trip, Noreen has begun to notice just how often Sylvie does this—laughs when she has no idea what is funny, her hand flying up to her mouth to hide the way that confusion tugs it downward.

Noreen suddenly feels tired, tired of the story itself as well as of the way that Sylvie keeps talking over her, keeps saying, "That's not what happened" when it is, in fact, what happened. Then, there's the way that Sylvie steered the story right past the particulars of Noreen's meeting with Deb, had somehow gotten her talking about Deb's thighs when the meeting was really the important part.

What had happened was that Noreen was sitting at the bar, Sylvie's stool empty beside her, when Deb sat down on it, leaned toward her, and said, "You know why the Jews didn't leave Germany?" Noreen had been put off at first, thinking that Deb was telling a joke, some one-liner about the Holocaust. After all, it was at this very bar that the DJ had, between songs, once asked, "How many Polacks does it take to rape a lesbian?" and when Noreen complained to the owner, a pudgy man in running shorts, he had said, "What? Are there Polacks here?"

But Deb was not telling a joke. She was relating an anecdote that she had read somewhere, a reply that a Jewish man had given after the war, after he had survived and been asked to explain, in retrospect, why it was that the Jews had not left when they had the chance. "Because we had pianos," the man had said, at least according to Deb. Deb was slightly tipsy but not at all drunk, and so she did not go on and on about this in an overly sentimental way, which Noreen appreciated, yet it was obvious that the man's response had meant something to her. Later, Noreen told Sylvie about the exchange and Sylvie had seemed impressed, so how, Noreen wonders, could Sylvie tell the story without beginning there, with the Jews and their pianos?

The others are still laughing at Calvin's Olivia Newton-John crack, everyone except for Noreen and Martin. They have just added Martin, so there are six of them now, sitting at a table beside a pool in a tiny hotel in Yogyakarta, drinking beer and taking turns describing their oddest brush with fame. When it was his turn, Martin, who grew up in Washington, had shrugged and said, "I don't know," and then, as though it were a question: "Ted Bundy used to be my parents' paperboy?" Martin is forty-five, the oldest of the group, and the others sense that he would not have joined them back home, that he has joined them now precisely because they are not in the United States.

The truth of it is, they are all tired of dealing with non-Americans, tired of having to explain themselves and of having to work so hard to understand what others are explaining to them. They are tired and what they want—crave, actually—is just to sit around with a bunch of other Americans playing silly games like this, games that do not require them to stop constantly and explain, to say things like "Ted Bundy? Are you kidding? He's famous." Because, of course, the explanations never stop there. If they were talking to an Asian, they'd have to explain the whole concept of serial killers (unless the person was from

Japan, of course) and if the other person was European, forget it—they'd spend the next half hour discussing why Americans were all so damn violent.

This tiredness is what had attuned them to accent as they heard one another soliciting directions from the hotel employees and ordering eggs sunny-side up, though it was Calvin who finally brought them together, yesterday afternoon as they lounged around the pool with the other hotel guests, eyeing one another. He had thrown out some ridiculous sports question, something about American football, and they had all clamored to respond—even those who had no interest in sports—because they understood that sports was not the point. They stayed up until midnight drinking and discussing where they were from, without having to stop to explain that Minnesota was cold, or worse, having to fumble around trying to figure out what thirty below Fahrenheit translated into for the rest of the world. And they would have kept going had the front desk guy not warned them that other guests were starting to complain.

"The loud Americans," they called out in stage whispers as they disbanded, laughing and giddy after a night of drinking, happy to have found one another, a feeling that they all share, though one that they haven't verbalized for various reasons— Noreen because she feels that it would make them seem provincial to acknowledge such a thing and Joe, on the other hand, simply because he sees it as a given, and Joe's belief is that people who state givens are either insecure or stupid.

That was last night, and now they have reconvened, adding Martin, whom Joe overheard discussing flight reservations with the front desk man when he got up to use the restroom. "That's the guy," Joe said, indicating Martin with a nod as Martin passed their table, and Sylvie called out to him, politely but with the slightly patronizing tone that people in groups some-times adopt when addressing someone alone. "Hey! Excuse me. May I ask where you're from?" she asked, even though they already knew where he was from, knew, that is, that he was American.

Martin turned and looked at them; *sizing them up* was how Joe saw it, which is how Joe generally sees such things, just to be clear about Joe. Joe is, as his name suggests, an average guy—moderate in habit and opinion with uninspired taste. He grew up in a rural, slightly-depressed-though-no-more-so-than-the-towns-around-it town in Minnesota, where he was a medio-cre student of average intelligence and in possession of no real talents that set him above others, that marked him, that is, as someone destined to rise above his humble beginnings (as such beginnings are always described after a person has done a little rising). But what Joe did possess was a desire to do just that, to leave that town behind entirely, a desire, moreover, that wed-ded itself to no one plan for doing so, which actually made the whole thing far more accomplishable than had he hoped to achieve it, say, by becoming a doctor or wowing everyone with his athletic prowess.

Instead, Joe accomplished it by lying, by packing his bags and moving to California, where he knew nobody, which meant that there was nobody to point out that he was lying. Once there, he lied his way into a progression of increasingly better-paying jobs, his favorite for the chamber of commerce, where he was the guy that got sent out with giant scissors to cut the ribbon when new businesses opened, from which he learned that women really gravitate toward a man with big scis-sors. When it was Joe's turn to discuss his brush with fame, he described meeting Dorothy Hamill, a lie, of course, and an easy one at that, for Joe knows the trick to lying well, which is either to go really big or, as is the case here, really small—to talk about sharing a ski lift with a figure skater who was last known for her haircut.

Besides lying, or perhaps hand in hand with it, what Joe does have a talent for is sizing people up. Thus, as he sat watching Martin size them up and sizing him up back, he sensed immediately that Martin was disdainful of them, of their need to be together. Disdain is one of those things that hits too close to home with Joe (perhaps because of the humble beginnings) and is, therefore, one of the few things that diminishes his objectivity, which is why he failed to consider that Martin might simply be distracted, might be focusing on his own problems to the exclusion of what is going on around him, a state of mind that can easily be mistaken for disdain.

This is precisely the case with Martin, who has come to Indonesia with his wife of thirteen years, a trip that the two of them began planning even before they were married and which it has taken them all this time to bring to fruition. Martin has always been vaguely distrustful of success, a disposition that allows him to now feel vindicated because here in Indonesia, things have fallen quickly apart for Martin, starting in Bali of all places, where he and his wife began their vacation because everyone back home told them that Bali was *the* place to start: Bali was paradise, they said, an Eden of smiling, happy people, and the dances, especially the *barong* dance, were simply the most beautiful things they would ever see.

During the long flight to Bali, his wife had started out in a state of wine-drinking jubilation, but as the hours went by, she developed a terrible headache, the result of caffeine withdrawal, which neither aspirin nor a belated cup of weak airline coffee could assuage. Then, as they flew over the turbulent Strait of Malacca, she became nauseated as well. Martin was sure that she would feel better once they landed, but as they entered the airport, they were met with the sweet, cloying smell of jasmine and the overwhelming humidity of the tropics, and she rushed to the nearest garbage can and exploded into it, the entire history of the flight recorded in her vomit as she held weakly to the can with one hand and pushed back her stringy brown hair with the other. And through it all, Martin stayed frozen where he was, perhaps fifty feet away, watching as several young soldiers looked on impassively from the exits and the other members of their flight, strangers with whom they had spent the last fifteen hours, passed by and stared at his wife, bearing witness to the contents of her stomach and seeing her hunched over, her mouth smeared with something pink, the wine that she had consumed thousands of miles ago when she was still feeling festive.

Finally, a saronged woman about his wife's age approached her and, in what sounded like an Irish accent, said, "Get it all out, luv. It's the only way." She handed his wife several tissues, looking discreetly away as his wife cleaned her face. "All better, isn't it then?" the woman said, his wife thanking her weakly as she went on her way. Only then had Martin spun into action, coming up behind his wife as though he had been there all along, whispering, "Do you need the bathroom?" and "No? Are you sure? Because there's one right here." Later, as they rode in a taxi through the streets of Denpasar, he had wanted to acknowledge his failure, or, even better, he had wanted her to acknowledge it, to scold him in the loud voice that he hated, but she had said nothing, her head thrown back, eyes closed, as the taxi sped along.

Three days later, they checked into a hotel in Singaraja, along the northern coast of Bali, a hotel that catered to Indonesian businessmen and where they were the only tourists and, as such, were accorded the dubious honor of being placed in a room directly across from the hotel desk. There, with the night receptionist just outside their door and Indonesian business- men snoring away behind the paper-thin walls on either side of them, his wife had wakened him in the middle of the night to tell him that she was thoroughly and profoundly miserable, that she had been for years and had been concealing it from him, and that she now understood that he was to blame for all of it, even the fact that she had been concealing it. He switched on the lamp next to the bed because it felt wrong to be discussing such things in the dark, and when he did, she began sobbing, but all Martin could think about was the night receptionist outside his door, listening to his wife cry.

Hoping to discuss the situation more rationally, Martin got out of the narrow bed and sat in a chair beside the armoire, leaning back with his arms crossed in front of him. He knew, of course, what crossed arms conveyed—inapproachability, an unwillingness to listen, outright hostility—for he had the sort of job, a middle-management position with a company that pro- duced copiers, where people were always going on about things like teamwork and communication and body language, but he also knew that his arms were incapable of doing anything else at that moment but reaching toward each other and holding on.

After listening to his wife sob and curse him for nearly an hour, he asked in a low voice that he hoped she might imitate, "What can I do?"

He had meant what could he do at that moment to make her stop crying, but she had looked up at him incredulously and said, "Can you learn to cry when you hear sad songs? Can you learn to articulate why you prefer radishes to cucumbers? Can you learn to appreciate irony? Wait. Can you learn to even *understand* irony? No? Well, then there is absolutely nothing you can do, Martin."

He slept sitting upright in the chair, and the next morning, with no mention of what had happened during the night, they packed and moved on to Ubud. During the day, they walked around the town, visiting the monkeys and stopping, it seemed to him, at every shop they passed. At one of them, his wife bought a carving that was heavy and round like a softball, the wood cut into the shape of a man with his legs pulled up to his chest, his head and shoulders curled over his knees.

"Is weeping Buddha," the shopkeeper told Martin's wife. She sighed and gave the man the exact amount of money that he asked for, and Martin kept his mouth shut.

That night, they ate dinner at an outdoor restaurant called Kodok, which, according to a poorly written explanation on the front of the menu, was the Indonesian word for *frog*. Martin supposed that the word was an onomatopoeia, and he marveled at the fact that *kodok* was nothing like the English word for the sound that frogs made, *rib-it,* yet both words seemed exactly right to him somehow. Normally, he would have shared this observation with his wife, but he didn't, just as normally she would have commented on how beautiful the garden around them was, with candles nestled in beds of woven banana leaves and flowers everywhere and a pond near their table, but she didn't.

In keeping with the restaurant's theme, Martin ordered frog legs, which he had never had before. Several minutes after placing his order, as the two of them sat rolling their bamboo placemats up like tiny carpets and letting them unfurl, he watched as a boy bent over the little pool and, hands flashing, grabbed two plump, kicking frogs and rushed back to the kitchen with them. Martin was horrified. He thought that if he hurried, he could change his order before the damage was done, but when he looked up, his wife was staring at him with such naked revulsion that he did nothing—nothing, that is, except suck the frog legs clear down to the bone when they arrived.

The trip had gone on like this, the two of them speaking only about small matters such as who should go to the front desk to request more toilet paper and what bus seats they had been assigned. They continued to sleep in the same bed, not talking, not touching, not even accidentally, and finally, after a week of this, Martin gathered his courage one morning at breakfast and asked, "Is it because of what happened in the airport?" For even though it was impossible to change things, he felt that he had to know.

His wife had stared at him blankly for a moment. She was eating papaya, which she loved but which they rarely had back home in Ohio.

"Maybe we should go our separate ways?" he said then, because as he watched her eat the papaya and smack her lips, he understood that she was content, perhaps even happy.

"Think about the money," she scolded. "How can we afford to keep traveling if we don't share expenses?" Then, after a moment, she added, "Besides, what's so different, Martin, really?" She asked this almost gently, which made it worse, for it meant that she felt secure enough to consider his feelings.

At least here in Yogyakarta they have begun spending their days apart. She has hooked up with four grown siblings, three sisters and a brother, who are staying at their hotel, and though Martin feels that she is intruding upon the siblings' family reunion, he does not say this to her, knowing that she would scoff at him, would say something like, "Poor Martin. How does it feel to always think you're in the way?"

In a few days, they are supposed to leave for Jakarta, and

from there, they are to fly to Sumatra, and it is not until two weeks from now, an interminable amount of time, that they are scheduled to return to Jakarta and begin their trip back home, but Martin has realized that he can't continue on like this. He simply cannot. That is what he had been speaking to the front desk man about when Joe wandered by. The front desk man, it turned out, was actually the manager, a helpful fellow with the unfortunate facial features of a toad: darting tongue, lidless eyes, and thin lips that cut far back into his cheeks. Martin felt immediately apologetic when he faced him, which he later understood to be residual guilt over the frog legs.

"I must change my flight," he told him, forming the story as he went along. He laid out his ticket, Garuda Airlines, Jakarta to Singapore, for the man to see. "I read about the Garuda crash in September, and quite frankly, I've become nervous." He began his request in this way to conceal his real motive, which was to change the flight date from two weeks hence to tomorrow, though why he felt he needed this bit of subterfuge, he could not say. However, as he spoke, he realized that there was truth to what he was saying. He had never been the sort that gave flying any thought, that questioned the ability of planes to stay aloft, but he saw now that things were not as he had always thought them to be.

"Sir, there is nothing to worry about. Garuda is our national airline. It is very safe. That accident, it was caused by the forest fires—the smoke—but that was months ago. I think there is no need to worry." The man studied the ticket. "Also, sir, your flight is not for two weeks." He added this quietly.

"I see," said Martin, quietly also. "Well, I was thinking that as long as I'm making such a big change anyway, perhaps I might change the dates as well. In fact, I would like to take a flight tomorrow afternoon, from Jakarta. Can this be arranged?"

"I am not sure, sir," the man said, flustered for some reason by the request. "You see, it is rather short notice. And your wife? Mrs. Stein?" he said, pronouncing Martin's surname so that it sounded like the mark that dropped food leaves on one's clothing, but Martin did not bother to correct him because he couldn't imagine that it made any difference to either of them.

"My wife will be staying. Only I must return early. You understand." And to be sure that the man did understand, he placed a twenty-dollar bill on the counter, which, he had read in his guidebook, was the way that things got done in Indonesia. The man seemed embarrassed by the bill's appearance and in no way acknowledged it, but neither did he return it. Instead, it sat on the counter between them as he made his calls, first to Singapore Airlines, arranging a shuttle flight from Yogyakarta to Jakarta for the next morning, followed by an afternoon flight to Singapore, and then to Garuda Airlines, canceling the original flight. Only after hanging up the telephone for the final time did he place his hand on the counter between them, over the twenty-dollar bill, and, still mispronouncing Martin's name, he declared, "Everything is arranged, Mr. Stein."

"Thank you," Martin replied, but looking at the kindly, toad-like features, he felt suddenly ill. He walked quickly away from the desk, and as he passed the nearby pool area, which doubled as a bar, a woman called out to him from one of the tables, asking where he was from.

He turned and stared at the woman and her companions for a long moment, thinking to himself, "Where *am* I from?" and finally, he took a deep breath and said, "Cleveland," and then, as though these people might not know where that was, he added, "Cleveland, Ohio," and they all nodded and smiled.

"Of course we know Cleveland. We're Americans," they said, and they invited him to sit down.

* * *

They are playing a game, the fame game. Martin hates games, and when it is his turn, he tells them about his parents' paperboy, Ted Bundy, though hesitantly, for he is still not sure that he understands the point of the game. The two lesbians go next, relating a very long and increasingly convoluted story about a woman with big thighs and an Australian who might or might not have been Olivia Newton-John. The thigh woman was raised by Satan worshippers in Minot, North Dakota, but had escaped when she was seventeen. Now, she raises horses and lifts weights and is a lesbian also.

Suddenly, or so it seems to him, Sylvie, the lesbian who is doing most of the talking, pushes her hands against her own throat as she explains that the thigh woman had threatened to kill the Australian woman with a pool cue, claiming that the Australian had been sent by the Satan worshippers to retrieve her. Martin is sure that he has missed something, some crucial detail, and he studies the others, hoping for a clue, but the waiter approaches their table with another round of drinks, and Sylvie pauses while everyone pays, a chaotic undertaking because they are all distracted by trying to convert rupiahs into dollars in their heads.

Joe, seeing an opportunity to get the conversation away from this god-awful story that, as far as he can tell, has nothing remotely to do with a brush with fame, turns to Martin and asks, "Did I hear you discussing flights with the desk guy?"

Martin considers explaining that the "desk guy" is actually the manager, but he is tired, so he simply says yes, he is leaving the next day. He does not mention that he moved his flight up two weeks, only that he has made the change to Singapore Airlines. "I'm feeling a little nervous about this Garuda

Air," he says. "They had a crash in September. Now, Singapore Airlines—you *know* how things are in that country. They cane pilots for crashing." They all laugh because it is the only thing they do know about Singapore—that it's that little country that's always caning people.

Amanda, the sixth and youngest member of the group, says softly, "I think you're very wise, Martin." She is the sort of woman that men describe as *sweet,* which simply means that she listens far more than she talks and that she is prone to comments like this, comments that reinforce their opinions of themselves in very uncomplicated ways. She is the only one who has not yet described a brush with fame and who is actually interested in Sylvie's story, partly because she has a cousin in Minot, North Dakota.

There is another thing to know about Amanda, a secret that she has maintained successfully over the last two days, largely by keeping track of her vowels. Amanda is not American. She is Canadian, though her mother is American, a Minnesotan who fell in love with Amanda's father years ago over the course of a weekend getaway to Winnipeg with a group of friends. "With my girlfriends," her mother says when she tells the story, though Amanda has told her mother repeatedly, and at times petulantly, to stop using *girlfriends* like that—to talk about the women with whom she bowls and shops.

"Only lesbians call other women *girlfriends* these days," she explains, "and they *don't* mean friends." But her mother disregards everything she says, every attempt she makes to offer advice that might save her mother from embarrassment.

Once, for example, during their annual visit to Minnesota, she overheard her mother telling a group of relatives that Warren— Warren was Amanda's father—had to "really Jew down" the used car salesman from whom they had just purchased a car.

Amanda was sitting on the sofa nearby reading a book about lighthouses. She always read books about strange topics when she visited her relatives because she secretly liked promoting the notion that they already had of her—as *different*. *Different* was not meant as a compliment, but because she considered her relatives backward, she clamored after the label as though it were. She lowered the lighthouse book and said, "Mother, I cannot believe you said that."

"What?" said her mother.

"'Jew him down.' I cannot believe you would use an expression like that."

The conversation had stopped as they all turned to look at her, seventeen-year-old Amanda, their flesh and blood, who was being raised in Canada. No wonder she had such odd ideas. No wonder she read books about lighthouses. But her mother just laughed. "Honestly, Amanda," she said. "Sometimes you have the most peculiar ideas. Next you're going to tell me that the Dutch are up in arms about 'going Dutch.'" The relatives laughed then also, laughed because even though Amanda's mother had moved to Canada, she still had her sense of humor.

Amanda hopes to sleep with Calvin, though Calvin is not yet aware of her interest, a state of affairs that would normally suggest that nothing is going to happen between them. Calvin, however, does not work that way, does not allow himself the luxury of choosing friends or sexual partners. Calvin waits to be chosen. Today is Calvin's birthday, but he has not yet decided whether he will tell the others, afraid that they might find him weird, even pathetic, if they learn that he is here celebrating alone. Back home in Michigan, the story of his trip to Indonesia will play differently. His friends and coworkers will say, "That's Calvin for you, trotting off just like that to celebrate his birthday in Java—wherever the hell that is." Back home, he is funny, risk-taking Calvin, spontaneous Calvin who runs off to places like Java and Florida and Belize, warm places, at the drop of a hat. Calvin has worked hard to create his own myth.

By the time the group begins to break up for the night, Calvin has finally noticed the way that Amanda's hand creeps across the table when she addresses him, the way it sits demurely in her lap when she speaks to everyone else. Then, too, there is the way that she laughs at his jokes, heartily, with a whispered, breathy "Oh, Calvin" at the end. He thinks that all they need is one more good session of drinking and chatting as a group, one more chance for him to showcase his humor for her, and so, as they stand to go off to bed, he says, "Tomorrow, folks? Same table? Fourish?"

Everyone nods except Martin, of course, who will be in Singapore by then. Even Noreen nods, though she is tired of everyone, but she is most tired of Sylvie—Sylvie, who never knows when to stop talking. Even when they are in bed, lying side by side with books in their hands, Sylvie cannot stop talking. "Do you see these books in our hands? That means we're reading," she said to Sylvie a few nights earlier, her voice straining to make it sound lighthearted, like a joke. And tonight will surely be worse because tonight, frustrated by having her story cut short, Sylvie will feel compelled to finish it again and again as they lie in bed.

Sylvie, she suspects, did not notice that the others were alternately puzzled and amused by the story, not to mention annoyed by the pace at which it was told. Noreen tries to imagine the story from their point of view, a story heard over drinks around a pool in a hot, bright country, and though she had sympathized with their impatience, she still cannot make sense of their reactions, for she cannot find amusement in anything about that night, certainly not in the fear she felt as Deb pressed the Australian woman against the bar, pool cue twitching in her red, meaty hands, and announced, "In two minutes, if you are still here, I am going to kill you," not screaming the words as an exaggerated expression of anger but stating them clearly and matter-of-factly, attaching a time frame, making of them a promise.

Is it possible, Noreen wonders, to locate the exact moment that fear (or hate or love) takes shape? And is there ever a way to convey that feeling to another person, to describe the memory of it so perfectly that it is like performing a transplant, your heart beating frantically in the body of that other person? That night, after the Australian fled, Deb turned to Noreen and Sylvie and remarked nonchalantly, "She knew," and Noreen, looking fully into Deb's eyes for the first time, saw in them something distant and unmoored, like a small boat far out at sea.

When it was Noreen's turn at the pool table, her hands shook as they held the cue, which felt different to her now—like something capable of smashing open a head or boring through a heart. As Deb racked the balls for the next game, her back turned to them, Noreen grabbed Sylvie's hand, and they fled the bar also, sprinting across the vast, dark parking lot, glancing around nervously as they fumbled to open the doors of Noreen's car. Once inside, they locked the doors and flung themselves on each other for just a moment, their hearts thudding crazily against the other's groping hands, before Noreen started the car and sped out of the parking lot, not turning on the headlights until they reached the street. Halfway home, they pulled over on a dark street and finished each other off quickly right there in the car, not even bothering to silence the engine.

On the third afternoon, shortly after the five of them convene and order their first round of drinks, a sweaty woman approaches their table and asks whether they have seen Martin. "Martin?" they repeat in a sort of lackadaisical chorus.

"Yes," she says impatiently. "Martin. I saw him having drinks with you yesterday. I'm his wife."

They look at one another nervously. Martin had not mentioned a wife. "We haven't seen Martin today," Joe says at last.

Martin's wife picks up a napkin from their table and wipes her face with it. "I've been out all day with friends," she explains. "Man, is this place muggy." She studies the napkin for a moment, then says, "Well, I better run up to the room and get myself into a shower." But she does not commit herself to action; instead, she continues to hover over them, and so they feel obligated to ask her to sit down.

"I must look a fright," she says, falling quickly into a chair. She eyes them suspiciously, as though she suspects them of harboring a loyalty to Martin, and then launches immediately into the story of how Martin ordered frog legs in Ubud. Amanda, with a drawn-out Canadian "oh" that almost gives her secret away, shrieks, "Oh no, the poor frogs." The others say nothing, especially Calvin, who does not think that Amanda would be impressed by a joke about the dead, legless frogs.

In the midst of this, the front desk man appears beside their table. "Mrs. Stein," he says quietly, addressing Martin's wife and mispronouncing her name.

"Stein," she corrects him curtly.

"Stein," he repeats dully. "I am very sorry, Mrs. Stein. I do not know how to say this, but the plane has crashed." He does not know when he decided to begin in this way, by referring to *the* plane, a pretense suggesting that they share between them the knowledge of her husband's departure.

"I'm afraid that you must have me confused with another

guest. I don't know anything about a plane," says Martin's wife, speaking stiffly, almost angrily.

He puts his hand nervously into his pocket, seeking out Martin's twenty-dollar bill, which feels different from Indonesian money, sturdier. Yes, it's there. It exists, which means that everything else exists—Martin, the flight change, the plane— but, he realizes as he gets to the end of this chain of associations, what this means is that none of them exists.

"The plane that your husband was on," he croaks. "I switched him yesterday because he was nervous about flying our local airline. I called the Singapore office myself. He flew to Jakarta this morning, and from there he was going to Singapore." His seemingly lidless eyes blink once, slowly, and then focus on the table.

"It's true," says Noreen. "Martin told us yesterday that he was leaving this morning, that he had just changed his flight because Garuda made him nervous."

"Why didn't you mention this a minute ago when I asked?" Martin's wife asks, widening the scope of her anger to include all of them.

"I guess we thought that maybe he'd changed his mind," explains Calvin.

"He did not," says the manager sadly. "I took him in the hotel van myself."

"It really was none of our business," adds Joe.

Martin's wife stands then, stands and takes another napkin from the table and passes it across her face, and when she is done, it is as though she has wiped away the angry expression, and in its place a new expression struggles to take shape, her face like a television screen as one fiddles with the antennae, all blurs and fuzziness and glimpses.

The manager has begun to cry, quietly and without embarrassment. "Come," he says to Martin's wife gently, reaching for her arm. "The families are gathering at the airport to grieve. I will take you."

The five Americans watch them walk away from the table together, too shocked to speak. They order one round of drinks and then another, and finally Calvin says, "That front desk guy's a heck of a nice guy," and because they are a little tipsy by now, they drink a toast to the front desk guy.

"His English is really good also," says Sylvie. "I mean, he knows a word like *grieve?*" She holds up her glass, and they drink a second toast—this time, to the front desk man's English.

Only then do they discuss Martin, shaking their heads finally at the irony of the situation: how Martin died as a result of his desire to live. "Yep, old Martin would have liked that," Calvin says, and they nod together, agreeing that their friend would have appreciated the irony, for that is how they have come to think of Martin—as a friend—because he is dead and they were the last to know him.

"Well," says Noreen after a moment, stretching to signal that she is done for the night. She stands, and Sylvie rises as well. "It was nice meeting you all. We're leaving for Bali tomorrow." She does not look at Sylvie as she says this.

"Idyllic little Bali," Joe replies.

"What?" says Noreen.

"Idyllic little Bali," repeats Joe. "Don't you remember yesterday, when Martin first sat down and I asked him where he was coming from? He said: 'I've just spent eight days in idyllic little Bali.'" From very far away, which is how yesterday seems now that it has become a time when Martin was still alive, Noreen can hear him intoning the words, like a man in a trance, like a man exhausted by the task of putting paradise into words.

Dr. Daneau's Punishment

Dr. Dunno. That is what the boys call me, what they write on desks and in bathroom stalls, a play on my name—which is Daneau—and on the fact that, day after day, that is how they respond to my questions. "Dunno," they say with an elaborate shrug and the limp, unarticulated drawl that has become ubiquitous among teenagers in a classroom setting; they cannot even be bothered to claim their ignorance in the form of a complete sentence, to say, "I don't know," a less than desirable response to be sure, but one that does not smack of apathy and laziness and disdain.

They arrive each day with matted hair and soiled faces, a lifetime of wax and dirt spilling from their ears. "Ear rice," the Koreans call it, referring, no doubt, to the tiny balls that a normal person, one who attends to his ears on a regular basis, is likely to produce—not to the prodigious amounts produced by thirteen-year-old boys oblivious to hygiene. However, I cannot sit beside them each morning as they prepare for school, coaxing them to apply just a bit more soap, to consider a cleaner shirt. No. My realm is the classroom, my only concern that when they leave it, they possess at least a modicum of proficiency in that much-maligned subject to which I have devoted my life: mathematics.

Would it surprise you to know that I have students who do

171

not understand the concept of ten, who, when given the task of adding some multiple of ten to a number ending in, let us say, four, cannot predict that the sum will also end in four? This, of course, suggests a much bigger problem—an ignorance of zero itself. The Romans developed no concept of zero and we see where that got them, the Roman numeral system in all its past glory relegated to the role of placeholder in complex outlines and on the faces of clocks.

"Imagine your lives without zero," I once challenged my students in a moment of folly, thinking that I was offering inspiration, a new window onto the world, but they had stared back at me blandly, no doubt wondering what zero could possibly have to do with eating and sleeping and unabated nose picking.

"You mean like sports?" said James Nyquist. I had not meant sports, for *sports* is a topic to which I never allude.

"Kindly elaborate, Mr. Nyquist. I have yet to see your point."

"Like in the beginning when no one's scored," he said.

"Yes," I said, and then, more forcefully, "Yes!" for I meant precisely this.

"We'd just start at one, I guess," he said.

"One?" I repeated. "But *one* implies that you've already scored."

"You said to imagine our lives without zero," he pointed out. "That means it doesn't exist, right? And if both sides start at one, it's the same as starting at zero."

It was as though I had eliminated Pringles from their lives. Fine, they would eat Ruffles instead. That easily was zero dispensed with.

This week, we are discussing averages, concerning ourselves only with *mean* averages, the general consensus among my colleagues being that *median* and *mode* would simply muddy the already none-too-clear waters. Toward this end, I gave young Mr. Stuart the following task: to average five test scores ranging from 77 percent to 94 percent. After much button pushing (for no task can be performed without a calculator firmly in hand), he announced that the average score was 264 percent.

"That, sir, is impossible," I replied. I have found that few things annoy an eighth-grade boy like being referred to as *sir* by a grown man.

He, however, was quick to provide me with incontrovertible proof. "See for yourself," he said, surprisingly smug for one whose chin still bore a dusting of toast crumbs, and thrust the calculator in my face. Indeed, through some mismanagement of the keys, he had arrived at 264 percent.

"Do you not understand what *average* means?" I asked.

"It means you're like everyone else," he said.

"Well," I replied. "Yes. Except for those who are above average. And, of course, those who are below." I did not make it personal, did not point out his obvious qualifications for the latter category; I am, after all, an educator. Moreover, I have been reprimanded for such things in the past. Just last month, it was brought to my attention that the names I had given to the three math groups in the class were inappropriate. The most proficient, and not incidentally smallest, group I chose to call the Superheroes, a name that I considered attractive (dare I say motivational) to boys of this age. The middle group was dubbed the Bluebirds, an innocuous but not unflattering moniker. It was the name that I selected for the third group that raised some ire. The Donkeys.

"But didn't you consider the implication?" the principal asked. "Donkeys are slow animals."

"I am quite familiar with the characteristics of the donkey," I replied indignantly. "In short, I found the comparison apt."

"Well, perhaps you would like to explain that to the boys' parents?" he said.

Although I was spared having to answer to that particular pack of irate mothers and fathers, I was required to submit a list of three appropriate replacements for "the Donkeys" by the following morning, a request with which I complied; by noon, I had been invited back to the principal's office to discuss my suggestions.

A word about Thorqvist, my principal. First, I find him an affable fellow, though a bit less affability would work wonders with some of these boys. I also cannot object to his sartorial choices, nor to the fact that he is always well pressed, a state of affairs that his wife is surely behind. He is somewhat of a malapropist, particularly in regard to clichés, which he uses liberally and generally manages to botch. On one occasion—and here I said nothing because I supported his cause if not his phrasing—he urged the faculty to be careful in making sweeping curriculum changes, lest they "throw the baby out with the dishwater." Another time, during an assembly when it would have been inappropriate to correct him, I had literally to take my tongue between thumb and index finger as he cautioned the boys not once but thrice: "Each of you must learn to take responsibility for your educations if you do not wish to find yourselves up a creek without a ladder."

Lastly, there is Thorqvist's habitual misuse of the reflexive pronoun "myself," which he insists on employing as a subject, a task for which it was never intended. (Forgive me for stating the obvious.) Thus, he began our discussion of my suggestions for a replacement name as follows: "The vice principal and myself have reviewed your list and find your suggestions no less objectionable than 'the Donkeys.'"

I removed my spectacles and cleaned them thoroughly,

and when I resumed wearing them, I found that my list had appeared in front of me. Across the top, I had typed "Suggested Name Replacements for the Slow-Learners' Group" and beneath this, in slightly smaller print, "Submitted by Dr. Michael Daneau." In the middle of the page, indented and prefaced by bullets, were my suggestions:

- the Mongrels
- the Chain Gang
- the Spuds

"I am not sure that I understand your objections, sir," I said, after pretending to review the list. "First, I doubt that the boys, or even their parents for that matter, will be familiar with the first two. Most people prefer the simpler term *mutt,* and chain gangs have long since fallen out of favor, at least in this country. That leaves only *Spuds,* and what, may I ask, is objectionable about the potato?"

He peered at me for a moment, hoping to decipher my tone. "Well," he said at last. "First, there is the question of why, out of all possible names, you are drawn to a nickname for the potato. There is also the matter of sound, Dr. Daneau. Have you not considered that *Spuds* sounds a great deal like *Duds*?"

"Surely you are not telling me that we must consider rhyming?" I gasped.

"I am not saying that we must consider rhyming per se, but we must consider implications." He sighed heavily, a familiar enough sigh, for it was the same sigh that I produce when dealing with some particularly obtuse student, Peterson, for example, to whom I had applied this sigh just the day before after a long and unsuccessful attempt to teach him basic test-taking skills.

"Quickly now, Peterson," I had cried out in a fit of exasperation. "If I were to wad this test of yours into a ball and throw it, where would it land? A. across the room, B. in North Dakota, C. in India." As you can see, I was not above stacking the deck, but Peterson looked back at me as though I had asked him to calculate the precise distance from his desk to the sun.

"Well?" I pressed him. "What strikes you as obviously wrong?" My point, as it always is in regard to multiple choice, was that he should begin by eliminating; therein lies my objection to the format, for when does life itself proceed in such a fashion, offering us just one correct option presented amid a limited number of others that are so patently wrong?

"I don't know, sir," he said. He was one of the politer boys, the type who gets along largely on manners, by jumping up after a movie to reopen the blinds or to rearrange the desks. He added miserably, "I'm sorry, sir. I've never been much good at geography."

That is when I produced the sigh, the sigh meant only to alleviate my own frustration. Still, as I sat in Thorqvist's office the next day, listening to him emit a similar sigh, I did experience a twinge of remorse regarding young Peterson.

Thorqvist and I are both great believers in civility, and so we chose to disengage briefly, to turn our attention away from the matter of names while we both calmed down. Casting around his office for a momentary distraction, I noticed a new sampler on the wall behind his desk. "More of your wife's work?" I asked. His wall had previously featured six of her embroideries, each containing a proverb whose message she apparently found so inspiring that she felt compelled to reproduce it in small, exact stitches.

Thorqvist nodded—sheepishly, dare I say? He is no genius, my principal, but neither, I believe, is he the sort to be swayed by the bland, lowest-common-denominator wisdom of proverbs. It is true that he has a fondness for clichés, but proverbs are a far different species. Clichés are a speaker's convenience, a linguistic shortcut uttered, in most cases, entirely without thought and received in the same fashion. They are like mosquitoes, ubiquitous and annoying but ultimately harmless. A proverb, however, is much stealthier: like the bite of a snake, it is meant to change a life.

I stood before his wife's seventh contribution, a Slovenian proverb according to the final line of stitches. "Thorqvist," I said, fumbling for words. "Have you actually read this . . . this Slovenian nonsense?" I proceeded to read his wife's sampler aloud: "An ant is over six feet tall when measured by its own foot-rule." Still he did not reply, and so I turned to him and spoke urgently: "Thorqvist, don't you see that this message is antithetical to our very mission as educators? Certainly our boys would all like to be measured according to their own *foot-rule* as it were, but that is precisely the point, is it not? The boys must understand that it is the world's *foot-rule* that matters."

The sampler hit on a sore spot with me, for it reinforced a growing trend in education—namely, the notion that we are the keepers of our students' self-esteem and, as such, must never allow them to feel that they have failed. Just recently, for example, we were expected to spend an entire day being lectured at by one of these ponytailed pedagogy types hired from the university for an exorbitant fee to beat the latest theories into us. He began the session by waving a handful of red pens about.

"Who can tell me what these are?" he asked, and when enough of my colleagues had taken the bait, calling out, "Red pens," he announced theatrically, "Ah yes, everybody is familiar with red pens, I see. Well, teachers, I am here to tell you that the red pen, bleeding its way across the students' work all these years, is finally and fully finished." With a flourish that underscored his rhetoric, he tossed the entire handful of pens into a nearby trash can.

"May I point out," I said, raising my hand, "that red allows the student to differentiate his work from my corrections and thus to see clearly his mistakes."

He regarded me for a moment, yanking on his ponytail as though, I could not help but think, trying to start a motor. "I believe that I hear a bit of the sage-on-the-stage mentality in your comments, Mr. . . ."

"Doctor," I corrected him. "Dr. Daneau. Mathematics."

"Dr. Daneau," he repeated, patronizingly of course, as though I were a child who had informed him that I was not six years old but rather six and a half.

"If by *sage-on-the-stage mentality* you are referring to the fact that I know math and they do not, then I must confess that I see no problem with that *mentality*. Indeed, I see no alternative."

"This," he said gravely, spreading his hands wide, "is why these professional development days are so important." The implication, of course, was that something I had said was the referred-to "this" that demonstrated his point.

He consulted his watch. "I was not expecting quite so much discussion on the topic of red pens," he quipped. A few of my colleagues chuckled—obedient, *baa*ing laughter—and he glanced in my direction to see whether I had noted it. I looked around at my colleagues, who fell largely into two camps: the older teachers, who viewed professional development as something to be sat through whilst offering up the least possible resistance, and the new teachers, impressionable, enthusiastic note takers who were having their beliefs shaped by ideologues such as this, this *sage on the stage* as it were.

"Gang," he called out. "Take ten minutes, and then we'll reconvene to role-play some of our new ideas."

I did not partake of the ten-minute break. Instead, I went

home and took to my bed for the afternoon, overcome with fever at the thought of role-playing.

After I had let Thorqvist know my opinion of his wife's sampler and he had refrained from replying, we returned to the matter of names. I was about to offer up the Penguins as a compromise when he said, "The vice principal and myself have come up with a name for the group in question. I hope that it will be to your liking, Dr. Daneau." He paused, and I knew what this meant—that the name would be so far from my liking that he hesitated even to speak it aloud.

"Well?"

"The Cheetahs," he declared.

"The Cheetahs?"

He nodded, presenting a wolfish smile.

"I am being asked to reward them for their sluggishness? No," I said, and then even more vehemently, "No, I cannot do it. I will not take part in this emperor's-new-clothes approach to education."

"I am afraid the decision has been made."

"By the vice principal and *yourself?*" I replied peevishly, making a jab that went unnoticed and thus afforded me no pleasure. A moment later, I turned desperate. "Can we not compromise?" I asked and, inspired by his smile, said, "How about the Jackals? I believe that they are also known for their speed."

He showed me the wolfish smile yet again, though I think that he considered it wistful, even worldly. As I rose to leave, he said, "One catches more flies with honey than with nectar, Dr. Daneau."

* * *

The Provinces, we called places such as this when I was a lad growing up in New York City, meaning it to sound sophisticated I suppose. Such are the foibles of youth. I have been living here, in the Provinces, almost twenty years. How I came to be here would be of little interest to most; suffice it to say that it involved love of an unrequited nature and that I brought myself here as a means of penance, penance for having allowed myself the folly of unrequited love. Here, to be more specific, is Minnesota, a stultifyingly cold place offset by good manners. I have been able to get by with a series of houseboys, young men who value age and education. Do not misunderstand me, though: houseboys must be paid.

Marcos, my current houseboy, is studying to become a teacher himself. I flatter myself to think that my influence has led to this career choice, though on more lucid days I understand that he has made this choice despite me, despite my constant complaining, despite the late-night phone calls, sometimes two or three in a week, filled with snickers and threats and commentary of a flatulent nature. At night, after he has served our meal and we have eaten it while speaking of our days, after he has washed the dishes and I have attended to my paperwork, we return to the table, where we spend an hour preparing him for the state teachers' exam. He will be leaving me soon, and though I do everything within my power to help him, I do so with the knowledge that I am working against myself.

The other night, he opened the exam book to a math question and looked up at me expectantly, as he always does. "Start with the extremes," I reminded him. Only then did I glance down at the question: "Which measurement would be most appropriate to use when discussing the weight of a pencil? A. ounce B. quart C. pound D. ton."

"But surely this is not a real question?" I said, pointing to the words *pencil* and then *ton* to make my point. In doing so, I brushed his hand where it rested on the page, a brief and largely accidental touch but deeply sustaining. He smiled at me gently because that is his nature. He is sweet and kind, more so than any other houseboy whose services I have enlisted, and so he did not begrudge me this fleeting touch of skin, this small morsel of pleasure. I worry about Marcos, worry about what kind of teacher he will be if he can so easily be convinced to give himself over in this way.

Marcos arrived from Brazil five years ago, and when I employed him two years later, he was still pronouncing his past tense verbs as though the *-ed* were an extra syllable to be emphasized emphatically as he spoke: "Yesterday, I talk-*id* to my friend and then I walk-*id* to the school." We spent the first months of his employment undoing this habit, but others have been harder to break, particularly his tendency to translate from Portuguese with no thought as to whether it will make sense in English.

"Doctor, truly I do not know whether to get married or to buy a bicycle," he will say when faced with a dilemma. He knows the English equivalent, which places one between a rock and a hard place, but does not care for it. "Why a hard place, Doctor?" he asks. "It is not very poetic, I think, to say 'a hard place.'" His tone, as always, is delightfully unsure.

Somewhere along the way, he has developed a penchant for the expression "Close, but no cigar," which he finds numerous opportunities to use. "Are we having lamb this evening, Marcos?" I will ask, and he will reply, "Close, but no cigar, Doctor," even when I am not at all close, when it is not lamb but fish that he has prepared. I do not have the heart to correct him, to tell him that this expression has gone the way of carnivals, from whence it derives, and cigars themselves.

Each evening when I arrive home, I sit in my armchair and flip through the paper, acquainting myself with the day's events while Marcos bustles about, making the final preparations for dinner and fixing my cocktail. Tonight, he appears promptly with my martini, carrying it on a tray as he has been taught.

"Doctor," he greets me, setting the drink down.

I nod. "Thank you, Marcos. What are you preparing for this evening's meal?"

"I am roasting a chicken," he says happily, and when I nod again, he sweeps back into the kitchen.

Certainly Marcos is not the most talented houseboy that I have ever employed. The chicken will be tough, the breasts, in particular, so dry that they will become edible only after being diced and tossed with mayonnaise and mustard. Jung was my most capable cook, though he favored garlic a bit too strongly. I do not like the smell of food on my body, and the garlic was always there, each time I opened my mouth or lifted an arm.

My martini is fine but not exceptional, for Marcos lacks consistency. I drink it anyway while passing through the first several pages of the paper, which I do quickly, as much of the news is devoted to the upcoming elections. I will vote, of course, for I am a firm believer in civic duty, but I do not wish to have these people intrude upon my daily life.

In the back section, which contains the local news, my eye is caught by a photograph of a young man standing beside an airplane, his hand resting on the wing in a proprietary manner. The headline attached to the article reads, "Pilot Plummets to Death," but I notice this only later, so struck am I first by the photograph and then by the text beneath it, which, incredibly, gives the young man's name as Thomas Jefferson.

One of my colleagues recently told me that his unusual first name, Gifford, was chosen by his grandparents, fanatical campers wishing to pay homage to Gifford Pinchot, the man largely responsible for establishing park conservation under Theodore

Roosevelt. It strikes me that living up to a name such as Gifford is possible and, more important, that not living up to it can at least remain a private defeat, for most people have never heard of Gifford Pinchot—which is not the case with a name like Thomas Jefferson, a name that would have always left this young man feeling hopelessly inadequate.

I skim the article, wanting to know what minor accomplishment this young Mr. Jefferson has achieved, and thus learn that the young man staring back at me, a twenty-four-year-old pilot from White Bear Lake, attempted his third solo flight yesterday. I say *attempted* because shortly after takeoff, a bird flew directly into Mr. Jefferson's cockpit windshield, shattering the glass and blinding Mr. Jefferson, ending his career as well as his life. I sip from my martini, but my hand is shaking, and I end up spilling far more than I consume. I try to imagine his final moments, how he felt as he went to his death in this way, sitting in his beloved cockpit contemplating the ineluctability of gravity, robbed of the one sense that could save him while the other four endeavored to offer assistance, all of them, even taste, focused single-mindedly on the moment of impact, his life reduced to that one certainty.

I am reminded of Miriam, a woman I knew many years ago in graduate school. Several years before she and I met, her husband was killed by a speeding truck after he pulled over on a Los Angeles freeway and stepped from his car. The police were not able to figure out why he had stopped that night, but Miriam said that she was haunted less by the mystery of this than by the constant replaying in her mind of the moment when her husband looked up and saw the truck nearly on top of him, saw reflected in the driver's eyes his imminent death. Miriam was a rational woman in every other way, a student of mathematics like me, but she could no longer drive on or near the highway—a main artery of Los Angeles—on which her husband was killed. She told me this story as we studied together over coffee late one night, by way of explaining why she had left Los Angeles, where even attending to simple errands had become complicated and draining.

I understood, of course, the way that memory worked, the way that one could see or smell or hear almost anything and be reminded of lost love. Passing a certain deli, I would think, *There, once, I purchased a bit of expensive cheese in hopes of enticing him to share my lunch*; and a few blocks later, *On that bench, we professed our mutual disdain for sentimentality while watching pigeons toss bread crumbs about*; and finally, awfully, *There, at that corner, as we walked together after a performance of what was to have been Mahler's ninth symphony but which Mahler, overcome by superstition, had called his tenth, hoping to trick death as Beethoven and Bruckner had been unable to—there we parted ways for the very last time.*

I sit for some minutes, staring at the face of young Mr. Jefferson, thinking to myself, "This beautiful young lad is dead."

"Doctor," says Marcos, and I drop the newspaper, startled by his presence.

"Dinner?" I say, struggling to my feet.

"Telephone," he replies.

"I did not hear it ring."

"Your principal," he mouths, his expression serious, for my principal never phones me at home.

I go into my study to take the call. "Good evening, Thorqvist," I say.

"Daneau. Sorry to trouble you at home. The, ah, your . . ." he says, struggling for words to describe Marcos, who undoubtedly introduced himself as my houseboy.

"My houseboy?" I say, attempting matter-of-factness.

"Yes," he says, clearing his throat directly into the phone.

"He assured me that I was not calling you away from the table."

"Not at all," I say.

"Excellent. I, listen, we must speak tomorrow. First thing."

"Very well. I will stop by your office. Seven thirty shall we say?"

"Fine." He sounds distracted, and in the background, I hear a woman, his wife no doubt, asking querulously, "Well, what does he say for himself?"

"Good evening then, Thorqvist," I say and hang up.

As usual, the chicken is dry, but I spend an inordinate amount of time praising it, sidestepping Marcos's questions regarding Thorqvist's call. After dinner, I beg off of our nightly study session. "Headache," I explain, touching my temples, and though it is only eight o'clock, I go off to bed.

In fact, my head is throbbing. I realize this only when the room is dark and I am lying very still, listening to the familiar sounds of Marcos's cleaning. When I interviewed Marcos three years ago, we walked through the house as I described his duties room by room, ending up here, in the bedroom, where two full-size beds sat side by side. "Yours would be the right one, though if you prefer the left, that would be fine," I explained nervously. This was the moment when interviews crashed to a halt, when the houseboy-to-be exploded angrily out the door or made some awkward excuse and left. With those few, like Jung, who stayed, a round of negotiations ensued, during which the salary crept upward while I assured them repeatedly that nothing more was required than their nightly presence in the other bed. This was true, though I did not mention that without it, I could not sleep. Only Marcos knows this—Marcos, who took in the two beds and my nervous fumbling and said, "Doctor, when I was a boy, we were very poor. My brothers and I slept in one room. I miss that very much." He smiled, and I clasped my hands together and smiled back.

Finally, I doze off, awakening when Marcos slips into his bed. Moments later, the room fills with the uncomplicated and reassuring sound of his snoring.

"Ah, Daneau," Thorqvist greets me heartily the next morning.

"Dr. Thorqvist," I reply, waiting for an invitation to be seated, but he is busy rummaging through papers, no doubt seeking out the newest bit of damning evidence. "Coffee?" he asks at last, looking up. I nod, and he rises and leaves quickly, almost, I think, gratefully. Out of habit, I glance at the row of his wife's samplers, noting that an eighth one has appeared. Its focus is also the ant, though this one offers an Iranian perspective on those troublesome creatures. In faulty English, it reads: "For an ant to have wings would be his undoing."

"Sit. Sit," says Thorqvist, bustling back in with two coffees.

"Thank you," I say, accepting one of them, and then, "Your wife seems quite enamored of the ant."

"Yes." He settles himself back behind his desk. "She finds them industrious and underappreciated and—" He waves his hand about to indicate that there is a third adjective he cannot recall.

"Iranian, this one," I say. "Have I told you my favorite Iranian proverb, Dr. Thorqvist?"

He stirs his coffee.

"He'd hang if it were free," I say.

"Who?" he asks, looking up quickly.

"No," I say. "That's the proverb. Well, it's not exactly a proverb. It's what one says of a cheapskate. He'd hang if it were free." I laugh suggestively, and he spits out a halfhearted chuckle that turns into a thundering bout of throat clearing, at the end of which we both fall silent.

"Dr. Daneau," he begins tentatively. "I wonder—" He falters when I hold up my hand warningly, for he knows how I feel about the word *wonder,* not the word itself but the usage that has been imposed on us by the Critical Friends, a nervous, giddy group of experts brought in by the school to help improve classroom performance. The Critical Friends is their actual name, a name far better than any I could devise by way of satire, and they employed it without a trace of irony when they introduced themselves at the first meeting of the school year. "We are here to help," they continued earnestly, the frequency with which they made this assertion calling it into question, just as the fact that they referred to themselves as *friends* when they were so obviously not underscored that discrepancy.

They would be coming into our classrooms to observe us, they explained, after which they would discuss with us what they had observed. This process, the process of discussing their observations with us, was referred to as *reflecting,* a word once used to define the capabilities of mirrors and perfectly still bodies of water. No more. Now, we cannot act, speak, or read without being obligated to reflect, publicly and aloud. Reflections have become the bookends to our days, the benedictions to our meetings.

At a meeting last month, for example, we were placed in pairs and told to reflect upon our days; after several minutes of this, we were instructed to reflect upon our partner's reflection, at which point I lost all patience and cried out, "Sir, we are fiddling as Rome burns. I have students who cannot say how many inches are in a foot, who do not understand that four times five begets the same answer as five times four." This outburst, as it was termed, merited a visit to Thorqvist's office, where he explained that the exercise had been intended to promote faculty camaraderie. How, he asked me, did I suppose Miss Thoreson felt about my outburst?

"She was telling me what she had for lunch," I replied. "A bologna sandwich. I can elaborate if you like, but please consider my feelings, being asked to *reflect* upon the inadequacies of her lunch. Quite honestly, I do not wish to know the details of my colleagues' lives nor to *share* with them the details of mine. I do not wish to hug my colleagues or reveal to them my favorite song. Certainly, I do not want them feeding me Jell-O from a spoon gripped between their teeth." These were all references to activities introduced by the Critical Friends, who emphasized closeness and frankness and transparency but who, in fact, operated like a secret society, sweeping in and out of classrooms, sequestering themselves with individual teachers, and introducing a whole new vocabulary, which I privately referred to as the Orwellian Code. Under their tutelage (and here I return to my point, having digressed), we are no longer to speak of our *concerns* or *dislikes,* freighted as these words are with negativity; we are instead, the Friends explained, to *wonder* about such things, or, reverting to the noun form, *to share a wonder*.

"But that has just the opposite effect," I had shouted, half-rising from my seat. "If one of my esteemed colleagues were to *wonder* at my idea, I would understand immediately that my idea was so poor, so ill-conceived, so beyond the pale, that he felt compelled to resort to euphemism in order to conceal his horror." Several of my colleagues chuckled, but their amusement did not keep them from complying, and eventually I was the only one left still speaking of weaknesses and concerns.

Thus, when I take umbrage at Thorqvist's use of *wonder,* he squeezes his eyes shut but quickly reopens them and says, "Fine, allow me to rephrase," and I know then that the matter before us is serious. He clears his throat and begins again. "Dr. Daneau, I am . . . concerned by reports from parents that you are making the boys hold hands with one another." He coughs excessively before asking, "Is this true?"

"Why, yes," I say. I do not know what I had been expecting, but it was not this. "I have been employing this punishment for some years, quite effectively I might add. When two boys insist on pummeling each other, punching and roughhousing and such as young boys are wont to do, I have found that nothing works better than to make them sit side by side for the rest of the period holding hands. If they can't keep their hands off each other, I advise them, then they shall spend the period with their hands directly engaged with each other. I, of course, impose this punishment judiciously."

Thorqvist stares at me, a look that I cannot fully decipher. "Parents have complained," he says at last.

"Parents complain about everything these days, except for the most troubling fact of all—that their children are lazy and spoiled and entirely ill-equipped to face the world."

"Dr. Daneau, I must say that I am surprised, surprised that you, of all people, have chosen to use such a method."

"I am afraid that I do not follow you."

He fidgets with his pen, somersaulting it from nib to end several times. "Well, Dr. Daneau, I prefer to address this delicately, so you will forgive me for being roundabout—it is simply that, given your personal situation as it were, I am surprised that you would consider such a thing . . . well, appropriate."

"Dr. Thorqvist," I say sharply, "I do not see your point. However, I do ask that you think carefully before pulling your support for discipline."

"I am afraid that you misunderstand the severity of this matter, Dr. Daneau, so let me be very clear: there will be an investigation. Furthermore, I must inform you that you have been officially placed on leave. A substitute has been called. You are to leave the building immediately without having any contact with the students. Do you understand what I am telling you?" I gather my energy to stage an angry rebuttal, but his soliloquy does not end there. "Please make this easy on both of us, Michael," he continues instead, quietly, using my given name for the very first time in our long acquaintance.

It has been years since anyone has called me Michael in this way, intimately, urgently. The last person to do so was he, the night that we walked together after the Mahler, a performance that left me in a precarious state. The baritone was a moody, Heathcliffian presence on the stage, and the words, sung in German so that I received them secondhand from a translation printed in the program, affected me profoundly. I began to shake and then, as the baritone repeated the final, haunting word, *Ewig,* to sob. In the half-lit hall, I reached out and gripped his arm, but it was as though my touch burned, so quickly did he pull away.

We left the concert hall and walked aimlessly, not speaking, not even exchanging small politenesses about the cellist who dropped her bow midmovement, until we reached the corner, *that corner,* where an elderly woman approached us carrying a metal lunchbox. It was clear from her eyes and the thickness of her lipstick that she was mad, and when she spoke, she held the lunchbox to her mouth as though it were a channel for her words.

"Please be so kind as to tell me where to go," she said.

I might have ignored her, but he was not like that. "Ma'am," he began, but she interrupted him, crying out, "I cannot hear you. You must speak into the box. Please," and she held the box to her ear, waiting. He, of course, leaned forward, doing as she asked. "Ma'am," he said, "you must take this money and find a place, a safe place, where you can eat and pass the night." He held out a five-dollar bill, which she regarded cautiously, as though trying to determine whether it was money or a snake. Finally, with a grunt, she seized it and gestured for him to listen.

"Only we can know," she whispered into the box, into his ear, and though there were numerous ways to interpret her words, which were nothing more than the words of a crazy woman after all, I could not help but hear them as a request, a request that I be excluded. She walked away, box in one hand, money in the other, and, as though heeding her directive, he turned to me immediately and said, "We must not mingle with each other, Michael."

He was Iranian, but his English was very good. Still, there was no way for me to know what he meant by this, to know why he had used *mingle,* which was something that people, *strangers,* did at cocktail parties. Of course, he might have been thinking of the word in a purely physical sense, for he was a scientist, my former chemistry professor in fact, and in this capacity, I had heard him use the word often to speak of the way that liquids came together, mingling in the beaker. He moved close to me one last time, shook my hand formally, and uttered the very same words that, twenty years later, my principal would use in asking me to leave the building: "Please make this easy on both of us, Michael."

Thorqvist concludes our meeting with one of his usual malapropisms, urging me to "keep my lip up." It is this, and only this, that keeps me from becoming emotionally indiscreet, that allows me the fortitude to walk out of his office and across the parking lot to my car. It is October, a likable month I have always thought. The air is chilly and crisp, and as I drive, I study the sky, imagining young Thomas Jefferson's family also gazing up at this moment, gazing at this very same sky and thinking, "That is where he died." It seems to me unjust, supremely and sublimely unjust, to have as a reminder such a vast, inescapable expanse.

Marcos is studying when I arrive home, studying with the stereo turned up loud to some awful music of a type that I have never known him to enjoy. He shuts it off immediately, looking concerned to see me home. "Are you ill, Doctor?" he asks.

"Yes," I reply. "I am unwell, Marcos. Help me into bed." He does, taking my arm and leading me to our bedroom, where I sit on the edge of my bed while he removes my shoes.

"Marcos," I say, "when I was a boy and feeling unwell, my mother allowed me to sleep in her bed during the day so that when I went to my own bed at night, it would feel fresh and cool and unfamiliar. May I rest in your bed today, Marcos?"

"That is an excellent idea, Doctor," he says, and he pulls back the covers of his neatly made bed and helps me in, then perches on the edge. "Is it the headache from last night, Doctor?" he asks with great concern.

"It is everything," I tell him. "It is everything in the world." I begin to cry then, cannot stop myself, and Marcos, who will be leaving me soon, takes my hand and holds it, stroking it gently with his thumb. Such torment, but I do not ask him to stop, for this punishment is what I need and what I deserve.

The Children Beneath the Seat

They had not expected the desert to be like this—just like the stereotypical images of it that they brought to Morocco with them—but, ironically (and disappointingly), it was. There were camels, one of which had chased them up the side of a gorge in a fit of misplaced anger, and the occasional oasis in the midst of kilometer after kilometer of rock and sand and dryness. The only thing that had really shocked them was the unwavering brownness of it all, consuming entire villages so that houses rose like intermittent lumps in a bedspread of brownness. Intellectually, of course, they had expected it, but the intellect cannot always sufficiently inform the senses, which was the reason that they had decided to travel in the first place. *Brownness* has thus become their new word, for there seemed no other way to express it except by giving it the weight, the concreteness, of nounhood—not just brown, but the *state* of being brown. Needless to say, they are from a lush place, Minnesota, a land with so many lakes that it feels compelled to brag about them on its license plates.

They are well into their forties, Bernadette older by thirteen months, but only now have they concluded, grudgingly, that there are things one cannot know except by seeing them. This realization has hit them hard, for they are English professors, both of them, women who have spent their entire lives reading, engaged in the world of heroes and plots, foreshadowing and epiphanies, and, perhaps without even realizing it, they had come to expect that life would follow literary extremes, would be either dazzlingly uplifting or stultifyingly tragic, but that was not the case at all. It did swerve occasionally toward one or the other, of course, but most of the time it occupied a vast middle ground, boring and relentless, a state of affairs that the world of literature had neither taught them to expect nor given them the tools with which to contend. Trapped within this vast middle ground, they graded papers and paid bills and slept, as did those around them, but it struck them, increasingly, that something was amiss.

It might have helped if they were religious by nature, but they were not, were, in fact, quite the opposite: their disinclination toward religion grew stronger, became more entrenched, as the years passed. Furthermore, in the nearly twenty years that they have been together, they have acquired a tendency to reflect, and thus intensify, certain traits in each other—cynicism and didacticism specifically. Finally, under the weight of their combined cynicism, each woman had begun to turn inward, away from the other, until there were times—increasingly more of them—that they crept into bed at night without having exchanged a single word all day. Then, when a simple "good night" or "sleep well" would have done much toward slowing this mutual sprint toward the end of their relationship, even then, or perhaps especially then, they could not speak, for the more language was required of them, the less each felt capable of producing it. Instead, they lay side by side, the silence between them like the pounding of waves, which is thought to be conducive to sleep but rarely is.

Thus, there is a subtext to this trip, unacknowledged but with the potential to rise up and overwhelm all others: in short, they hope to subject themselves to something so beyond the scope of what their lives have thus far encompassed that they will find themselves, in the face of it, free of pretense—able to rescue themselves and, in turn, their flagging relationship. The trip will be like an electric jolt to the heart, thinks Bernadette, for as English professors, they are enamored of metaphors and not always able to recognize trite ones, particularly those of their own making.

The desert has been introduced to them largely through the windows of various buses, which they don't mind, for there is something comforting about being on the move in this country. At the moment, for example, they are headed for Tafraoute, having spent two sweaty, interminable days in Agadir, the most depressing place they have visited thus far, its beach overflowing with Europeans and beer gardens and restaurants with signs outside all proclaiming, via a diversity of spellings: smorgasbord.

"We could have stayed home if we had wanted a smorgasbord," Bernadette had complained bitterly.

This was true. For nearly fifteen years, the two women have lived in Fergus Falls, a stagnant town along I-94, nearly an hour from Fargo-Moorhead. When they first moved here, colleagues at the community college where they are both employed had presented this proximity to the interstate as some obvious asset, the value of which remained unquantifiable because nobody required that it be quantified, but they eventually came to understand that the highway's presence was neutral—it brought nothing in, but neither did it take much out. Beyond the community college, the town is known for its small shopping mall and a park with a large statue of an otter in honor of the fact that Fergus Falls is the county seat for Otter Tail County.

Only in the last few years have they discovered that another world exists just beyond the Fergus Falls town limits and that, in this world, it is often possible to locate a smorgasbord (or a potluck or a meatball dinner) on a Sunday morning. Such events are generally affiliated with local churches, but the women did not let this bother them. They wore their teaching garb, which blended in well enough with the Sunday-morning attire favored by the locals, particularly as neither woman was prone toward drama or excess, but, still, they attracted attention. Two or three parishioners would approach them during the course of a meal under the pretense of welcoming them, each inevitably inquiring, "So, where are you girls from?" They were always *girls* in these settings—despite their ages and professions, neither of which they mentioned—because they were two women alone together on a day reserved for family.

Bernadette was the more talkative at these events, partly because the presence of food made her so, but she was excited also by the sense of adventure that these outings brought to their lives. As long as she could remember, they had awakened each Sunday morning at seven and dressed for the day in their standard casual wear, button-down shirts with sweatpants, a combination favored by both, for they agreed that a matching sweat suit was monotonous and neither liked T-shirts, Bernadette because they encroached on her neck and Sheila because she believed they made her forearms, which were unusually short, appear even more so. Together, they prepared coffee and a plate of liberally buttered toast, which they consumed over the course of the morning while reading; precisely at noon, they closed their books, opened a can of salmon, and made salmon melts, the last bite of which marked the end of their weekend. There were dishes to be done, of course, but on Sundays they completed this chore without any of their usual bickering,

Bernadette accusing Sheila of daydreaming as she washed and Sheila complaining that Bernadette only dried the outsides of things. As they faced the remains of the greasiest meal of the week, they interacted more like colleagues than lovers, observing the other's work with professional detachment. Then, they retreated to their respective studies and began the business of preparing for the coming week's classes.

And so, it was no overstatement to say that the smorgasbords and potlucks had changed everything, turning Sunday from a day of predictable introspection into one of intrigue and hastily graded papers, certainly as far as Bernadette was concerned; Sheila, who had spent every Sunday of her childhood in church, did not share Bernadette's enthusiasm but enjoyed observing it. She sat beside Bernadette at these outings, quietly troubled by an uneasiness for which she could not fully account, though she understood it to be rooted in distrust, which bothered her, for she did not consider herself an arbitrarily distrustful person. Certainly, she was routinely skeptical in her dealings with students, but that was only because she had witnessed numerous dishonesties over the years; thus, her reasoning went, it would be imprudent as well as professionally remiss to attend to her duties without a measured degree of vigilance. She prided herself, however, on never counting change in stores or asking workmen to put estimates into writing.

More unsettling for her was the fact that she believed this distrust to be mutual, believed that these strangers whose hotdishes and pies she consumed shared her misgivings, though in more generous moments, she understood that it was barely possible to know the workings of one's own mind, let alone those of a group of strangers, even strangers who, when considered as an abstraction, made up the all-too-familiar backdrop of her Iowan youth. That youth has, by design, become a detached

memory—she gave up corn when she was twenty and lost her
faith shortly thereafter, and then her parents had died, which
made visiting unnecessary. She now thought of her young self
as a character whom she had once encountered in a book: she
looked back upon her with fondness and a degree of pride, but
she felt also that this *character,* her younger self, had simply
ceased to be, had not died but merely ended, the way a book
did, with obstacles overcome and lessons learned, the turning
of the final page, and then the cover closing.

Perhaps because of the literary overtones with which she has
imbued her small-town upbringing, she is fond of assigning the
works of Willa Cather and Sherwood Anderson, though her
semesterly staple is a short story titled "The Lottery," in which
a group of villagers gathers together each year to draw lots,
with the loser, the one drawing the shortest lot, being stoned to
death by the others, for no reason other than to fulfill this particular tradition.

"What, exactly, does this story imply about traditions?"
she would begin the conversation each semester, thinking the
answer both obvious yet necessary to the formation of her students' worldview, but the students, masters at commandeer-
ing the question and leading the discussion safely away from
the text at hand, would invariably counter with listings of their
favorite traditions, each of which began the same way: "My
family always . . ." They would discuss their way through the
major holidays without her, comparing notes, a friendly rivalry
developing between those whose families always opened gifts
on Christmas Eve and those who held out for the actual day.
She would go home that evening, shattered, and fall into bed
at nine o'clock, but she could not help herself—she felt that her
students, most of them from the very communities whose potlucks and smorgasbords she partook of each Sunday, needed to

be taught the story's lesson, and so she was willing to ignore the fact that her teaching of it had become its own tradition.

"They need to learn to examine themselves—their milieu, their beliefs—critically," she would defend herself to Bernadette. "'The Lottery' is a parable, and that's what they're used to after all—parables." This was the way that the two of them spoke with each other, with the fervency of two middle-aged academics perpetually engaged in defending the obsolete theories of their youth. They used grammatically complete sentences, always, and when others inquired how they were, they refused to go along with the current convention of purporting to be *good*. "I'm well," they would reply in precise tones to anyone who cared to ask—grocery store cashiers and telemarketers as well as students and colleagues. Sometimes their students giggled at this response, and they suspected that the students, subjected to years of careless language, believed the two of them were the ones guilty of grammatical indiscretion.

"Of course it sounds funny to them," Bernadette grumbled. "How are they supposed to know any better when even their other professors claim to be *good*?"

So had begun their brief campaign to correct what they perceived as a grave injustice against the English language. "You're good?" they would query when presented with this response. "Have you been engaged in philanthropic activities?"

It was not in their natures to press the point, however, and so they generally stopped there, with this rather bewildering question hanging in the air, making further small talk unlikely. Thus, the campaign had been short-lived, though they continued to be "well" with all who still dared to ask.

"Even if we are the last two people in the country using *well,* we shall refuse to cave in. Actions speak louder than words, after all," Bernadette rallied, though she rarely employed clichés.

"But *well* is also a word," Sheila had reminded her, though she rarely began sentences with coordinate conjunctions.

"In this instance, however, the speaking of it is an action," Bernadette had countered, and their fretfulness had been abandoned as they debated whether *well,* in this particular case, constituted a word or an action.

So, of course, they did not blend in at potlucks and smorgasbords, despite their stolid dress, for they carried about them, in gesture and speech, the look of women who confronted daily the signs of steady, incontrovertible decay in the world around them.

Then, at a potluck last spring, they had been approached by a woman with large bones and an authoritative bearing, the latter established, in part, by the former. Unlike most people who approached them at these events, people who enjoyed their meal first, nestled among family and friends, before turning their prying attention to the two strange women in their midst, the big-boned woman approached them with a full plate, settling between them like a colleague who hoped to complain about a new departmental policy.

"Hello, ladies," she announced. She turned her plate carefully clockwise, stopping when the meager helping of three-bean salad sat precisely at twelve o'clock, and then, perhaps feeling that the unusually large mound of scalloped potatoes and ham on her plate required comment, she said, "Clara Johansson makes the best scalloped potatoes," adding, by way of clarification or maybe enticement, "All cream."

"I missed those," replied Bernadette apologetically, though technically she had avoided them, for she disliked foods that grew underground. "I shall have none of Eliot's 'dried tubers,'" she generally declared when potatoes were mentioned, to the bafflement of those around her, and Sheila looked at her, waiting for it, but Bernadette merely turned to the big-boned woman and explained, "There's so much to choose from at potlucks."

"Yes, that's the truth, isn't it," said the woman. Then, after a pause that, in retrospect, they both agreed had been an "artful pause," she added, "Anyhow, this is the church's last potluck."

"The last potluck! What a shame," Bernadette had cried out, not at all disingenuously though certainly with greater audible enthusiasm than she normally displayed. "It seems to be a popular event," she observed in quieter tones.

"Oh no, it's not the *event* we'll be changing," said the big-boned woman. "Just the name. From now on, it will be called a *pot God's will*. We want to make it clear, especially to some of the younger parishioners, that there is no such thing as luck, not when God is in charge."

Because the woman spoke without a trace of irony, Bernadette was nervous to make eye contact, fearful that such intimacy might provoke a response that she had no way of predicting and therefore suppressing; she was not a giggler nor the sort to weep publicly, but she felt that either reaction was possible, and so she smiled cautiously at the woman's scalloped potatoes instead. *Writing well,* Bernadette heard herself telling her students monotonously, semester after semester, *requires the ability to become your audience—knowing what they know, seeing as they see, feeling what they feel.* She looked up at the big-boned woman, who sat regarding the two of them, potatoes growing cold in front of her, and she understood what terrifying and ridiculous advice she had been meting out all these years. She recalled a joke that she had made once as they approached the front doors of one of these churches. "I'm so hungry I could eat the Eucharist," she had told Sheila, and they had laughed together smugly, glancing around to make sure that nobody stood within earshot. She almost wished that the big-boned woman would stand and publicly denounce them, swinging her big-boned fists like wrecking balls in their direction. How much easier and nobler, she thought, to depart amid cries of "Heretics!" or calls to be burned at the stake.

Instead, they left quietly.

"You knew it was a church," Sheila pointed out once they were in the car.

"Yes, but we were just there to eat," Bernadette answered sorrowfully, and Sheila did not reply, for despite her feelings of unease, she too had believed that they were welcome, at least for the time it took to eat a plate of hotdish and Jell-O.

"It's not as though we didn't pay for what we ate," Bernadette said a moment later, indignantly this time, but this position was problematic as well, for it made of them contributors, contributors to the promotion of the belief that God oversaw everything, guiding one's hand through the cookbook of life to stop at just the right hotdish recipe. When Bernadette offered this analogy, it sounded like a thesis straight out of the freshman composition papers that they graded day after day, and so they were able to laugh about it, but there was no ignoring the fact that the conversation with the big-boned woman had changed everything. They thought back over every potluck and meatball dinner and smorgasbord that they had ever attended, and in doing so, they were overcome with self-consciousness, as though it had suddenly occurred to them that they had attended each of these events unclothed, but unclothed the way that one is in a dream, where one is aware of one's nakedness not as the person sitting there naked but as the viewer of the dream, those two one in the same except for an overwhelming difference—the inability to act, to change one's nakedness.

"Which would you rather have if you had to choose—

knowledge or the ability to act?" Sheila asked, trying to change the mood in the car to a more philosophical one, but it had not worked, for they understood immediately how futile one was without the other. Then, because the mood in the car still needed changing, they had tried irony next, laughing at the fact that they now understood how Adam and Eve must have felt, naked and suddenly ashamed of it.

In the midst of this bit of levity, Bernadette had broken in, anguished, asking, "But how can they *believe* such a thing?" and this question, rhetorical though it was, had demanded a bit of thoughtful silence. They had not really acknowledged it then, but that had been the beginning of things: this sudden feeling that books were no longer enough, that the world was vastly different than they believed it to be, which is why Agadir, with its beer gardens and smorgasbords, had galled them so, for they found that now that they had finally done it, broken away from the lakes and their teaching and the routine of their days, they expected nothing to be familiar and, in fact, took great offense when it was.

Agadir had been filled with overpriced tourist hotels, its streets lined with tour buses, air-conditioned and fumeless, shocks and springs obsessively intact, nothing like the decrepit buses that the women have become used to, buses whose only virtues are cheapness and the ability to teach patience. In fact, because Agadir fell several weeks into their trip, they felt qualified to scoff at these tour buses with their two-people-to-a-seat, keep-the-aisles-clear policies. They have come to enjoy rolling through this landscape with people who are going about their daily business, hauling chickens and goats to market, people who seem thoroughly unmoved by the harsh brownness outside their windows.

They are particularly enamored of the fact that the drivers of these buses have assistants—*henchmen,* they have taken to calling them, part carnival barkers, part airline stewards—whose job it is to hang from the bus calling out destinations, to settle luggage and riders, to pump gas and fetch cigarettes for the driver, and, finally, to doze off, crouched in the small stairwell of the bus, during the brief moments when one round of duties is finished and the next, yet to begin.

They had stopped in Agadir, in fact, only because their guidebook claimed it had an English bookstore, which they never found, and now they are fleeing Agadir as well, its smorgasbords and carefully queued buses. They are going to Tafraoute because they have read in this same guidebook that Tafraoute is a place run by women, the men having gone off to work elsewhere and returning only when they are old enough, or wealthy enough, to retire. The book also had presented it as a place with color, pink granite and flowering almond trees (albeit not at this time of year) and, somewhere outside of town, a series of gigantic rocks painted blue and red and purple by a Belgian who had felt compelled—by the overwhelming brownness they suspect—to alter the desert in some basic but significant way. Their desire to leave Agadir propels them onto the first available bus, which is neither the fastest nor the cheapest, and while there will be ample opportunity during the trip to regret their haste, at first they are simply relieved.

Somewhere after Tiznit, in the tiny market of a village where they stop to take on passengers, an old man climbs onto the bus before it has fully stopped and makes his way back to them as though he has been awaiting their specific arrival. He looks from Sheila's face to Bernadette's, back and forth, confused, as though he expected to recognize them but does not. Then, he raises his fist in the air and lets it spring open, revealing a flimsy watch, which he swings like a pendulum in front of them.

"Is he trying to hypnotize us?" Sheila asks worriedly, for, in fact, she cannot take her eyes off the watch.

"He wants us to buy it," says Bernadette.

"How much?" asks the old man suddenly, in English.

Sheila shakes her head vehemently, but the man continues to dangle the watch with a confidence that they both find alarming.

"Where are we?" Bernadette asks him in English in order to assess his fluency but also because she would like to know. "What town is this?"

"How much?" he says again, patiently, and they cannot tell whether his response indicates a lack of English skills or an unwillingness to be distracted from commerce. In the midst of this comes a tapping at their half-open window, which they turn toward and then pull immediately back from, for directly on the other side of the glass, pressed up against it, is a retarded boy of an indeterminate age. He has an abnormally fleshy face that spreads out in strange, fat waves against the glass, and behind his ears are thick, lumpy growths that resemble wads of gum piled on top of one another. When he pulls back from the window, his lips leave behind snail-like tracks on the glass. Their fellow riders, who have been watching their interactions carefully, chuckle at their reaction to the boy while behind him a group of vendors has gathered, no doubt egging him on so that they might enjoy a bit of fun in the midst of the heat and the tedium of selling the same wares day after day.

"I love you!" the boy calls out to them in a deep, unformed voice, and they do not realize at first that he is speaking English. "I love you!" He begins to dance then, frantically, while the men behind him cheer and clap their hands in some vague semblance of rhythm. Even as the bus pulls out of the market, the boy is still dancing; he pulls off his shirt, either in response to the heat or the coaxing of the men, and dances, and their last glimpse of him is of a large white mound twisting and writhing, the final, energetic gasps of a fish set down in the desert.

They do not speak until the bus is well outside of town, allowing the dexterity of the henchman, who hangs from the bus with one hand, to command their attention. "I was just so . . . so . . . taken back," Sheila says at last, weakly, testing this position aloud, sensing that their claim to indignation on the retarded boy's behalf is compromised by the fact that everyone had witnessed their repulsion.

"An odd place," Bernadette agrees, feeling safest with small, inconsequential commentary, and then they are quiet again, aware of the continuing stares of their fellow passengers and the increasingly tortuous nature of the road.

Perhaps an hour later, although they are seemingly in the middle of nowhere, the bus stops, and a family climbs on board, the parents, plodding and silent, accompanied by three children of varying heights but with a uniformly androgynous appearance— dull, sunken eyes and shaven heads covered with scabs and even a number of open sores to which red slashes of Mercurochrome have been applied, giving them the appearance of strange, colorful warriors from some remote tribe that is not in the habit of taking the bus. The parents settle heavily into the seat in front of the women, the only empty seat, while the children pause mutely in the aisle until the father makes a gesture, a downward slice with his hand, and the children drop obediently to their knees and crawl beneath the seats, the two youngest curling together under the parents' seat like twins waiting side by side to be born, while the other, the tallest of the three, huddles beneath the women's seat.

Before the family's arrival, the women were quite aware of being the oddest thing that the other riders had expected to encounter on this trip, but now they are fairly sure that they have acquired competition, a fact that relieves them greatly, for it is a tiring thing already, this trip through winding mountain roads in 115-degree heat with the smell of diesel fuel and vomit everywhere. An occasional, vomit-ripe plastic bag rolls past their feet on inclines, like a water balloon in search of a target, but most of the riders have given up on bags and are simply emptying their stomachs directly onto the floor. At several particularly curvy points, Sheila thinks that she might be forced to join them, but she concentrates on restraint, mindful of the attention that her particular nausea is sure to attract. Each time the bus begins a steep climb, Sheila and Bernadette pull their feet up, holding them off the floor while vomit flows beneath them like an incoming tide, and then again on the downward grade as the tide goes out. They have only backpacks with them, cradled in their laps. Early on, they had removed the packs from beneath their seats, and it is this vacated space that the boy occupies, for, though still unsure of his gender, that is how they have decided to think of him—as a boy, or more specifically, and purely for ease of reference, as a pronoun: *he*.

"What do you think he's doing down there?" Sheila asks.

"Nothing, I imagine. He's probably just staring at our ankles." For some reason, this thought—of the small, strange boy fixated for hours on their ankles—unsettles both of them, and they begin to fidget, keeping their legs in restless motion.

"What if he bites us?" asks Sheila, who has unusually fleshy calves.

"Why would he bite us?" Bernadette responds, but sharply, in a way that suggests that she too has entertained such thoughts.

"It must be so hot down there," Sheila says eventually. "And they'll be covered with vomit."

"Well," says Bernadette, whose practical nature often gets misread as apathetic. "What can we do really?" She looks out the window, finding the barrenness consoling. Many of the other passengers are still watching them, some turned fully around in their seats, apparently unconcerned about the havoc that this may wreak on their already compromised stomachs. It is too soon to tell whether their interest has shifted to this strange family, three-fifths of which has taken up quarters under the seats, or whether people simply wish to see how the two women will respond to them.

"Why does everybody feel the need to stare at us?" complains Sheila. "Why don't *they* say something if they think it's so awful?"

"Maybe they don't think it's so awful," says Bernadette reflexively.

"Then why are they staring like that?"

"Like what?" Bernadette asks, more loudly than necessary despite the breeze from the open windows, which she knows she will later blame for her elevated tone. Her voice contains a surprising level of irritation, and their immediate neighbors look quickly at Sheila, expecting a response, the way that spectators follow a tennis ball that has been sent, with some force, back into an opponent's court.

"Like they're just waiting for *us* to do something," Sheila says.

"You know what I think?" Bernadette says tiredly. "I think they're just testing us. I don't think that anyone really cares whether something gets done or not. I think they're just wondering what we think about it all, whether we find it wrong or important or"—and here she pauses, searching for one last adjective—"or worthy," she says at last, unconvinced and disappointed by the vagueness of these options.

"Well," replies Sheila after a moment, "maybe you're right. Maybe we should just close our eyes right now and go to sleep, and when we wake up everybody else will be sleeping also." Sheila is calling her bluff. Bernadette understands this, just as she understands that she has put herself in a position to have it called.

"And we just leave them under there like little caged animals?" she asks, underscoring her words with an outrage that she does not really feel. Logic, for which she possesses a great and natural capacity, has deserted her; she notes its absence distantly, by attempting to catalog the things that have replaced it—the heat, of course, and the stench of diesel, which has created a ringing in her ears. "Well," she says dully, "there are probably worse things than riding under the seat of a bus."

"Of course there are *worse* things," Sheila explodes. "What are you suggesting? That we determine the absolute worst thing in the world and fix only that?"

As this discussion is taking place, the parents of the children have begun to devour a packet of fried fish, dropping the heads and bones onto the floor between their legs. They eat without speaking, though both are unusually loud chewers, and without offering anything to their children, who must surely be watching the steady rain of scraps. At last one of the children pops up between them—fish bones and greasy smudges of breading across the left side of his forehead—and extends his hand, urchin style, but the father pushes him back beneath the seat with a greasy hand of his own. A man leans over and says something to the parents in Arabic, something loud and unmistakably angry, and then another man adds to it, gesturing to the children beneath the seat for emphasis. The parents continue to eat without acknowledging any of them, and finally a third man rises and calls out to the driver, who pulls obediently to the side of the road. He and the henchman come back and stand in the aisle while various passengers offer statements, and in the end, it is the couple's passivity—they continue to eat without showing any interest in the proceedings against them—even more than their actions that seems to turn everyone against them. The henchman kneels and extricates the children, and because there are still no seats available, the three of them crouch together in the aisle, lined up like tiny members of a chain gang.

Bernadette and Sheila settle in at the only decent hotel in Tafraoute, a clean, unusually quiet place run by a graceful man in his sixties who never leaves the premises, relying, he explains, on a nephew to bring him everything he needs. They have seen the nephew only once, the first evening, when they arrived so exhausted from the trip that Bernadette had been unable to carry her backpack the half mile from the market, where the bus had left them, to the hotel. Instead, much to her embarrassment, she had been obliged to pay a boy to carry the pack for her, and he had served as their guide also, leading them through the dark streets with a backpack slung over each shoulder, for he had insisted on carrying Sheila's as well. When they arrived at the hotel, however, the boy had refused to accompany them inside, and they had paused just outside the door to hand him four dirhams and, for good measure, a handful of pennies that they were tired of carrying. He held the door for them, and even as it swung closed, they could hear him running away in the darkness—bare feet thudding, coins clinking reassuringly in his pocket.

"Welcome," the hotelier cried out warmly when they

stepped into the foyer, rising effortlessly to greet them from where he knelt in front of an extremely hairy man who was seated, trouser legs rolled, bare feet soaking in a basin of water. "Rest your bags," said the hotelier, as though the bags were the ones exhausted from the trip, but they set their backpacks down and then stood awkwardly nearby as the hotelier knelt once again and continued with his task, washing the hairy man's feet, which were also hairy and looked like two spiders resting in the basin of water.

The hairy man was in his forties perhaps, though his excessive hairiness had a way of obscuring his age, making him appear older at first glance and then, perhaps because hair suggested a certain vitality, younger. In any case, he was a good deal younger than the hotelier, and he smoked with elaborate disinterest as the hotelier lifted his feet from the basin and dried them tenderly with a white towel that hung down from his shoulder, handling them as one would delicate china at the end of a very long dinner party. As he worked, the hotelier asked the women polite questions about where they were from and whether they had become ill on the bus, and he chuckled pleasantly at their descriptions of people vomiting all around them.

"My nephew," he said suddenly in the midst of this discussion, indicating the hairy man with an elegant inclination of his head, and they had both stared at the nephew, waiting, for it seemed as though the hotelier had been planning to tell them something, perhaps about the nephew and vomiting, but after a lengthy silence it occurred to them that the hotelier had simply been introducing his nephew, and he, coming to the same realization, grunted belatedly in their direction.

Later, once they had filled in the register, shown their passports, and paid for the night, the hotelier escorted them to their room, gliding along ahead of them in his ghostly white djellaba.

The nephew had not moved from his chair as the three of them completed the paperwork, though he did rise as they left the room, in what they had imagined was a gentlemanly gesture, but in fact, he was simply moving himself nearer the desk, upon which sat a bell that he began to tap impatiently even as they made their way down the hallway to their room. Each time they admired some aspect of their room—the tightness with which the sheets had been tucked, the coolness of the tiles, the way that sparseness translated into beauty—the hotelier bowed slightly in their direction while the bell punctuated their comments like a series of exclamation marks, lending urgency and falseness to everything they said.

"My nephew," the hotelier said at last. "He requires my assistance." And with a final bow, he was gone.

Each morning when they go out, the hotelier waves at them from the courtyard, where he can always be found hanging sheets and towels to dry, and when they return in the afternoon, he insists in his gently assertive way that they drink tea with him in his quarters, which they do, the three of them stumbling along in French while he shows them, day after day, the same collection of six or seven magazine photographs of Richard Chamberlain, whose face he strokes absentmindedly with his thumb as they converse. Beyond these photographs, there is nothing about his room that suggests an individual presence, but it is beautiful nonetheless, with a bed in one corner, prayer mat tucked beneath it, and a living area to the other side, which is where they drink their tea, sitting close together on cushions made from old saddlebags around a brass table, round like an oversized plate, with spindly wooden legs that hold it several feet off the ground.

"Please stay tomorrow," the hotelier urges them each day as they are backing toward the door, having finished their sweet mint tea and finished looking at the photos of Richard Chamberlain and discussing his performance in *The Thorn Birds,* which neither woman has seen and the hotelier has seen only in English, a language he does not understand. And they do stay. They had planned to spend just two days in Tafraoute, two days in which to view the Belgian's rocks and the pink homes, but they have been here seven, a full week, and still they have no plan to leave. It is not the hotelier's daily invitation that holds them but an overwhelming lethargy unlike anything they have ever experienced and to which both women have succumbed, blaming it on the bus trip with its endless curves and vomiting. But they both know that it is more than that.

They stay even though they have run out of tourist activities—or perhaps *because* they have run out of them. Sometimes, they begin a game of dominoes with their breakfast and play through the morning until lunchtime, looking around the café in wonder to realize that hours have passed, that customers have come and gone, that bread and jam have given way to brochettes and soup. Other days, lying side by side on the twin beds in their room, they read books that the hotelier has given them, no doubt to keep them here, books left behind by other travelers, the sorts of books that they privately scoffed at their colleagues for reading back home, books about espionage and romance and mystery novels that pulled one along out of a simple need to know who had committed the murder and why—neatly answerable questions that did not beget other questions, which meant that once the book was finished, it stayed finished. They read quickly, skimming the pages for relevant facts, though neither of them has ever read in this way before, without regard to style or details, to the nuances of description. They finish two or three books a day, but after several days of this, they find themselves shocked at how easily they have been drawn back into a routine, as though routine were an addiction that their bodies held fast to even as their minds plotted an escape.

When they return to the hotel on the eighth afternoon, the hotelier is not waiting for them with tea, and though they have made a point to complain to each other about his presumptuousness and the sickly sweetness of the tea, they feel strangely offended by his absence, offended and disappointed. When he still has not made an appearance by the time they return from dinner, they are worried as well, for he can always be found washing out the bathroom sinks or rinsing down the foyer tiles or, once these tasks are completed, sitting quietly at his window seat, watching the world outside, the world from which he has exiled himself. Bernadette and Sheila have wondered aloud what it is he thinks as he sits there—whether he is thinking regretfully about his decision to leave the world or feeling vindicated by it. Never has it occurred to them that he still considers himself a part of it, considers himself the one whose job it is to sit and watch.

Because they have grown to expect his presence, they do not know how to respond to his absence, and they stand uncertainly in the foyer for several minutes, talking more loudly than usual in hopes that he will hear them and appear, but finally they decide that they better check on him, so they rap quietly at the door to his quarters, quietly because they are from Minnesota and this act goes against all they believe in. They can hear activity inside—the swish of fabric and voices, low and urgent—but when the hotelier finally comes to the door and peers out, they see that he is crying, and neither of them knows what to say.

"Yes?" he asks finally, and Sheila blurts out something about missing their afternoon tea. He studies them impassively for a moment and says, "Fine, I shall make tea. Please wait in the foyer." Though they both try to explain that that is not what

Sheila had meant, he closes the door, and they have no choice but to go to the foyer and wait. When he enters carrying a tray and bends to place it on the table in front of them, they see first that he has brought only two cups and then that his right eye, which he had made an effort to turn away from them before, is puffy with the first traces of bruising.

"What happened to your eye?" asks Bernadette before she can think better of it.

"Please do not study my eye," replies the hotelier, and neither woman can decide whether he has used the word *study* accidentally, because his French is limited, or intentionally, a purposeful attempt to infuse the conversation with a formality that would preclude further discussion. In any case, it achieves the latter effect, and the two sit drinking their tea, which is so sweet that their teeth and tongues thicken with sugar and feel too large for their mouths. As they walk down the hallway to their room, they pause beside the hotelier, who has settled in at his window seat, and though they call out a mumbled good evening, he does not return their greeting, does not even turn toward them, and once they are back in their room and changing into their nightshirts, they do not discuss the hotelier because they are both too overcome by sadness.

They awaken early the next morning, and though they have slept well, the sadness has only intensified, has become so powerful that each woman feels the room cannot accommodate the two of them and it, and so they dress quickly and, without speaking about it first, pack their bags and set them by the door.

"Well," says Bernadette, "I guess this is it."

"Yes," Sheila agrees, "I guess it is."

"Ladies," the hotelier sings out when they appear in the foyer with their backpacks. His eye is in full color now, but he makes no attempt to hide it as he had done the night before.

"Please, let us have some tea together." He gestures toward his quarters, and, because they are leaving, they feel that they cannot say no. They find his low table set with three teacups as well as a loaf of bread, jam, and a small plate of olives, the three cushions arranged neatly around it, and he allows them to survey it for a moment before urging them, with a graceful sweep of his arm, in the direction of it all.

"I am sorry, ladies, about the difficulties," he tells them once they are seated, his voice strangely animated. "My nephew, you see. He came for a visit." He turns his attention to pouring the tea, and the women look around the room one last time, trying not to fidget, though they are anxious to leave, to make a first step toward departure, even one that will mean sitting in the market for another two hours awaiting the arrival of the bus. Nearby, so close, in fact, that they wonder how they could not have noticed them immediately, are the Richard Chamberlain photographs, in shreds, laid out on the open prayer rug. Somebody, presumably the hotelier, has attempted to mend them, but with limited success, the resulting composites bringing together features of the actor from conflicting decades, drastically differing hairstyles and clothing, a facial topography of wrinkles that appear and disappear and then appear again.

The hotelier acknowledges the damage with a shrug. "My nephew," he says sadly but then, perhaps because they both look guiltily away from the photographs, he adds almost cheerfully, "There is nothing that can be done, but he will bring me others. Better ones. He is sorry for what he has done." Giving a small, authoritative clap of his hands first in Bernadette's direction and then in Sheila's, he orders them, "Eat, please," and they both take up their bread, on which he has spread jam, and begin the process of chewing and swallowing.

Nothing more is said as they finish eating, drink one cup of tea, and accept, though do not drink, a second, but when they stretch their legs in anticipation of leaving, the hotelier rises first and prepares to speak. He stands before them for perhaps forty seconds, clearing his throat repeatedly until both women fear that he might have a piece of bread lodged in it, but at last he stops, gasps once, and his hands, twin birds that generally flutter about excitedly when he speaks, dart inside the sleeves of his djellaba and are still.

"You see, I love him, and that must be considered," he announces, ceremoniously and with great finality, and only now do the women understand how much they have come to rely on his hands, their fluttering, distracting lightness. He smiles at them both then, sweetly, and in the awkward silence that ensues, the women begin to move away from each other, distractedly, their buttocks rotating on the scratchy woolen cushions until they are sitting with their backs nearly touching, faces cast in opposite directions, as though they can no longer bear the thought of their eyes resting on the same things. To a third party, not the hotelier but a casual observer, one able to take in, from a measured remove, both women at once, they might resemble a pair of matching bookends that have drawn more closely together in order to accommodate the steadily depleting collection of books that they once held between them.

All Boy

Later, when Harold finally learned that his parents had not fired Mrs. Norman, the babysitter, for locking him in the closet while she watched her favorite television shows, he could not imagine why he had ever attributed her firing to this in the first place, especially since his parents had not seemed particularly upset by the news of his confinement. His father had said something vague about it building character and teaching inner resources, and his mother, in an attempt to be more specific, said that it could not hurt to learn how the sightless got by. Nor had Harold minded being in the closet, where he kept a survival kit inspired by the one that his parents, indeed all Minnesotans, stored in their cars in winter, though his contained only a small flashlight, several books, water, and a roll of Life Savers, chosen because he liked the surprise—there in the dark—of not knowing which flavor was next.

Furthermore, he understood Mrs. Norman's motivations, which had to do with the fact that if he were allowed to watch television with her, he would inevitably ask questions, which she would feel obligated to answer, thus diminishing her concentration and so her pleasure. Her concerns seemed to him reasonable: he had a tendency to ask questions, for he was a curious child (though awkwardly so), a characteristic that his teachers cited as proof in making comments both positive and negative.

Mrs. Norman, it turned out, had been fired because she sometimes wore his father's socks while she watched television, slipping them on over her own bare feet. It was the *bare* part that completely unhinged his father, who did not like to drink from other people's glasses or sit in the dentist's chair while the dentist stood close to him smelling of metal. One night, Mrs. Norman left a pair of his father's socks on the sofa instead of putting them back in his father's drawer, and when his father asked her about it, she said, "Oh my, I took them off when my toes got toasty and forgot all about them," apologizing as though the issue were the forgetting and not the wearing. This had further angered Harold's father, who considered the sharing of socks—his naked feet where hers had been—an intimacy beyond what he could bear, and after he talked about it "morning, noon, and night for two days," as Harold's mother later put it, they fired Mrs. Norman.

Harold was quite familiar with Mrs. Norman's feet. They were what old people's feet should look like, he thought, with nails so yellow and thick that she could not cut them by herself, not even with his assistance. Instead, her daughter, who occasionally stopped by on one of the two nights each week that Mrs. Norman stayed with Harold, cut them using a tool with long handles and an end that looked like the beak of a parrot.

"May I watch?" Harold asked because he was the sort of child who differentiated between *may* and *can* and found that adults often responded favorably to this, granting him privileges that they might not otherwise have offered. He did not feel that he was being dishonest because he cared deeply about grammar and would have gone on using *may* even without such incentives.

"You may," replied Mrs. Norman, inclining her head toward him as though she were a visiting dignitary granting him an audience, and Harold sat down next to her. Her daughter, a powerful-looking woman in her thirties, stood over them with the device, holding it in a way that suggested that she enjoyed tools and was looking forward to using it. Harold did not like tools, which he thought of as destructive, even though his father told him that he needed to learn to view the bigger picture: it was true that tools were used to cut and bore and pound, but these small acts of destruction generally resulted in a much bigger act of creation. "Like our house," his father said, as though their house were an obvious example of the way that creation came out of destruction.

Mrs. Norman's daughter was what his parents called jolly. There were other words that they used, words that he did not yet know despite his extensive vocabulary, but he knew *jolly* and felt that she was. She drove a very old motorcycle, which she had to roll to start, and once when his father, who knew nothing about motorcycles, made polite conversation, asking, "Is it a Harley?" she replied, "More like a Hardly," and then she thumped his father on the shoulder and laughed. His father had also laughed, surprising Harold because being touched by people he didn't really know was another thing his father considered too intimate.

Mrs. Norman's daughter grasped her mother's foot and positioned it on her thigh, but this gave her no room to wield the device properly, so she helped her mother onto the floor, where Mrs. Norman sat with her back braced against the sofa while her daughter squeezed the ends of the cutting device together and the tips of the nails broke free with a loud snap and flew into the air like tiddledywinks.

"Can you please pick those up, Harold?" said Mrs. Norman. "They're sharp, and I don't want anyone stepping on them."

Harold crouched on the floor around Mrs. Norman's newly

trimmed feet and began to collect the nail clippings, gathering them in his cupped left hand. He studied one of them, flexing it between his fingers, surprised at its sturdiness. "May I keep it?" he asked, thinking that it would make a welcome addition to the contents of his pocket, which already included a small snail shell, an empty bullet casing, a strip of birch tree parchment, and several dried lima beans, items chosen because they offered a certain tactile reassurance.

"Ish, no," said Mrs. Norman. "I want you to throw them away this minute and then scrub your hands. You too," she admonished her daughter, who was using the hem of her shirt to brush away the chalky residue that clung to the tool's beak.

Harold went into the kitchen and emptied Mrs. Norman's toenail clippings into the milk carton filled with compost—all except the large one, which he slipped into his pocket. As he scrubbed his hands at the sink, Mrs. Norman's daughter came and stood beside him, so close that he could smell her, an oily smell that he suspected came from the Hardly. Harold did not like to be this close to people, close enough to smell them, though his mother said that this was simply his father rubbing off on him and that he needed to focus on the positive aspects of smell, the way that it enhanced hunger and rounded out memory. Harold tried to embrace his mother's perspective, but he could not get over the way that odor disregarded boundaries, wrapping him, for example, in the earthy, almost tuberish smell that hung in the air after Mrs. Norman had spent time in the bathroom.

"How old are you these days?" asked Mrs. Norman's daughter as she scrubbed vigorously at her hands.

"Ten," he said. "Well, eleven."

"Which is it?" asked Mrs. Norman's daughter, still scrubbing. "Ten or eleven? Age is a very clear-cut thing, you know.

When you become eleven, you lose all rights to ten." She said this in a serious tone, looking him in the eye rather than down at her soapy hands, but then she laughed the way she had when she said "more like a Hardly" to his father, and Harold instinctively stepped away from her.

"Eleven." This was true. He had turned eleven just two weeks earlier.

"And what sorts of things do eleven-year-old boys like to do these days?"

"I'm not sure." He knew what *he* liked to do. Besides reading, which was his primary interest and one that he would not belittle by calling a hobby, he liked very specific things: he enjoyed making pancakes but not waffles; he took pleasure in helping his mother dust but could not be convinced to vacuum; he kept lists of words that he particularly liked or disliked the sound of. At the moment, he thought that *vaccination* and *expectorate* were beautiful but could not bear the word *dwindle*.

He did not, however, know what boys his age liked to do, for he had no friends. At school, he interacted only with adults, who, he had learned, were subject to many of the same foibles he witnessed in his classmates, especially Miss Jamison, his homeroom teacher, who cared deeply about having the approval of her students and found ways to ridicule Harold in front of them, not overtly as his classmates did but making clear her intention nonetheless.

For example, after he had been home with a cold for two days, she asked, "Harry, how are you feeling?" She was the only teacher who called him Harry, though all of his classmates did, and he hated it, convinced that they were really saying "hairy," but when he complained to his mother, she told him to explain that he "did not care for the diminutive," and so he did not mention the problem to her again.

"I'm better," he said.

"Better?" Miss Jamison repeated loudly. "So you're feeling *better?*" She said this with a smirk, exaggerating *better* as though it were wrong in some fundamental and obvious way, and his classmates all laughed knowingly. He spent the rest of the morning thinking about it: hadn't she been asking him to compare how he felt today with how he felt yesterday? Ultimately, he decided that there was nothing wrong with saying *better,* but that night at dinner when his father asked how he was feeling, he said, "Well," just to be safe.

Shortly after Mrs. Norman's firing, it seemed that Harold might acquire a friend, a boy named Simon, who transferred into his class just after Thanksgiving. When Simon came over to his house to play, however, he announced to Harold that his mother had a lustful look.

"I don't know what that means," Harold replied grudgingly, for he was used to being the one who knew words that his classmates did not.

"You know. Like she wants sex," Simon said matter-of-factly, as though this were a perfectly normal observation to make about a potential friend's mother. Harold did not reply, and the two boys sat on the floor in his room chewing summer sausage sandwiches made for them by his mother, who had chatted away with Simon as she cut and buttered the bread, trying, Harold knew, to be overly gay as a way of making up for his inability to say and do the sorts of things that would make Simon want to visit again. This was what her hard work had earned her, Harold thought sadly, the indignity of being described as lustful by an eleven-year-old boy who then gobbled up the sandwiches that she had so lustfully prepared.

Simon's comment struck him as particularly unfair because he knew that his parents did not have sex. He had heard his mother telling Aunt Elizabeth as much on the telephone. His aunt lived in Milwaukee, and because it was a long-distance call, she and his mother talked just once a month, generally when his father was at work, though lately they had begun to talk more often, and his father had started to complain about the higher bills. "Why doesn't she ever call you?" asked his father, adding, "Goddamn hippies."

Harold did not know what hippies were, not exactly, but his aunt had spent two days with them in August, and so he had his theories. Prior to this visit, he had not seen his aunt since he was six because she and his father did not get along, and throughout the visit, he felt his father's unspoken expectation of loyalty, but he could not help himself: he had liked his aunt, who wore fringe and waited until both of his parents were out of the room to say, "Harold, I'm deeply sorry about your name. I should have tried to stop them."

Harold didn't know how to respond, for he thought of his name as who he was, a feature that could not be changed without altering everything else. Still, he liked the earnest, conspiratorial way in which his aunt addressed him.

"What do your friends call you?" she asked. "Harry?"

He did not tell her that he had no friends. "No, I don't really care for diminutives," he said instead.

She laughed. "Well. Now I can certainly see why they chose Harold."

He smiled shyly then and offered to make her iced tea.

"Groovy," she said. "I like a man who can cook," and when he explained that iced tea did not actually involve cooking, she laughed her throaty, pleasant laugh yet again.

Eventually, Harold understood that his mother called his

aunt more frequently because she and his father argued more frequently, their arguments sometimes taking root right in front of him but over things so small that he did not understand how they had been able to make arguments out of them. Thanksgiving was a perfect example. As the turkey cooked, his parents sat together in the kitchen drinking wine and chatting, their faces growing flushed from the heat and the alcohol, and when everything was ready, his father seated his mother and then placed the turkey in front of her with a flourish.

"Le turkey, Madame," he declared, pronouncing *turkey* as though it were French.

His mother giggled and picked up the carving knife. "Harold, what part would you like?" she asked.

"White meat, please."

"I'll give you breast meat," his mother said, adding with a small chuckle, "God knows your father has no interest in breast."

For the rest of the meal, Harold's father spoke only to Harold, asking *him* for the gravy when it actually sat in front of his mother. His mother was also silent, and when the meal was nearly over, she dumped the last of the cranberries onto Harold's plate even though all three of them knew that cranberries were his father's favorite part of Thanksgiving. Later, as Harold sat reading in his room, he heard his parents yelling, and he crept down the hallway and perched at the top of the stairs, letting their voices funnel up to him.

"You know *exactly* what I'm talking about," his father shouted.

"Come on, Charles. Lighten up." Harold heard a small catch in his mother's voice, which meant she wanted to laugh. "He thought I was talking about the turkey breast." She paused. "Which, of course, I was."

There were five words that were forbidden in their house-

hold, words that, according to his father, were not only pro-
fane but aesthetically unappealing. Harold heard his father say
one of these words to his mother, his voice becoming low and
precise as it did when he was very angry. His mother did not
reply, and a moment later, Harold heard his father open the
front door and leave.

When his mother came to tuck him in, her eyes red from
crying, he asked where his father had gone. "To the pool hall,"
she said, which made her start crying again because this was
an old joke between them. When his father occasionally disappeared after dinner, slipping out unannounced, Harold's
mother always said, "I guess he's gone to the pool hall." She
had explained to Harold what a pool hall was, and they both
laughed at the notion of his neat, serious father in such a place,
there among men who smoked cigars and sweated and made
bets with their hard-earned money.

"You have a lot of books," Simon said after he had proclaimed
Harold's mother lustful and they had finished their sandwiches
and there seemed nothing left to do.

"Yes," said Harold. He almost added that he was a "voracious reader," but remembering what his father always said,
that words were meant to be tools of communication but just
as often drove wedges between people, he opted for triteness
instead. "I love reading," he mumbled.

"Have you read all of these books?" asked Simon with a shrug.

"Yes. Now, I mainly check them out of the library. The limit
is three at a time, but Mr. Tesky lets me take five." Mr. Tesky was
his favorite librarian because, in making recommendations, he
never relied on expressions like *the other boys* and *kids your age*.

"Yes," replied Simon. "That's because he's a fag."

Harold had no idea what *fag* meant, but he regretted terribly not using *voracious*. "Figure it out from context," his mother always told him after he had bothered her one too many times to explain words. He considered the context and decided that *fag* had to do with being helpful.

"Yes," he agreed. "He is."

Simon laughed and threw a pillow at him. "You're a fag also," Simon said.

It turned out that *fag* meant to work really hard: "toil," said his dictionary. Which made sense, for Mr. Tesky did work very hard. Of course, Harold normally would have noticed that this *fag* was a verb while Simon had used it as a noun, but Simon's visit had left him feeling tired and unmoored, and so he overlooked this obvious distinction. He set the dictionary back on the shelf in the spot that it always occupied and surveyed his room, looking for something out of place, something to explain his uneasiness. Finally, he decided to calm himself by slipping into his kimono.

Harold had purchased the kimono that summer at a yard sale at which his mother had been convinced to stop only because there were books for sale. Overall, his parents did not approve of yard sales, for they felt that there was something *unsavory* about putting one's personal belongings outside for strangers to see, and not just to see but to handle and even buy. Harold, however, liked wandering amid carpets with dark, mysterious stains and mismatched cutlery and stacks of clothing that had presumably once fit the people selling them, people who seemed in no way embarrassed to be associated with these dingy socks and stretched-out waistbands.

The kimono, by contrast, was the most beautiful piece of clothing he had ever seen, black with a white crane painted across the back, and his mother, who lent him the two dollars to purchase it, told him that it was from Japan and that in Japan everyone wore such things, and though he found this hard to believe, Mr. Tesky later showed him a book from his personal collection with pictures of Japanese people wearing kimonos as they walked in the streets and sat around drinking tea. Harold wore his kimono only at home, but he felt different when he slipped it on, more graceful and at ease, though whether this meant that he felt more himself or less, he could not say.

He stopped wearing the kimono quite abruptly when he overheard his father referring to it as his "dress," though there had been issues before that: as he ate, the sleeves dragged across his food and became sullied with red spaghetti sauce and pork chop grease, and as he descended the stairs one night, he tripped on the hem, toppling down the last three steps and wrenching his ankle. For days afterward, he worried that he had inherited his mother's clumsiness, though she tended to fall only in public, usually on special occasions. On his first day of school this year, for example, she turned to wave at him and caught her foot where the tile became carpeting. She flew forward, upsetting an easel at which one of his classmates stood painting, and landed facedown on the floor, her skirt hiked up along her thigh. Miss Jamison rushed to help, and his classmates gathered around her in awe, shocked and excited to see an adult splayed out on the floor. His mother always attended carefully to his cuts and fevers and upset stomachs, and he knew that he should go to her, but he did not because he could not bear being regarded as the boy whose mother fell. Instead, he stayed at his desk with the top up against the sight of her, arranging his books. When he got home that afternoon, his mother teased him about it so relentlessly that he knew he had hurt her deeply.

His mother knocked at his door and came in. If she was surprised to see him wearing his kimono again, she did not say so. Instead, she got right to her point, which was that she felt he should invite Simon for a sleepover.

"I don't think that's a good idea," said Harold.

"Why not?" asked his mother, ready, he knew, to tell him yet again that he would have more friends (using "more" as though he actually had some) once he learned not to be so hard on people. "He seemed like an affable fellow."

"Yes," agreed Harold, trying to think of a way to turn his mother against Simon without having to use the word *lustful*. "He is affable, but he's also a Democrat."

His mother sighed loudly and stood up. "I thought you'd had enough of that thing," she said, meaning his kimono, and she went downstairs to make dinner.

Harold's parents were Republicans. For Halloween, they had insisted that he go as the Gallup Poll, a costume requiring two people, one to be Jimmy Carter and the other, Gerald Ford. He wanted to be Carter because he liked the slow, buttery way that Carter spoke, but his parents had forbidden it, instead phoning the parents of a girl in his class whose father was his father's subordinate at the bank. The girl, whose name was Molly, had been dropped off the afternoon before Halloween, and the two of them sat in his living room, where, with the help of his mother and several newspaper photos, they sketched the two candidates. He was surprised at how well the masks captured the two men—Carter's sheepish smile and Ford's large, bland forehead—and after cutting small slits for the eyes and stapling elastic bands to the sides, he and Molly slipped them on and practiced trotting around the living room side by side, pretending to jockey for position and calling out, "We're the Gallup Poll."

Later, after Molly had gone home, his mother told him that

he needed to be sure to finish first, and so, as they paraded in front of the judges the next afternoon, he made a halfhearted surge at the very end, nosing ahead of Jimmy Carter. After the prizes had been given, predictably, to a witch, a robot, and a farmer, Mr. Tesky came up to Harold and complimented him on his costume. "Do you follow politics?" Mr. Tesky asked, his Adam's apple bobbling playfully. As usual, he wore corduroy pants with a belt so long that it actually made another half turn around his body. Harold wondered whether Mr. Tesky had once been fat, a man better suited for this belt, but he did not ask because he knew that it was impolite to ask questions about health. Actually, his parents included money, religion, and politics on this list as well, so Harold did not know how to respond to Mr. Tesky's question.

"No," he said finally. "I'm too young to follow politics."

Mr. Tesky laughed and reached out as though to ruffle his hair, then seemed to think better of it and retracted his hand, thrusting it into his back pocket as though putting the gesture literally behind him.

At dinner, Harold's father asked nothing about Simon's visit, which Harold took as an indication that his mother had been sufficiently convinced of Simon's unsuitability. Instead, the conversation centered on back-to-school night, which they would all three be attending the next evening. Harold did not understand why his parents required him to participate, but the one time that he had protested, explaining that none of his classmates would be going, his father berated him for his apathy. As his parents chewed their roast beef, Harold went through the list of his teachers again, making sure that they understood that Mrs. Olson taught science and Miss Olson, social studies, because his parents tended to mix up the two women, expecting Miss Olson to be young when, in fact, she was just a few years from retirement.

"You should also meet Mr. Tesky," he said, and then, because it was his habit to utilize new words immediately, he added, "He's a fag."

"Harold," said his mother in her severe voice. "I don't want to hear you ever talking that way about people. That's a terrible accusation." His father said nothing.

Harold did not reply because he had found that when his mother became angry like this, it was best to remain silent and let the moment pass, even when he did not understand what had caused her outburst, for his confusion often provoked her more.

The next night, as his mother stood in his homeroom talking to a group of other mothers, his father announced, "I think I will have a talk with your Mr. Tesky. Perhaps you can escort me to the library, Harold."

Mr. Tesky was on a ladder when they arrived, wearing his belt and a half, the tip of it sticking out at them from behind like a tongue. He did not seem to realize at first that they had come to talk to him, and so while they stood looking up at him, he continued to shelve books, sliding himself nervously along on his rolling ladder. When he finally came down and shook hands with Harold's father, Harold saw that his collar was twisted inward on one side; it occurred to him that Mr. Tesky's collars were always askew but that he had never thought to note it until now, now that he was viewing Mr. Tesky through his father's eyes.

For nearly ten minutes, the two men discussed Harold and his reading habits, his father comporting himself as though he were gathering information on a new hire at the bank, revealing nothing about himself while asking questions that sought to lay bare gaps in Harold's knowledge or abilities, weaknesses in his approach to reading. Then, shifting the conversation suddenly away from Harold, his father asked, "Say, what do you make of these speed-reading courses?"

"Speed-reading?" repeated Mr. Tesky.

"I've been doing some research," said his father. "Apparently the Carters are big fans and so was Kennedy," adding with a snort, "For what that's worth," as though speed-reading, like opinions on communism or the economy, must be discussed along party lines. "I'm thinking about holding a seminar at the bank, maybe bringing in a specialist."

Mr. Tesky sawed his index finger vigorously back and forth beneath his nose.

"Did you know that the average person reads just two words a second?" his father continued. "But with training, that can be increased to five, even seven. I've just been reading about the Wood method. Ever heard of it? You move your hand across the page as you read, and apparently the motion catches the eye's attention and stimulates it to work faster." He opened a book and demonstrated, sweeping his hand across the page as though blessing it or driving out demons.

Mr. Tesky regarded him the way that Harold's mother regarded guests who added salt to the food before tasting it. "Mr. Lundstrom," he began, his neck growing blotchy. "The point of reading is to luxuriate in the words, to appreciate their beauty and nuance, to delve fully into their meaning."

"Speed-reading maintains comprehension," insisted Harold's father.

"Understanding has its own rhythm, Mr. Lundstrom," said Mr. Tesky. "Waving your hand about? Well. That is merely a distraction."

Harold had never heard Mr. Tesky speak with such severity,

not even when children ignored basic library rules, laughing loudly or moving books around so that others would have trouble finding them. In turn, he had always been impressed with his father's ability to make conversation with all sorts of people: when the electrician came to update the wiring in their kitchen, his father asked him why electricians made less than plumbers when their work was so much more dangerous, and when the plumber came the next week to unclog the toilet, he told the plumber that he deserved every penny he charged and then some, given what he had to endure. His father deftly calculated people's interests and needs, drawing them out by soliciting their advice, by making them feel knowledgeable and competent, yet with Mr. Tesky, he had failed. He had asked him about speed-reading but said nothing about the stacks of books that he kept on his nightstand and read faithfully from each night.

Harold and his father made their way back down the half-lit hallway to his classroom, where his mother was still deep in conversation with the other mothers, standing in a circle near the bulletin board on which Miss Jamison had placed examples of what she considered their best work. In Harold's case, she had tacked up an uninspired summary of the process of photosynthesis, something he had dashed off one morning before school. Harold knew that people would assume that science was his favorite subject, particularly given the correctness of the writing, but the truth was that he hated science and had written about it correctly only because it would have required more effort to write incorrectly, to misplace commas or choose less exact words.

His mother, unaware that he and his father had returned, was indeed pointing to his paragraph as she described a boy fascinated by earthquakes, the solar system, and creatures without legs, speaking for several minutes but never mentioning that his fascination was a function not of curiosity but of fear. The other mothers chuckled politely, and then, her voice rising toward closure, his mother announced, "I guess Harold's just all boy," invoking his name to refer to a boy who seemed to him as unknowable as God. His mother turned and saw Harold behind her, and her words became a door shutting between them.

By Minnesota standards, the winter was mild, meaning that the temperature hovered just above zero rather than dipping precipitously below. Still, as they drove home, the road stretched before them treacherously, the icy patches more difficult to detect at night. His mother, who was better on ice, was behind the wheel, Harold beside her because his father had climbed into the back, indicating his wish to be left alone. His mother did not take heed of this, however, instead offering comments about the other mothers that would normally have made his father laugh. Harold wondered whether he would someday grow to care about the sorts of things that his parents did, things like whether a person was missing a button or had applied slightly more mascara to the right eye than the left.

"Oh," she blurted out, as though suddenly remembering a missed appointment or forgotten birthday. "The librarian. How was he?"

"Ichabod Crane," said his father tiredly. "Skinny. Bookish. Disheveled."

Harold's father did not approve of skinniness in men. He believed that men should be muscular, and though he himself was not, he had established a workout space in a small room at the back of the house, filling it with variously sized barbells and two weight machines and covering the walls with pictures of men flexing their muscles. Harold knew that his father had taped up the pictures to provide inspiration, but the men frightened Harold because they had a hard, geometric quality: they wore V-shaped swimming suits, and their torsos—small waists and broad shoulders—were inverted triangles topped off by square heads. Often, his father came home from work and went directly into this room without even changing out of his suit and tie, and when Harold was sent to call him for dinner, he always paused at the door and then left without knocking because he could hear his father inside, groaning.

A week later, Harold entered the house to the now familiar sound of his mother speaking to Aunt Elizabeth on the telephone. School had been dismissed an hour early because it was the start of Christmas break, but his mother seemed to have forgotten this, and Harold set about quietly preparing his favorite snack, Minute Rice with butter. "Before we even met, apparently," he heard his mother say as he waited for the water to boil, "but do you suppose he thought to tell me about it? I'm just the wife—the blind, convenient, little banker's wife."

She listened a moment, then cut in sharply. "Don't patronize me, Elizabeth. I know that." She snorted. "In the closet," she said derisively. "Where do you even get these terms?" She slammed down the receiver, and as Harold ate his Minute Rice with butter, he could hear his mother sobbing in her bedroom upstairs.

When she came down an hour later, she looked surprised to find him sitting at the kitchen table. He had washed his rice bowl and pot and put everything away, and he let her believe that he had just arrived.

"Should I make you a snack?" she asked.

"No," Harold said. "I'm not really hungry." He waited until she took out the cutting board and began cutting up apples for a crisp. "Remember when you fired Mrs. Norman for putting me in the closet?" he said in what he hoped was a casual voice.

His mother turned toward him quickly. "That's not why we fired Mrs. Norman," she said, and she explained in great detail about the socks. "He's always been like that. So particular." She paused. "Harold, your father is leaving. I'll let him explain it to you." She turned back around and continued cutting.

That night, after the three of them had eaten dinner in silence, Harold walked outside with his father, who was carrying two suitcases and a garment bag. His father stowed the luggage in the trunk of his car, and then told Harold that he had something to say.

"Okay," said Harold.

His father cleared his throat several times, sounding like a lawnmower that would not turn over. "According to basic economic theory," he began, "human beings always work harder to avoid losing what they already have than they do at acquiring more. You see, loss is always more devastating than the potential for gain is motivating. I want you to remember that, Harold."

Harold nodded and thrust his hands deep into his pockets, seeking out Mrs. Norman's toenail, which he flexed between his thumb and index finger.

"I have a new friend," his father said, "and I'm moving in with"—he hesitated—"him."

"Does that mean that you won't be checking the windows and doors anymore?" Harold asked. Every night before shutting off the lights, his father walked through the house, staring at each window and each door, checking to make sure that they were properly closed. His mother had always been annoyed by the practice, by the time it took his father to inspect the entire house, but it was something that he had done every night of

Harold's life and so Harold considered it as much a part of bed-time as brushing his teeth and closing his eyes.

"I guess not," his father said, sounding disappointed at Har-old's question. He reached out and placed his hand on his car door, and Harold knew what this meant: that his father was ready, even impatient, to leave, that as he stood there explain-ing himself to Harold, he really wanted to be in his car driving away, away toward his new friend and his new house—while Harold stayed behind in this house, where he would continue to brush his teeth and close his eyes as he always had, except from now on he and his mother would sleep with the windows and doors unchecked all around them. The thought of this filled him with terror, and as he stood there in the driveway watch-ing his father leave, Harold found himself longing for the dark safety of the closet: the familiar smells of wet wool and vacuum cleaner dust, the far-off chatter of Mrs. Norman's television shows, the line of light marking the bottom of the locked door, a line so thin that it made what lay on the other side seem, after all, like nothing.

Acknowledgments

I am grateful for the Flannery O'Connor Award for Short Fiction and the publication of this collection. I would like to thank Nancy Zafris, the Flannery O'Connor Award series editor and a wonderful writer, who was generous with both her knowledge and her enthusiasm as she guided me through the process of publishing my first book. I am also deeply indebted to the staff at the University of Georgia Press. Finally, I would like to thank everyone at Scribner for deciding to give this collection a second life and working with their usual care and dedication to do so.

Many of these stories have appeared, sometimes in slightly different form, in other publications. I would like to acknowledge and thank them: "The Bigness of the World" in *Bellingham Review* (2009); "Bed Death" in *The Kenyon Review* (2009); "Talking Fowl with My Father" in *New England Review* (2009); "The Day You Were Born," *New World Writing* (2011); "Nobody Walks to the Mennonites" in *Blue Mesa Review* (2007); "Upon Completion of Baldness" in *Hobart* (2009); "And Down We Went" in *Five Chapters* (2009); "Idyllic Little Bali" in *Prairie Schooner* (2009); "Dr. Daneau's Punishment" in *The Georgia Review* (2009); "The Children Beneath the Seat" in *New England Review* (2006); and "All Boy" in *New England Review* (2009); the latter was reprinted in *Best American Short Stories 2010*; "Bed Death" was selected for *The PEN/O. Henry Prize Stories 2011*.

I have appreciated the careful attention that the editors at these publications have brought to my work; I would especially like to thank Carolyn Kuebler and Stephen Donadio at *New England Review,* who were the first to publish a story from this collection back in 2006 and have lent support in many ways.

I am also indebted to friends and family in various places, including though by no means limited to the following: New Mexico, where I wrote half of these stories; San Francisco, where I wrote the other half; and Minnesota, where I grew up in a town of four hundred people, an experience that shaped me as a writer. Specifically, I thank friends who provided feedback, enthusiasm, and fodder. They know who they are.

Also, many of the stories are set in countries where I have either lived or traveled. I appreciate the tremendous hospitality that was shown me in these countries.

Finally, I am grateful most of all to my partner of many years, the novelist Anne Raeff. Kurt Vonnegut said, "Every successful creative person creates with an audience of one in mind." Anne has always been my *one.*

Please turn the page for an excerpt from Lori Ostlund's
debut novel,

AFTER THE PARADE

"Lori Ostlund's wonderful novel *After the Parade* should
come with a set of instructions: Be perfectly still. Listen
carefully. Peer beneath every placid surface. Be alive to
the possibility of wonder."
> —Richard Russo, author of the
> Pulitzer Prize–winning novel
> *Empire Falls*

December

1

Aaron had gotten a late start—some mix-up at the U-Haul office that nobody seemed qualified to fix—so it was early afternoon when he finally began loading the truck, nearly eight when he finished. He wanted to drive away right then but could not imagine setting out so late. It was enough that the truck sat in the driveway packed, declaring his intention. Instead, he took a walk around the neighborhood, as was his nightly habit, had been his nightly habit since he and Walter moved here nine years earlier. He always followed the same route, designed with the neighborhood cats in mind. He knew where they all lived, had made up names for each of them—Falstaff and Serial Mom, Puffin and Owen Meany—and when he called to them using these names, they stood up from wherever they were hiding and ran down to the sidewalk to greet him.

He passed the house of the old woman who, on many nights, though not this one, watched for him from her kitchen window and then hurried out with a jar that she could not open. She called him by his first name and he called her Mrs. Trujillo, since she was surely twice his age, and as he twisted the lid off a jar of honey or instant coffee, they engaged in pleasantries, establishing that they were both fine, that they had enjoyed peaceful, ordinary days, saying the sorts of things that Aaron had grown up in his mother's café hearing people say to one another. As a boy, he had dreaded such talk, for he had been shy and no good at it, but as he grew older, he had come to appreciate these small nods at civility.

Of course, Mrs. Trujillo was not always fine. Sometimes, her back was acting up or her hands were numb. She would hold them out toward him, as though the numbness were something that could be seen, and when he put the jar back into them, he said, "Be careful now, Mrs. Trujillo. Think what a mess you'd have with broken glass and honey." Maybe he made a joke that wasn't really funny, something about all those ants with bleeding tongues, and she would laugh the way that people who are very lonely laugh, paying you the only way they know how. She always seemed sheepish about mentioning her ailments, sheepish again when he inquired the next time whether she was feeling better, yet for years they had engaged in this ritual, and as he passed her house that last night, he felt relief at her absence. Still, when he let his mind stray to the future, to the next night and the one after, the thought of Mrs. Trujillo looking out the window with a stubborn jar of spaghetti sauce in her hands made his heart ache.

Aaron picked up his pace, almost ran to Falstaff's house, where he crouched on the sidewalk and called softly to the portly fellow, waiting for him to waddle off the porch that was his stage. At nine, he returned from his walk and circled the truck, double-checking the padlock because he knew there would come a moment during the night when he would lie there thinking about it, and this way he would have an image that he could pull up in his mind: the padlock, secured.

A week earlier, Aaron had gone into Walter's study with a list of the household items that he planned to take with him. He found Walter at his desk, a large teak desk that Walter's father had purchased in Denmark in the 1950s and shipped home. He had used the desk throughout his academic career, writing articles that added up to books about minor Polish poets, most of them long dead, and then it had become Walter's. Aaron loved the desk, which represented everything for which he had been longing all those years ago when Walter took him in and they began their life together: a profession that required a sturdy, beautiful desk; a father who cared enough about aesthetics to ship a desk across an ocean; a life, in every way, different from his own.

Though it was just four in the afternoon, Walter was drinking cognac—Spanish cognac, which he preferred to French— and later Aaron would realize that Walter had already known that something was wrong. Aaron stood in the office doorway, reading the list aloud—a set of bed linens, a towel, a cooking pot, a plate, a knife, cutlery. "Is there anything on the list that you prefer I not take?" he asked.

Walter looked out the window for what seemed a very long time. "I saved you, Aaron," he said at last. His head sank onto his desk, heavy with the memories it contained.

"Yes," Aaron agreed. "Yes, you did. Thank you." He could hear the stiffness in his voice and regretted—though could not change— it. This was how he had let Walter know that he was leaving.

Walter had already tended to his "nightly ablutions," as he termed the process of washing one's face and brushing one's teeth, elevating the mundane by renaming it. He was in bed, so there seemed nothing for Aaron to do but retire as well, except he had nowhere to sleep. He had packed the guest bed, a futon with a fold-up base, and they had never owned a typical couch, only an antique Javanese daybed from Winnie's store in Minneapolis. Winnie was Walter's sister, though from the very

beginning she had felt more like his own. Sleeping on the daybed would only make him think of her, which he did not want.
He had not even told Winnie that he was leaving. Of course, he
could sleep with Walter, in the space that he had occupied for
nearly twenty years, but it seemed to him *improper*—that was
the word that came to mind—to share a bed with the man he
was leaving. His dilemma reminded him of a story that Winnie
had told him just a few weeks earlier, during one of their weekly
phone conversations. Winnie had lots of stories, the pleasure—
and the burden—of owning a small business.

"I'm a captive audience," she had explained to him and Walter once. "I can't just lock up and leave. People know that on
some level, but it suits their needs to act as though we're two
willing participants. Sometimes they talk for hours."

"They are being presumptuous, presumptuous and self-
involved," Walter had said. Walter hated to waste time, hated
to have his wasted. "Just walk away."

Aaron knew that she would not, for he and Winnie were
alike: they understood that the world was filled with lonely
people, whom they did not begrudge these small moments of
companionship.

The story that Winnie had called to tell him was about a customer of hers, Sally Forth. ("Yes, that's really her name," Winnie had added before he could ask.) Sally Forth and her husband
had just returned from a ten-day vacation in Turkey, about
which she had said to Winnie, pretrip: "It's a Muslim country, you know. Lots of taboos in the air, and those are always
good for sex." Sally Forth was a woman impressed with her
own naughtiness, a woman endlessly amused by the things that
came out of her mouth. The first morning, as she and her husband sat eating breakfast in their hotel restaurant and discussing the day's itinerary, her husband turned to her and requested

a divorce. Winnie said that Sally Forth was the type of person who responded to news—good or bad—loudly and demonstratively, without considering her surroundings. Thus, Sally Forth, who was engaged in spreading jam on a piece of bread, reached across the table and ground the bread against her husband's chest, the jam making a red blotch directly over his heart. "Why would you bring me all the way to Turkey to tell me you want a divorce?" Sally Forth screamed, and her husband replied, "I thought you'd appreciate the gesture."

Winnie and Aaron had laughed together on the phone, not at Sally Forth or even at her husband but at this strange notion that proposing divorce required etiquette similar to that of proposing marriage—a carefully chosen moment, a grand gesture.

Sally Forth and her husband stayed in Turkey the whole ten days, during which her husband did not mention divorce again. By the time the vacation was over, she thought of his request as something specific to Turkey, but after they had collected their luggage at the airport back home in Minneapolis, Sally Forth's husband hugged her awkwardly and said that he would be in touch about "the details."

"I feel like such an idiot," she told Winnie. "But we kept sleeping in the same bed. If you're really leaving someone, you don't just get into bed with them, do you?"

And then, Sally Forth had begun to sob.

"I didn't know what to do," Winnie told Aaron sadly. "I wanted to hug her, but you know how I am about that, especially at work. I actually tried. I stepped toward her, but I couldn't do it. It seemed disingenuous—because we're not friends. I don't even like her. So I just let her stand there and cry."

As Aaron finished brushing his teeth, he tried to remember whether he and Winnie had reached any useful conclusions about the propriety of sharing a bed with the person one was about to leave, but he knew that they had not. Winnie had been focused solely on what she regarded as her failure to offer comfort.

"Sometimes," he had told her, "the hardest thing to give people is the thing we know they need the most." When he said this, he was trying to work up the courage to tell her that he was leaving Walter, but he had stopped there so that his comment seemed to refer to Winnie's treatment of Sally Forth, which meant that he had failed Winnie also.

He went into the bedroom and turned on the corner lamp. The room looked strange without his belongings. Gone were the rows of books and the gifts from his students, as well as the Indonesian night table that Winnie had given him when he and Walter moved from Minnesota to New Mexico. It was made from recycled wood, old teak that had come from a barn or railroad tracks or a chest for storing rice—Winnie was not sure what exactly. For Aaron, just knowing that the table had had another life was enough. When he sat down on his side of the bed, Walter did not seem to notice. That was the thing about a king-size bed: its occupants could lead entirely separate lives, never touching, oblivious to the other's presence or absence.

"Walter," he said, but there was no reply. He crawled across the vast middle ground of the bed and shook Walter's shoulder.

"Enh," said Walter, a sound that he often made when he was sleeping, so Aaron considered the possibility that he was not faking sleep.

"Is it okay if I sleep here?" he asked, but Walter, treating the question as a prelude to an argument, said, "I'm too tired for this right now. Let's talk in the morning." And so Aaron spent his last night with Walter in their bed, trying to sleep, trying because he could not stop thinking about the fact that everything he owned was sitting in the driveway—on wheels nonetheless—which meant that every noise became the sound of his possessions being driven away into the night. He was reminded of something that one of his Vietnamese students, Vu, had said in class during a routine speaking exercise. Vu declared that if a person discovered an unlocked store while walking down the street at night, he had the right to take what he wanted from inside. Until then, Vu had struck him as honest and reliable, so the nonchalance with which Vu stated this opinion had shocked Aaron.

"That's stealing," Aaron blurted out, so astonished that he forgot about the purpose of the exercise, which was to get the quieter students talking.

"No," Vu said, seemingly puzzled by Aaron's vehemence as well as his logic. "Not stealing. If I destroy lock or break window, this is stealing. If you do not lock door, you are not careful person. You must be responsibility person to own business." Vu constantly mixed up parts of speech and left off articles, but Aaron did not knock on the desk as he normally did to remind Vu to pay attention to his grammar.

"But you did not pay for these things," Aaron cried. "I did. We are not *required* to lock up our belongings. We do so only because there are dishonest people in the world, but locking them up is not what makes them ours. They are ours because we own them."

Vu regarded him calmly. "When the policeman comes, he will ask, 'Did you lock this door?' If you say no, he will not look very well for your things. He will think, 'This man is careless, and now he makes work for me.'"

"I'm not saying it's a *good* idea to leave your door unlocked, Vu. I'm only saying that the things inside are mine, whether I remember to lock the door or not." Belatedly, he had addressed the rest of the class. "What do you guys think?"

They had stared back at him, frightened by his tone. Later,

when he tried to understand what had made him so angry, he had come up with nothing more precise than that Vu had challenged the soundness of a code that seemed obvious, inviolable.

Aaron got out of bed to peek at the truck parked in the driveway. He did this several more times. Around three, having risen for the sixth time, he stood in the dark bedroom listening to Walter's familiar wheezing. Then he put on his clothes and left. As he backed the truck out of the driveway with the headlights off because he did not want them shining in and illuminating the house, the thought came to him that he was like his mother: sneaking away without saying good-bye, disappearing into the night.

All along their street, the houses were lit up with holiday lights. That afternoon, as Aaron carried the first box out to the truck, Walter had blocked the door to ask, "Whatever is going on here?," adding, "It's nearly Christmas." In the past, Aaron would have made a joke along the lines of "What, are you a Jew for Jesus now?" They would have laughed, not because it was funny exactly but because of the level of trust it implied. Instead, Aaron had continued loading the truck without answering, and Walter had retreated to his study.

It was quiet at this hour. Driving home from the symphony one night several years earlier, he and Walter had seen a teenage boy being beaten by five other boys in the park just blocks from their house. Though Albuquerque had plenty of crime, their neighborhood was considered safe, a place where people walked their dogs at midnight, so the sight of this—a petty drug deal going bad—startled them. Walter slammed on the brakes and leaped from the car, yelling, "Stop that," as he and Aaron, dressed in suits and ties, rushed toward the fight. The five boys in hairnets turned and ran, as did the sixth boy, who jumped up and sprinted toward his car, a BMW, and drove off.

Later, in bed, Walter joked, "Nothing more terrifying than two middle-aged fags in suits," though Aaron was just thirty-five at the time. They laughed, made giddy by the moment and by the more sobering realization that the night could have turned out much different. Walter got up and went into the kitchen and came back with two glasses of port, which they sat in bed—the king-size bed—drinking, and though Walter insisted on a light-hearted tone, Aaron took his hand and held it tightly, reminded yet again that Walter was a good man who cared about others.

When Aaron got to the park, he pulled the truck to the curb and turned off the engine, which seemed very loud in the middle of the night. He sat in the dark and cried, thinking about Walter asleep in their bed down the street.

Aaron was in Gallup buying coffee when the sun rose, approaching Needles, California, when he fell asleep at the wheel, awakening within seconds to the disorienting sight of the grassy median before him. He swerved right, the truck shifting its weight behind him, and found himself on the road again, cars honking all around him, a man in a pickup truck jabbing his middle finger at him and screaming something that he took to be "Asshole!" He was not the sort who came away from close calls energized, nor did he believe in endangering the lives of others. He took the next exit, checked into a motel in Needles, and was soon asleep, the heavy drapes closed tightly against the California sun.

But as he slept, a series of thuds worked their way into his dreams. He awoke suddenly, the room dark and still, and he thought maybe the thudding was nothing more than his own heart. It came again, loud and heavy, something hitting the wall directly behind him. *A body,* he thought, and then, *Not a body. A human being.*

He reached out and felt a lamp on the table beside the bed, then fumbled along its base for the switch. From the next room, he heard a keening sound followed by the unmistakable thump of a fist meeting flesh. He slipped on his sneakers. Outside, it was dusk. He ran down a flight of steps and turned left, into the motel lobby. The woman at the desk was the one who had checked him in. He remembered the distrustful way she looked at him when he burst in and declared that he needed a room, so exhausted he could not recall his zip code for the paperwork.

"Call the police," he said.

She stared at him.

"You need to call the police. A man in the room next to me is beating someone up—a woman, I think, his wife or girlfriend. Someone." He could see now that beneath her heavy makeup, she was young, maybe twenty, the situation beyond anything for which either her receptionist training or meager years of living had prepared her. "Nine-one-one," he said slowly, like he was explaining grammar to a student. He reached across the counter, picked up the receiver, and held it out to her. She looked left and right, as if crossing the street. He knew that she was looking for someone besides him.

At last, a switch seemed to flip on inside her. She took a breath and said, "Sir, you're in room two-fifty-two, correct?" He shrugged to indicate that he didn't know, but she continued on, his uncertainty fueling her confidence. "It must be two-fifty-three, that couple from Montana. But they had a child with them? Is there a child?" she asked.

"Just call," he said, and he ran back outside. When he got to room 253, he hesitated, the full weight of his good-fences-make-good-neighbors upbringing bearing down on him. He raised his hand and knocked hard at the door. The room went silent, and he knew that something was very wrong.

"Hello?" he called, making his voice louder because he had learned early on in teaching that volume was the best way to conceal a quaver.

The receptionist came up the steps and stood watching, afraid, he knew, of the responsibility they shared, of the haste with which she had wedded her life to his. "Key?" he mouthed, but she shook her head. He stepped back until he felt the walkway railing behind him and then rushed at the door, doing this again and again until the chain ripped away and he was in.

The receptionist's name was Britta. He had heard her spelling it for the policeman who took down their stories as they stood outside the door that Aaron had broken through minutes earlier.

That night she knocked at his room door. "It's me, Britta," she called, without adding qualifiers—"the receptionist" or "we saved a boy's life together this afternoon."

When he opened the door, she said, "I came to give you an update on Jacob," but she was carrying a six-pack of beer, which confused him. Still, he invited her in because he could not sleep, could not stop picturing the boy—Jacob—lying on the floor as though he simply preferred it to the bed, as though he had lain down there and gone to sleep. There'd been blood, and the boy's arm was flung upward and out at an angle that only a broken bone would allow. The mother sat to the side, sobbing about her son from a distance, from the *comfort* of a chair. She was not smoking but Aaron later thought of her that way, as a woman who sat in a chair and smoked while her husband threw her son against the wall. It was the husband who surprised him most: a small, jovial-looking man with crow's-feet (*duck feet* a student had once called them, mistaking the bird) and a face that seemed suited for laughing.

He and Britta did not drink the beer she had brought,

though he could see that she wanted to. "It's still cold," she said hopefully as she set it down. She would not go further, would not slip a can from the plastic noose without his prompting. She was an employee after all, used to entering these rooms deferentially. Aaron was relieved. He had left behind everything that was familiar, but at least he recognized himself in this person who would not drink beer with a teenager in a cheap motel room in Needles, California.

The beer sat sweating on the desk between the television and the Gideon Bible. "Were you reading the Bible?" Britta asked, for of course she would know that it was generally kept tucked away in the bottom drawer of the desk. He felt embarrassed by the question, though he could see that she considered Bible-reading a normal activity, one to be expected given what had happened earlier.

"Not really," he said, which was true. He had spent the last three hours *not really* doing anything. He had tried, and failed at, a succession of activities: sleeping, reading (both the Gideon Bible and *Death Comes for the Archbishop,* his least favorite Willa Cather book, though he periodically felt obligated to give it another chance), studying the map of California in an attempt to memorize the final leg of his trip, mending a small tear that had appeared in his shirtsleeve, and watching television. When Britta knocked, he had been sitting on the bed listening, the way he had as a child just after his father died and he lay in bed each night straining to hear whether his mother was crying in her room at the other end of the house. Some nights he heard her (gasping sobs that he would be reminded of as an adult when he overheard people having sex) while other nights there was silence.

"Where are you going?" Britta asked him.

"San Francisco," he said.

She nodded in a way that meant she had no interest in such

things: San Francisco specifically, but really the world outside Needles. He tried to imagine himself as Britta, spending his days interacting with people who were on the move, coming from or going to places that he had never seen, maybe never even heard of. Was it possible that she had not once felt the urge to pack up and follow, to solve the mystery of who Britta would be—would *become*—in Columbus, Ohio, or Roanoke, Virginia? It seemed inconceivable to him, to have no curiosity about one's parallel lives, those lives that different places would demand that you live.

They sat in silence, he at the foot of the bed and she in the chair beside the desk. He did not know what to say next. "Do you like working at the motel?" he asked finally.

"It's okay," she said. "It's kind of boring most of the time, but sometimes it's interesting."

"Give me an example of something interesting," he said, his teacher's voice never far away. "Other than today, of course."

"Today wasn't interesting," she said. "It was scary. I threw up afterward. Weren't you scared at all?"

"Yes," he said. "Actually, I was terrified."

She smiled, and then she began to cry. "Do you think we did the right thing?" she asked.

"What do you mean?"

"I don't know," she said. "My boyfriend—Lex—he said that it was none of our business. And my boss is this Indian guy—he's all in a bad mood now because he said it's bad for business for people to see the cops here."

Aaron's first impulse was to ask what her boss's ethnicity had to do with the rest of her statement, but he did not. He sensed no malice, and the question would only confuse her. "Listen," he said sternly. "We definitely did the right thing. Okay? We saved a boy's life."

His voice broke on the word *saved*. It seemed he had been

waiting his whole life to save this boy, though he did not believe in fate, did not believe that everything in his forty-one years had happened in order to bring him here, to a run-down motel in Needles, California, so that he might save Jacob. No. They were two separate facts: he had saved a life, and he was alone. He had never felt so tired.

"I need to go to bed," he said, and he stood up.

Britta stood also and picked up her beer, leaving behind six wet circles on the desktop. "He's in a coma," she announced as she paused in the doorway. "Jacob. So you see, we might not have saved him. He might die anyway."

Aaron leaned against the door frame, steadying himself. "At least we gave him a chance," he said. Then, because he did not have it in him to offer more, he offered this: "You're a good person, Britta, and that's important."

They were standing so close that he could smell alcohol and ketchup on her breath. He imagined her sitting in a car in an empty parking lot somewhere in Needles with her boyfriend, Lex, the two of them eating French fries and drinking beer as she tried to tell Lex about Jacob while Lex rubbed his greasy lips across her breasts.

"Good night," Aaron said, gently now. He shut the door and pressed his ear to it, waiting to slide the chain into place because he worried she might take the sound of it personally, though later he realized that she would not have thought the chain had anything to do with her. It was a feature of the room, something to be used, like the ice bucket or the small bars of soap in the bathroom.

When the telephone rang, he sat up fast in the dark and reached for it. "Hello," he said.

"Front desk," said the man on the other end. He sounded

bored, which reassured Aaron. "You have the U-Haul in the parking lot."

"Yes," said Aaron, though the man had not inflected it as a question. "Is something wrong? What time is it?"

"You'll need to come down to the parking lot. Sir." The "sir" was an afterthought, and later Aaron knew he should have considered that, should have weighed the man's reassuring boredom against that pause.

"Now?" said Aaron. "Is something wrong?" But the line had already gone dead.

He looked at the bedside clock. It seemed so long ago that he had been lying beside Walter, worrying about the truck, yet it had been only twenty-four hours. He dressed and ran down the steps to the parking lot, where a man stood beside the truck. Aaron had parked under a light—not intentionally, for he had been too tired for such foresight—and as he got closer, he could see that the man was young, still a boy, with hair that held the shape of a work cap.

"What's wrong?" Aaron asked. The boy lifted his right hand in a fist and slammed it into Aaron's stomach.

As a child, Aaron had been bullied—punched, taunted, bitten so hard that his arm swelled—but he had always managed to deflect fights as an adult. It was not easy. He was tall, four inches over six feet, and his height was often seen as a challenge, turning innocent encounters—accidentally jostling someone, for example—into potential altercations. He did not know how to reconcile what other men saw when they looked at him with the image preserved in his mind, that of a small boy wetting himself as his father's casket was lowered into the ground.

The boy hit him again, and Aaron dropped backward onto his buttocks. "What do you want?" he asked, looking up at the boy.

"I'm Lex," said the boy.

"Ah, yes, Britta's friend."

"*Boy*friend," said the boy.

"Yes, of course," said Aaron, but something about the way he articulated this angered the boy even more. He jerked back his foot and kicked Aaron hard in the hip. Aaron whimpered. He had learned early on that bullies liked to know they were having an effect.

"What was she doing in there?" asked the boy.

"Where?" said Aaron. "In my room, you mean? We were talking. She was telling me about Jacob, the child we saved this afternoon."

"So why was she crying then?"

"Crying?" said Aaron.

"She was crying when she came out. I saw her. I was right here the whole time, and I saw her come out of your room. She was crying, and she wouldn't talk to me."

"Well," Aaron said, trying to think of words, which was not easy because he was frightened. He could see the fury in the boy, the fury at being in love with someone he did not understand. "You do realize that people cry. Sometimes we know why they are crying, and sometimes we do not. Britta had an extremely hard day. She saw a child who had been beaten almost to death."

The boy looked down at him. "She was in your room. You can talk how you like, mister, but she was in your room."

Aaron realized only then what it was the boy imagined. "I don't have sex with women," he said quietly. He thought of his words as a gift to the boy, who did not have it in him to add up the details differently, to alter his calculations. Behind him, Aaron could hear the interstate, the sound of trucks floating past Needles at night.

"What?" said Lex. "What are you saying? That you're some kind of fag?" His voice was filled with wonder.

Later, when he was in the U-Haul driving away, Aaron would consider Lex's phrasing: *some kind of fag,* as if fags came in *kinds*. He supposed they did. He did not like the word *fag,* but he knew where he stood with people who used it, knew what they thought and what to expect from them. He had nodded, agreeing that he was *some kind of fag* because the question was not really about him. Lex's fist somersaulted helplessly in the air, his version of being left speechless, and he turned and walked away.

Aaron's wallet was in his back pocket, the truck keys in the front. He could simply rise from the pavement, get into the truck, and drive away. He wished that he were that type of person, one who lived spontaneously and without regrets, but he was not. He was the type who would berate himself endlessly for leaving behind a much-needed map and everything else that had been in the overnight bag. He went back up to his room, checked beneath the bed and in the shower, though he had not used the latter, and when he left, he had everything with which he had arrived. He drove slowly away from Needles, waiting for the sun to catch up with him.